Also by **Roxie Noir**

Never Enough *A Rockstar Romance*

Slow Burn *A Bodyguard Romance*

Torch *A Second Chance Romance*

Convict *A Bad Boy Romance*

Reign *A Royal Military Romance*

Loaded *A Bad Boy Romance*

Ride *A Bad Boy Romance*

Find them all on RoxieNoir.com!

Never Enough

Dirtshine Book One • A Rockstar Romance

**It's a simple enough transaction.
Marisol needs the money, and I need a nice girl to
parade in front of the cameras.
No feelings. No strings. No *falling* for anyone.**

I've been clean for months, but my record company's not
satisfied. Apparently it isn't enough to *only* kick a heroin
addiction - they're insisting that I find a girlfriend as well.

If I don't, they pull Dirtshine's massive record deal.

It's supposed to show that I've *changed my ways*, that
I've *turned over a new leaf*, all that rubbish. But I've had it with
suit-wearing wankers telling me what I'm to do, so I'm on
the verge of telling them to go fuck themselves.

And then *she* shows up.

Marisol locks me out of my own concert by accident. She's
wearing a suit at a rock show, searching for her lost law
school textbook, has *no* idea who I am...

...and for the first time in *years*, I'm hooked.

She's smart, driven, and utterly gorgeous. The sort of girl
who earnestly believes in following the rules and hates when
others don't.

I'm a huge rock star, recovering addict, and general fuckup.

Our relationship is for show, and that's *all*. But with every
smile, every laugh, and every breathtaking glance at her
curves, I want her more.

Two months is all we agreed to. But it's never going to be
enough.

Available now on RoxieNoir.com!

SLOW BURN

A Bodyguard Romance

I was hired to protect her, not make her scream my name.

From dodging bullets in Afghanistan to working for the Secret Service, I know danger *pretty* well.

Or I thought I did. That was before my latest assignment came with a whole *new* kind of danger.

Her name? Ruby.

She's the gorgeous-as-hell, opinionated, spitfire daughter of Senator Burgess. Her family's *beyond* strict, but for a girl who's so innocent, she's *anything* but sweet.

Wicked green eyes, curves that beg me to touch them, and a smile that makes me think dirty, *dirty* thoughts.

Her father's a *nightmare* — a totalitarian who rules his family with an iron fist. He decides what clothes his daughters wear, what books they read, where they can go — hell, who they *marry*.

Ruby can pretend with them, but she can't pretend with me. I can tell there's more to her than the demure southern belle she has to be in public.

But I'm a professional, hired to be her bodyguard. I know better than to fall for someone I'm supposed to protect, but with every glance, every accidental touch, every word she says to me, I just want her *more*.

I want to tear away the innocent good girl veneer, and make the *real* Ruby scream my name as she rakes her nails down my back.

It's fucking dangerous. If we get caught, there will be *hell* to pay — and it'll be worse for her.

But I don't think I can stay away.

Available now on RoxieNoir.com!

TORCH

A Second Chance Romance

Playing with fire gets you hot, but playing with a fireman gets you wet.

Fighting wildfires is dangerous as hell. If I fuck it up I get a hundred-foot wall of flame coming at me with nowhere to run, no escape, and no rescue - but it's still the best damn job in the world.

And women? They practically line up to slide down my pole. I never did like repeating myself. Not since she broke my heart into a thousand pieces, anyway.

Clementine's that ex. The one I thought I was going to marry until she dumped my ass while I was on active duty.

The one who's suddenly next door. She's still hotter than any fire I've ever fought.

We already went down in flames once, but I've never wanted anyone like I want Clementine. Not even close.

Fuck it. I need to have her again, even if it's just one more time, and to hell with the consequences.

I've already gotten burned once.

Hunter and I were over a long, *long* time ago, and there was a good reason why. Actually, there were a hundred good reasons, and I remember them *all*.

Until he shows up in my town. He's left the Marines to become a wildlands firefighter. He's rugged, hardened, dangerous, and...

...he looks at me *just* like he used to. He makes me laugh just like he used to, like the last eight years may as well have been eight minutes.

And when he gets close, I can't help but think of everything *else* we used to do - the sweaty, naked, toe-curling things. The way he could take me from laughing to moaning in half a second.

Playing with *this* kind of fire may get me hot — my *God* does it get me hot — but it also gets me burned, and once was enough.

...or was it?

Available now on RoxieNoir.com!

CONVICT

A Bad Boy Romance

I never wanted to be good. Not until I met her.

Five years in prison was supposed to reform me, but it didn't teach me shit.

I tried to start fresh: new name, new town, new *life*. No more raising hell, no more women whose names I don't bother learning, no more running from the law.

Yeah, I fucked *that* up in no time at all, but it doesn't matter. I've never liked anything but trouble - and Luna is trouble with a capital T.

She's whip smart, headstrong, fucking *gorgeous*... and a cop.

I know I can't have her. She'll see through my lies in seconds. She deserves a happy ending I know I can't give her.

Hell, with the demons from my past chasing me down, I can't even keep her *safe*.

All I can give Luna is trouble. But I can't stay away.

I don't mind being a little bad.

I date nice men. If I keep saying it, it'll be true, right?

That means I *don't* date the sexy, rakish, tattoo-covered mechanic who's got one dimple and a lifetime of working with his hands. I don't need a man who lies to the police, *obviously* has problems with authority... and who growls *filthy* things into my ear when we're alone.

It doesn't matter if one glance from Stone makes me want to tear my clothes off, I *don't* fantasize about someone who's a suspect in a double arson.

Even if the way he calls me *detective* turns me into a puddle.

I can spot trouble from a mile away, and trouble's the last thing I need.

...right?

Available now on RoxieNoir.com!

To Phylis—

Always You

Dirtshine: Book Two

by

ROXIE NOIR

Cover: Coverlüv
Photographer: Sara Eirew
Editor: Sennah Tate

ISBN: 1976424992
ISBN-13: 978-1976424991

PROLOGUE
Trent

Darcy's hand is freezing, so I fold mine around it.

This is dangerous, I think.

Dangerous because I don't know if I can stop myself much longer. Dangerous because I don't want to.

"You're an ice cube," I tell her.

"I'm not *that* cold," she protests, but I can see goosebumps rise on her arms. We've been out here for hours, sitting on the hood of the car, talking, eating pie straight from the tin like savages.

"Bullshit," I mutter.

I give in. I slide my hands up her arms, to her shoulders, and I pull her against me. I've wanted this for longer than I can remember, and being this close is fucking *intoxicating*, even if there are a million reasons I shouldn't do it.

"If anything else happens to you, Gavin might murder me," I tell her.

1

"So you're warming me up to save your own skin," she teases.

"If that's what I say, will it work?"

"It's in the sixties out here at least," I point out. "I'm not gonna get hypothermia."

Even as she says that, she leans her head into the hollow of my throat, her body pressing against mine. I close my eyes, my hands still careful on her shoulders, avoiding the bandages on her back so I don't hurt her.

Don't ruin this, I tell myself. *You won't forgive yourself if you do.*

But Darcy slides her arms around me, holding me closer. I know it's nothing, just a friendly hug, but *Jesus* it feels like it's something, but maybe only because that's what I want.

"Thanks for this," I finally murmur.

I mean the afternoon. I mean her somehow knowing exactly what to do when my brother called with the news. I mean her being the closest thing I've ever had to a soulmate, even if it's purely platonic.

But I also mean *this*. Standing here in my arms, just like this.

"I wish I knew how to really help," she says.

"You did."

She pulls back, looks up at me, her arms still around my waist.

"I thought this was dumb," she teases.

"Throwing rocks as anger management is pretty dumb," I say. "It's also exactly what I needed."

There's something in her wide blue eyes I don't recognize. Something I can't name but that makes me want *more* from her yet again, and I let one hand drift down to her hip, always careful of the bandages.

Darcy doesn't move, but her breathing gets faster. Every nerve in my body is singing, *screaming* not to do this, and I ignore them all. It feels inevitable, like everything's been leading me to this point.

Then my fingers are in her hair, running along her cheekbone. Darcy swallows, still looking me dead in the eye, her lips slightly parted. I feel like I'm in a black hole, falling unstoppably toward her.

This isn't what friends do.

This is fucking dangerous.

"Darcy," I whisper, my face an inch from hers.

I know this is how I change everything, how I risk losing her, how I shift both our worlds in one second, but I can't keep acting like it's not what I want. I can't keep acting like *she* isn't what I want, like she isn't what I've wanted all along.

I tilt my head toward hers, one last pause, one last moment like this.

She takes a deep, shaky breath.

"Don't," she whispers.

CHAPTER ONE
Trent

Ten Days Earlier

Darcy's fucking *nowhere* to be found. We're on in five minutes and she's wandered off somewhere and left no discernible trace, at least not that I can find. Her phone's going to voicemail. None of the small army of people wearing black and talking into earpieces has seen a dark-haired, blue-eyed girl in a vintage dress, ripped fishnets, and combat boots, so I don't know how the fuck I'm supposed to find her.

"Call time was ten minutes ago," Nigel is saying, as if telling *me* will magically make Darcy appear. "I told her this morning—"

"I know," I say, cutting him off.

"Is she lost?" he says, his graying eyebrows knitting together with a level of concern only our manager can produce. "She hasn't gone to the wrong stage, has she? She knows it's at the main one?"

If I fucking knew I'd have found her by now, I think, but I manage not to say it out loud.

4

"I'm gonna go look for her again," I say. "Text if you or Gavin find her."

"I'll check the loo!" he calls after me.

Backstage at Grizzly Fest is a throbbing mass of people. There's the assistants and coordinators who make everything run, all wearing headsets and carrying clipboards. There are the festival-goers who somehow got backstage passes and then wandered out of the designated 'backstage' area so they could stare around, goggle-eyed, and get in everyone's way.

There's the 'talent,' half of whom are dressed more or less like me — shirt, jeans, shoes — and half of whom look like they're from a Vegas show about Ziggy Stardust.

Darcy, our bass player, is somewhere in this shitshow when she's *supposed* to be going on stage in less than five minutes, and since everyone knows we're best friends, finding her is now *my* job.

I step out of the stream of humanity and into an alcove, just for a moment, letting some stagehands carry a huge upholstered pair of lips past. She's obviously not here. One, I would have found her already, and two, despite having played arenas for a couple years now, she still gets nervous before every single show. She's probably somewhere quiet, by herself, and lost track of time.

With that in mind, I head away from the zoo. I open a door, push through some curtains, go around some set pieces, and suddenly it's quieter. I can still hear the hubbub — they can probably hear the hubbub two hours away in Seattle — but it's a dull roar, not ear-piercing. I've got the feeling I'm closer.

I walk past a tiger painted on plywood, a cage with a stripper pole in it, a giant plastic cloud, and suddenly I hear her voice.

"The graduation ceremony from explosives school must really be something," Darcy says.

There's a pause. I duck around an enormous painting of a half-naked woman giving the finger, and *there* she fucking is, talking to some guy. He's got his arms full with spent fireworks, and he looks like he might drop one at any moment.

"We didn't really have a graduation ceremony?" the guy says, sounding kind of baffled. "We just, like, got the certificate and went home the last day."

I don't think he got the joke.

"Darce," I say. "We're on."

The guy jumps a little, and Darcy turns toward me.

"Oh, shit," she says. "Already?"

"Ten minutes ago."

"Fuck, I'm sorry," she says. "I already turned my phone off and I lost track of time."

"Hey, wait!" the guy says, so excited he drops a cardboard tube that he's holding.

Darcy flinches, and I look at the side of it. Definitely a spent firework, which you're definitely not supposed to just fucking drop.

"Listen, I know you're like, going on tour and stuff, but if you're ever in Tallwood again and you want to hang out or something..."

He leans down, depositing the rest of the spent fireworks ungracefully on the floor. Darcy takes a step back, toward me, as he searches his pockets.

"Fireworks school didn't teach you not to drop those?" I say.

I fucking know not to just throw those things around, and the extent of my education was lighting bottle rockets off in the desert until the cops showed up.

"Sorry," he mutters, then rips a label off of one, then scribbles something on it against his leg, stands up, holds it out to Darcy.

"But, like, call me if you're ever in town again?"

She takes the torn label. It's got a phone number and a name: Phil.

Phil. Fucking *Phil*.

"C'mon," I say to her, shooting him a glare. "We've got a show."

"Um, thanks," she says, folding the scrap of paper between two fingers. "Nice meeting you!"

Phil smiles hopefully as Darcy turns and ducks behind the naked lady painting, shoving the phone number into her pocket. I can hear Phil fumbling with the cardboard tubes as we walk away and I wish I could tear his fucking number up.

I'm not jealous, he's just clearly a fucking idiot, so there's obviously no reason for Darcy to bother keeping his number. That's all.

CHAPTER TWO
Darcy

"Nigel might skin you alive," Trent says. "The poor man is having kittens right now."

Shit.

"Sorry," I say. "I went back there to chill for a few minutes, and then that guy was there and we were talking and I kinda just forgot what time it was."

Trent just grunts. He's not particularly talkative at the best of times — last year, *Rolling Stone* actually called him 'broody and mysterious,' and while I don't think he's exactly either, I can see where they get it — but he usually does better than grunt.

We don't say anything else as we walk to meet Gavin and Eddie, the rest of the band, both waiting just off-stage in the wings. I'm nervous, because I *always* get nervous, cracking my knuckles and repeating the set list to myself in my head.

Tidal, Charcoal Teeth, Cage Rattler...

When we get to the side of the stage, he's standing there, both his hands stuck in his pockets, staring out at the crowd. All day he's been walking around tensely, nitpicking roadies and backstage managers over this or that because it turns out that when he's not high all the time, he can be a little uptight. That, and he's just nervous.

Eddie's doing jump squats in his flip-flops, and every time he lands, before he squats again he shakes all his limbs out like he's a dog.

It's... interesting.

Eddie, in general, is *interesting*.

And there's the shadow, of course. The shadow that hangs over everything that we do as a band, the shadow that's gotten lighter every day since it very nearly suffocated us over a year ago, but I don't think it'll ever go away, not completely.

The shadow's named Liam, and he's why Eddie is our *new* drummer, why we still think of him that way even though it's been something like fourteen months. Liam's not dead, just gone, *very* gone, the sort of gone that no one talks to or interacts with.

At least, I think he's not dead. But I've got zero proof.

We all look at each other. Eddie shakes his head side-to-side and his cheeks flap while he says "HUMMMNGNGN," and we all look at him and then look at each other one more time, trying not to laugh.

"You lot ready?" Gavin asks.

"How many people?" Trent asks.

"Dammit, Trent," I say.

He looks down at me, a smile teasing the corners of his mouth. Eddie peeks out.

"There's, like—"

"Eddie, don't," Trent says. "I was just messing with Darcy."

"Oh," Eddie says.

"So that's a yes to being ready, or would you like to keep fucking around?" says Gavin.

I roll my eyes at him.

"Who made you the fun patrol?" I tease.

"Oh, fucking come *on*, it's the first massive show with the new songs, I've got every right to be a little—"

"Guys," Trent says. "Can we say *kumbaya* or whatever, hug it out, and go play some rock and roll?"

"Kumbaya," Eddie responds instantly.

"There. Now you, Darcy," he says, that smile at the corner of his mouth again, and I can't help but smile back because Trent *always* somehow knows the right thing to say to me.

"Okay," I say, refusing to say *kumbaya* because that's just fucking silly. "We gonna go do this?"

Eddie pumps one fist in the air and hollers, because of course he does. Gavin reaches one hand out to me, and when I take it, pulls me in for a quick hug, then does the same to Trent.

Trent puts an arm around my shoulders and pulls me against his big, warm body, and for just a split second I close my eyes because this is *nice*. So nice.

Then it's done. The lights on stage go down. The crowd starts cheering and the noise escalates to a fever pitch, a roar, and then they're stomping on the muddy ground and my heart is beating in time with the stomping and we walk onto the stage.

Madness. Cacophony. Pandemonium in the crowd and it's like I'm floating across the stage, my feet not touching the floor because there's nothing like this in the world, nothing at all.

My bass is on a stand already, and I pick it up, slinging it over my shoulder, silently sliding my fingers along its thick strings and suddenly I feel right at home because this is what I do best, this is what I know and I love, and now the rest of the night is on smooth autopilot and I get to enjoy myself.

Trent and I look at each other from across the stage. Gavin glances from me to him and then finally to Eddie, who nods.

He counts off, and then we all come down on that first note at the same time, the crowd screaming as it washes over them and we launch into the first song.

And it's pretty much the fucking best.

CHAPTER THREE
Trent

If there's a heaven, it probably feels a little like this, playing in perfect time with three other people while thousands more cheer for you. Suddenly everything that we went through to get here is *worth* it: ironing out guitar and bass licks in the studio at three in the morning, heading home as the sun rose. Arguing over a chord progression for three hours, practicing the tricky parts until I got blisters.

We end the first song and slide into the second without even stopping for a beat, just like we practiced. Darcy's bass swoops low and then rises, the only sound for a couple of bars, and I look over at her.

She's fucking mesmerizing. Every single fucking time, all eyes on her for these few bars, and even though I know she doesn't like being the center of attention it's glorious when she is. The curve of her neck as she tosses her dark hair back, the line of her shoulders in her dress, her fingers on the bass.

And her legs in that short dress, covered in ripped fishnets, wearing boots. Jesus *Christ*, man. One hundred percent pure rock chick, loud and careless and brash and don't-give-a-fuck as *hell*.

I'm gonna be honest: Darcy's crazy hot all the time, but *right now* is when she's the hottest. Right now's the time when I wonder *again* what would happen if I finally stopped pretending that I don't want her and just fucking did something about it.

But then I join back into the song and the wild, nearly-uncontrollable urge fades back to its normal level, always there but under control. As I do she glances over at me, a little smile on her face like we've got some kind of secret, just the two of us, even across the space and the noise of the stage.

I smile back because we do. We've got lots of secrets. Darcy knows things about me that no one else does, and vice-versa.

We finish that song, and the momentum only builds. The crowd gets louder, stompier, and we move again into the third song without stopping. This one's slower, not exactly a ballad but not as hard as the first two. I'm already sweating under the stage lights, playing a little slower, a little softer.

It's a lull, a respite, a brief meditation from the madness. I let the air buzz around me and find this quiet place, my hands on autopilot for a moment.

And then there's a *bang.*

It's loud as hell, behind us and way overhead where there shouldn't be a bang and I flinch, then whirl around wondering what the *fuck* that was.

Then there's a second bang, the fizzle and flash of a lone firework.

I keep playing on autopilot, but my stomach turns uneasily because Dirtshine doesn't *have* fireworks.

There shouldn't be fucking unannounced pyrotechnics, I think, glancing toward the side of the stage. *Is that left over from the band before us, or did someone fucking forget to tell—*

The bass line cuts out in a jumble. I jerk my head over.

She's on fire.

Her hair and the back of her dress are ablaze and I'm already running before I even know what's happening, tearing my guitar off over my head and throwing it somewhere else with a horrible clang.

I tackle her, pushing her roughly to the floor and beating at the fire with my hands. Darcy is *screaming*, and I feel like the sound is tearing me in half but the fire won't go out, it's not enough, it's not working and she's screaming in pain and holy fuck I have to do something *I have to do something.*

I pull off my shirt and throw myself down on top of her. I'm praying that it works, that someone *fucking* gets here with a fire extinguisher.

That *please God stop make it stop I don't know what else I can do.*

And then the fire's out. It takes me a second to realize that it's gone, that it's just me awkwardly on top of Darcy and she's half-gasping, half-sobbing but she's *breathing*, alive, hurt but alive and I think I might fucking cry with relief.

Instead I get blasted in the face with thick white foam that gets into my mouth and stings my eyes. I inhale some of it by accident and nearly choke, and when it's finally over I'm on my side on the floor next to Darcy, water streaming from my burning eyes, both of us totally covered in fire extinguisher foam.

"Are you okay?" someone shouts, and I don't even fucking answer.

Darcy's moving her hands underneath herself, like she's trying to push herself off the floor, her breathing still shallow and fast, but it's slippery and she fails with a pained gasp.

Everyone is running, shouting stupid bullshit like *what happened* and *is she okay* and I don't fucking

14

know the answer to either so I just take her hand in mine.

Darcy looks at me, her blue eyes wide and terrified, bright with tears, her breathing ragged and shallow.

"You're okay," I tell her, getting slowly to my elbows and knees. "You're fine. You're gonna be fine. Take a deep breath."

"Darcy," Gavin shouts, sliding to his knees in the foam front of her. "Trent, Jesus fucking Christ what the bloody fucking—"

I shoot Gavin a *shut the fuck up please* look and he falls quiet. After a moment, he takes her other hand in his.

Darcy squeezes my hand but she doesn't take the deep breath, just keeps gasping shallowly. Something black and twisted, ugly beyond belief unfurls in my chest and I swallow, trying to keep it down.

"Darce," I say, forcing my voice calm even though she was just *on fire* and now everyone's running around like chickens with their heads cut off. "I need you to take a deep breath before you hyperventilate and faint. Come on."

She looks at me steadily, and I hold her hand tighter in mine. After a few more moments of gasping she finally takes a deep, shuddering breath, her eyes going closed as they leak tears. Then she takes another, and another.

I'm going to fucking *murder* that fireworks clown. I don't mean that figuratively. I'm going to find him backstage and I'm going to beat the living *fuck* out of him for doing this to her, and then I'm going to take his broken, lifeless body and I'm going to—

"I wouldn't mind fainting," Darcy whispers, still shuddering with each breath but at least breathing normally. "Sounds okay."

Now I'm on my knees, and I lace my fingers through hers, holding her hand so tightly in both of mine I'm afraid I'll hurt her more. I don't think she even notices.

"It's really more trouble than it's worth," I say, just to say something, keep her calm.

Two paramedics are at the edge of the stage now, and they run toward the three of us. From the corner of my eye, I see Eddie hovering somewhere, but he's not really important right now.

"If you faint it'll be whole fucking production," I go on.

"Well, I wouldn't want *that*," Darcy says, her voice still weak and quavering, and relief floods through me, at the sarcastic edge in her voice.

The paramedics reach us. I whisper that I'm still there, and I let her hand go so they can do their jobs, standing off to the side with Gavin. We don't talk, just watch as they ask her questions, cut her clothes away, cut her bass strap off her.

After a few moments, they lift her and she *gasps*, the sound so filled with anguish and pain that I take an involuntary step forward before Gavin grabs my arm.

"They've got to get her to the ambulance somehow," he points out.

They lift her onto a stretcher, still on her stomach, and we follow a few feet behind as they wheel her toward the vehicle, red lights blazing.

I follow. Just before they hoist her in, I grab her hand one more time. I don't say anything, just squeeze, and she squeezes back. Her eyes are going hazy because I think they've already given her something for the pain.

The door shuts. The paramedics climb into the front and hit the sirens a few times before lumbering off across the muddy field, the crowd gawking, the loud *whoop whoop whoop* lost in the wide-open space as it drives away.

I watch it go and take a deep breath. Then I take another one, and another one, but all the fucking breathing exercises in the *world* aren't going to help because the anger's already there, buried in my chest, coiling and writhing and ready to strike.

I turn around and start walking back toward the outdoor stage. There are probably hundreds of people watching me right now — when stray fireworks light someone on fire it's fairly noteworthy — but I don't see any of them.

I just see Darcy, terrified and in pain and hyperventilating, lying on the stage and squeezing my hand.

"Trent!" calls Gavin, and he jogs up to me, a hand on my shoulder.

I shrug it off, jerking away from him.

"Mate—"

"I gotta take a leak," I say. My voice comes out flat and affectless.

"A leak."

"It's American for piss," I say, still walking fast through the squishy grass. We're turning heads as we half-walk and half-argue, onlookers with wide eyes and mouths shaped like O's just goggling at us.

"I fucking know what — goddamn it, Trent," he says, as we reach the stage. "Don't be fucking stupid."

I clench my jaw, already thinking of the sweet crunch of that kid's face against my knuckles.

Do I know better than to find this guy and kick his ass? Fuck yeah.

Do I give half a shit about that right now? Fuck no.

"Gavin, fuck off," I growl. "Unless you'd like to come hold it for me at the urinal?"

I turn away, still walking fast and angry, and this time he doesn't follow. Good.

I head toward the VIP porta-potties, but after fifty feet I veer away, opening a door to the back of the stage and shoving through a line of black curtains.

The way he was practically juggling those spent fireworks. Too fucking busy ogling Darcy, fucking *flirting* with her, to bother checking that there weren't any live ones left on stage.

He's sitting on a back staircase to the stage, his face in his hands. I think he's crying.

Good. He should feel bad. He'll feel fucking worse in a minute. There's no one else around, and I flex my right hand, a righteous cocktail of fury and excitement and revenge all slithering through my veins.

The guy looks up as I walk toward him, relief and recognition crossing his face.

"Hey, you're in the band too, right?" he says, his voice coming out high-pitched and eager. "Is she gonna be okay? Was it really a firework, or maybe an electrical—"

My fist hits his face with a crunchy *thump* and the guy cries out, falling backward against the stairs. He puts up one arm like he can defend himself that way, but I'm fucking *lit*, rage sizzling over my skin, down every nerve.

The next hit gets him in the solar plexus and knocks the wind out of him. He doubles over, eyes practically bugging out of his head, nose already swelling and trickling blood, not even making a sound as he slides to the ground.

Somewhere in the back of my mind I know this isn't a fair fight. I know it wouldn't be a fair fight if he had a baseball bat.

But you know what else wasn't a fair fucking fight? Darcy versus fire.

He looks up, face turning colors because he still can't breathe, but I'm not a fucking patient man. I grab the front of his shirt and haul him up against the back of the stage so his toes are barely on the ground

He *finally* gasps in a breath I slam him backwards.

"She was *on fire*," I growl. "You lazy fucking son of a *bitch*, you had—"

An arm wraps itself around my neck, taking me by surprise, and I'm hauled backward off the kid, stumbling a few steps before I can fling my attacker away and spin around, ready for whoever the fuck *this* is.

This is Gavin, standing a few feet away, hands up and palms out.

"Trent," he says, breathing hard. "Don't fucking *do* this, mate, you're not going to help Darcy by punching this arsehole—"

I just turn back to the asshole in question, but I only get about two steps before Gavin full-on tackles me, throwing both of us to the ground.

"Fuck!" I shout. "Get the *fuck* off me—"

He's got a knee in my back, but I throw him off and to the ground as he grabs my arm, yanking me off balance. It's an ugly wrestling match, neither of us prepared for it, and as angry as I am I know it's not *Gavin* I want to hurt.

But I still knee him in the back by accident. He elbows me in the mouth, and after a few minutes he's on his back and I'm on my hands and knees next to him feeling fresh bruises swell under my skin, my lip split, everything covered in grass and mud.

I spit blood onto the dirt below. Gavin coughs, rolling over, his shirt torn in three places. I'm still not wearing a shirt, because I put Darcy out with the one I had on.

The guy's gone, clearly the right fucking choice for him. Instead, Eddie's standing at the edge of the small space, back to a black curtain, eyeing Gavin and I warily.

"Everything cool?" he asks.

Gavin and I both look up at him, and a long moment of silence stretches out in between the three of us before Gavin finally speaks up.

"Yeah, mate," he says, sitting up on the ground, covered in mud and bruises. "Everything's totally fucking *cool*."

Eddie nods once, then disappears through the curtain. Fine with me. He's been wary of Gavin ever since Gavin punched him last year — long story — so it's just as well he doesn't get involved.

I heave myself to my feet, then hold my hand out to Gavin. I'm still angry, *furious*, but the deep black edge is off it, the void that I fell into for a minute there has gone for now.

He takes it and I haul him up, and for a moment, we just look at each other. I swallow, the taste of copper in my mouth.

"Thanks, man," I say softly. I don't know how Gavin Lockwood, Noted Junkie, has somehow become more reasonable and responsible than me in the past year, but it's happened. Sobering up and falling in love probably had something to do with it.

He puts his hand on my shoulder again and squeezes.

"I know the feeling," he says simply. "But I couldn't have you breaking a hand or something, right?"

I flex both my hands in response, just checking. Not broken.

"Right."

He smiles faintly, then claps my shoulder once before letting it go.

"Come on. Let's get you a shirt and go see Darcy in the hospital, yeah?"

I just nod in agreement.

CHAPTER FOUR

Darcy

I'm on something. I don't know what. Feels opioid, maybe, because I've got the sensation that the pain's not *gone*, just far away, but not so far that I can't see it. Just within vision.

I think I used to do this for fun, sometimes, back in the dark ages that were also the fun times, when Gavin and Liam were usually high and the four of us drove around the country in a van playing shitty little venues until suddenly we were playing huge venues, our album cover everywhere, and women's magazines were asking what my favorite lip gloss was.

I never fucking knew. It was the one in my bag already, probably vaseline or chapstick, but if I ran an interview saying *that* every lip gloss company on the fucking planet would send me actual dump trucks filled with lip gloss, more lip gloss than one person could possibly use in her whole entire life, and what was I...

"*Miss*," a woman is saying, crouching down, her face right in front of mine. I blink. "Your complete first and last name."

I stare at her. I think this might not be the first time she's asked.

"Miss," she says again, and I clear my throat. I swear I mean to say my name.

"Why are you being such a *bitch*?" I ask, my voice coming out weak and whispery, like I'm about to cry.

Wait. What?

The woman sighs.

. . .

At the hospital, they give me a sedative on top of whatever I'm already on, and then I may as well just not fucking be *there*. I'm dimly aware that I'm on some sort of gurney, still lying on my stomach, and there's a bright light behind me and people in masks talking about fibers and particles and degrees and scarring and damage, and I couldn't care less. Taped to the side of a cart are lovely pictures of a forest, a waterfall, a place I'm fairly sure is Yosemite Valley, the Grand Canyon.

My mind wanders while doctors do *something* to my back, and I keep getting everything jumbled up. Trent on the floor, next to me. Trent's hand in mine as he told me to quit making a production, the one person who knew exactly what to do.

Then Trent and I lying in the grass in Yosemite Valley, under the trees, my hand still in his, Trent saying *just breathe* and there's a campfire somewhere behind me. Somewhere in the back of my mind I'm unsettled but Trent is right there. Holding my hand.

And I float right the fuck away into the landscape.

CHAPTER FIVE
Trent

I stare at the flowers for sale in the hospital gift shop, arms crossed. There's a huge hole in my jeans, and they're still stained with grass and mud from my little tussle earlier with Gavin, not to mention whatever's in fire extinguisher foam, but it's too fucking bad. I washed my face. That's good enough.

All these flowers are bullshit. They're stupid, ugly carnations dyed in weird colors, or they're half-dead lilies, or they're multi-colored daisies. I don't know flower names. I just know I hate these.

There's also an entire section of roses, but I can't even look at roses. The smell alone makes me sweaty and nauseous. *Fuck* roses.

Fuck *hospitals*. Just being in one, just that hospital *scent* brings everything back. The terror, the shame, the *guilt*. That feeling of complete and total powerlessness.

Ever lied your face off to a doctor? I have. Dozens of times, starting when I was barely old enough to talk. Even *then* I understood what the alternative was.

They didn't believe me. I could see it in their faces, but I never cracked, no matter how many kindly nurses and gentle-faced CPS workers they sent in.

I never told them shit. It's fucked up, and it's probably even more fucked up that I'm a little proud of how I never cracked, but there it is.

I take a deep breath, ignoring the rose scent, and I just grab the biggest fucking flower display they've got. It includes a teddy bear and everything, and even though Darcy is anything but the teddy bear type, maybe she'll get a kick out of how dumb it is.

The girl behind the counter smiles up at me as I set the flowers down, rifling through my pockets.

"Will this be all?" she asks, batting her eyelashes a little.

I *think* she might recognize me, but it's hard to tell, and my face is kinda dinged up at the moment. And frankly, I'm out of patience for flirting, chit-chat, social niceties, or anything that isn't *getting out of here and seeing Darcy already*.

"Yeah."

"That'll be eighty-five forty-four."

I almost shout *for this shit?!* but I own a house in the Hollywood Hills with a pool and *two* luxury cars, so I pay for the fucking flowers.

"Thanks," I say, and get the hell out of there.

They moved Darcy from the emergency room to the regular hospital a little while ago, but they wouldn't let me see her yet. Said she was *resting*, so I sit myself and my huge fucking flower display in the waiting room.

And I *wait*. In the hospital. With a hole in my jeans, a torso still covered in dirt even though I did put a shirt on, and a lip that feels like it's the size of a softball.

It's excruciating. The waiting, not the injuries. The injuries I got used to a long, long time ago.

Gavin's not even there, because once we heard that she was all right but it would still be a while, he went

24

back to the venue to deal with *that* mess. Someone had to and there was no way I was leaving the hospital. And God only knows where Eddie is.

After forever, my phone rings with a number I don't know, so I jump to my feet and answer it.

"Trent Ryder."

"Hi, Trent, this is Tallwood Memorial Hospital. You're listed as the emergency contact for Darcy Greene?"

I'm out of my chair and at the waiting room door, flowers in hand, before she finishes Darcy's name.

"That's right."

"I'm sorry to be the bearer of bad news, but she had an incident today, and—"

I round the corner to the nurses' station. There's a woman on the phone with her back to me.

"I know all about it," I say, and she turns around.

"Oh," she says, putting down the phone.

"She awake?"

The nurse gives me a long, slow up-and-down, and I can't tell if she's checking me out or wondering what the hell I've been up to. Probably a little of each. It's a look I get a lot.

"Are you family?"

"I'm her emergency contact," I say, avoiding the question. I'm *technically* not family, but I'm what Darcy's got, so if the nurse wants to fight about this I'll fight about it.

But she glances over my flowers, then over my ring finger, and shrugs.

"Room two-thirty-one," she says, and points down the hall.

I'm strangely nervous. I can feel everyone's eyes on me, and I try not to think about what this looks like: huge guy with a swollen lip taking an *enormous* flower bouquet to a badly hurt woman. My mom used to get huge bouquets, too.

Everyone here knows what happened, I remind myself. *It's been running on the news for hours. They know it was nothing to do with you.*

Her door's partly open, and I knock softly before I push it open.

CHAPTER SIX
Darcy

The door to my hospital room opens, and an enormous flower display walks in. For some reason, even though for a moment I honestly think that flowers have learned to ambulate and are coming directly toward me, I don't panic.

Drugs are *great*.

"Yeah?" I ask the flowers, because it seems as good as anything else.

But then the flowers lower and Trent's head pops over the top, and *now* this makes sense.

"They wouldn't let me in while you were asleep, so I wandered to the gift shop and got you something," he says.

I'm pretty sure he means *I paced restlessly to the gift shop and glared at everyone and everything until I bought something and finally left*, but I don't argue.

"Are there any flowers left down there?" I ask, still feeling kind of sleepy and hazy, but at least my back mostly stopped hurting. "Jesus, Trent."

He half-smiles, which is pretty good for him.

"There are, but I can fix that if you want," he offers, looking around for a place to put the gargantuan display down. "Just say the word."

He puts the flowers on the sink, then brushes his hands off, comes over, and sits by the bed. His lip is all fucked up, and I frown.

"The hell happened to you?" I ask.

"I could ask you the same thing."

"You *know* what the hell happened to me."

"Do you know you have a black eye?"

I sigh. I'm on my stomach, propped up on some kind giant foam pillow wedge, and while it's better than lying on my back my face is all squished, my boobs are squished, and the whole thing is kind of uncomfortable. Plus, I've got the constant sensation that, despite the sheets being adequate cover, *everyone* is looking at my ass.

"Yeah, my face got banged up when I hit the floor," I say.

My left eye's swollen nearly shut and there's a big scrape down the side of my face, but it could be way worse.

"Sorry."

I just start laughing, or at least, I kinda try even though that *also* somehow makes my back hurt. Turns out you use your back for a whole lot of things.

"Yeah, you're a real asshole," I say. "You should've let me keep burning."

"Next time I'll make sure I ask first."

I take a deep breath and try to re-adjust myself a little. Trent sits up straighter, his hands on his knees.

"You need help?"

"No," I say grumpily. "This sex wedge is gonna be uncomfortable no matter what, I'm just moving to a different uncomfortable spot for a while."

I thrash a little while he looks on, half worried and half amused. My new position isn't much better than the old one, but at least it's new.

"Sex wedge?" he finally says. "That what the hospital calls it?"

"It looks like one of those fuck pillows," I explain.

Trent just leans back in the chair, crosses his thick arms in front of himself, and looks at me, *waiting*.

Shit.

"You know those kinda triangular pillows that they advertise on late-night TV, and you can fold them and flop them in all these different positions and, I don't know, accomplish the whole Kama Sutra at once?"

"I don't," he says.

"Yes you *do*," I say, even though I wish I would just shut up. "They've got a shirtless guy in weird boxers and the woman in, I think, a black bikini and she's got huge tits and they simulate sex on the fuck wedge really slow while she makes a crazy-ass O face?"

Both of Trent's eyebrows are raised.

"I've *never* seen this," he says.

"Well, you should have," I say, giving up. "And anyway, this looks like a big version of the Fuck Wedge. But less sexy, because I'm pretty high and my back hurts and I keep saying *fuck wedge*."

"You look kinda like a beached mermaid," he says. "Do mermaids use fuck wedges?"

I sigh and bury my face in the fuck wedge. My puffy black eye complains, and I wince.

"I'm sorry I brought up the fuck wedge," I say, my voice loud but muffled.

God, am I sorry I brought up the fuck wedge, and I don't think I would have except, you know, *extenuating circumstances*.

Trent's my best friend. I've told him things that I've never even *dreamed* of telling anyone else, from my deepest, darkest secrets to the fact that my very first crush as a kid was on Robin Hood from the animated Disney movie.

Robin Hood was a cartoon fox.

Trent makes me laugh. He hugs me when I cry, he talks me down when I get upset, and when I can't find something in my kitchen I call him because he usually *does* know where it is. And that all works in reverse, too. I've driven to his house at four in the morning, still in pajamas, because he had another nightmare and called me.

For fuck's sake, he's my emergency contact. I'm his. He doesn't know this, but after Dirtshine hit it big and then Gavin and Liam nearly fucking died, I made a will and put him in it.

But we don't talk about sex, or dating, or our love lives, or *any* of that stuff. The most we talk about that stuff is casually mentioning dates that we've been on in passing or something, but honestly, I hate even *that*. Hearing another woman's name in Trent's mouth gives me an uncomfortable, squirming feeling that I can't stand. And having to imagine him smiling and laughing with someone else or kissing them or *anything* makes me a little nauseous.

Likewise, I go on dates and shit and don't tell him. I mean, not often, and it has been a *long* time since someone got invited into Darcy's Special Cavern, but if I so much mention a guy hitting on me Trent gets grumpy and sullen.

And I don't hate that. I don't hate it at all, and that fact scares the shit out of me because, okay, yes, I've thought about going *there* with Trent more than once. More than a couple of times, actually, because he's sweet, protective, makes me laugh, and Trent *gets* me in a way no one else does. For fuck's sake, he just *saved my life*, or at least saved me from way worse burns.

Plus, have you ever seen a guitar player's forearms? Not to mention the *rest* of Trent? Jesus Christ.

But people who bang break up. They break up *all* the fucking time.

30

"I'm not really sure what part of the mermaid you fuck," I say, and turn my face back toward Trent. "Do they lay eggs?"

He's smiling.

"And you still haven't explained why you look like you got run over by an entire rugby team," I say. "Did you have to cross a rugby field to get here?"

"I think they call it a *pitch*."

"Don't fucking avoid the question."

He sits up straighter. He rearranges himself in the chair, taps the armrest, glances out the window, but I just keep watching him because I know he'll tell me if I just *wait*.

"Gavin and I got into it a little," he finally admits.

I'm not exactly *surprised*, but I can already tell that's not the whole story. The four members of Dirtshine — well, five, I guess, if you count both Liam *and* Eddie — have always had somewhat tumultuous relationships with each other. You know, the way you do when you're close with three other people but also spend a *lot* of time in a van, often high or drunk, and you know each other way, way too well?

"You and Gavin," I say, waiting for a better explanation.

Trent glares out the window.

"I had some words with the fireworks guy, and Gavin didn't think I should be having words with the fireworks guy, so I had words with Gavin instead."

I stare at him. I know what he means by *words*, because I've seen Trent angry. Even if I've never seen him actually get violent.

To anything living, at least. I've watched him punch some inanimate objects. They never fared well.

"Words didn't get your lip split," I say.

"No, that was Gavin's elbow."

I swallow hard, just watching his face, a knot forming in my stomach. I have a bad feeling that he might have actually *done* something to that guy, and that Gavin stopped him, or at least tried.

And I don't hate it. I hate that I don't hate it, because violence is bad and punching people is bad, but there's a secret part of my heart that gets warm and tingly at the thought of Trent going on a revenge crusade for me.

It's fucked up, but sweet. In a fucked up way.

"Is everyone okay?" I ask.

"Yeah, everyone's fine," he says, pushing his hair back from his forehead. "Well, except you."

"I'll *be* fine," I offer. "Two to three weeks."

"In the hospital?"

"Until it's healed. I think they want me out of here ASAP, something about burns getting infected easily and hospitals being a great breeding ground for super-MRSA and shit."

Trent takes a long, slow look at my back. I'm not wearing a shirt or anything, just bandages, but they are *definitely* not sexy. Unless mummies are sexy.

"How bad is it?" he finally asks. "Really."

I try to rearrange myself again and mostly just flop around a little on the sex wedge until different parts of me are uncomfortable.

"They're fairly serious second-degree burns but no third degree," I finally tell him. "So it looks super gross, probably, and the doctors said there are huge blisters and it's gonna hurt for a while and take a couple weeks to heal, but I don't need skin grafts or anything."

I pause for a moment. Trent's looking serious again, his eyes on my bandages like he can heal me with the force of his glare.

"And they said that if it hadn't been put out when it was it would have been way worse, so, thanks," I say.

Trent just half-smiles and looks down, like he doesn't know what to say. He's not really good with gratitude or compliments, like he never thinks he deserves them.

"Of course," he says. "Now you owe me."

I laugh.

"If you're ever on fire, I promise to do my best to put you out," I say.

CHAPTER SEVEN
Trent

Half an hour later, the nurses finally chase me out. Darcy's fallen asleep anyway, and I'm just sitting in the vinyl-covered arm chair next to her bed while she snores slightly, watching her back rise and fall. Thinking about how small and fragile and *hurtable* she looks right now, and how different it is from her normal loud, brassy, fuck-the-world-I'm-Darcy-fuckin'-Greene self.

I've never seen her like this. I told her once that she was an inside-out iron maiden — the torture device, not the band — because her spikes are on the outside. Not that I blame her. She's been through some shit and seen some shit that no one should have to see or go through, and if becoming a medieval torture device is how she did it, that's just fine.

But I hate leaving her, even though I know she's perfectly safe and she's where she needs to be, and I know that if something happened right now I'd be worth fuck-all in the help department. It's not like I can punch an infection.

For the record, I would. I'd punch MRSA right in the goddamn face.

It's past one in the morning. When I walk out of the hospital and into the parking lot, the air is cool and the night's dark, so dark I'm disoriented for a moment. Tallwood, Washington is a pretty small town with a pretty big music festival every year, but that means that I can see twice as many stars as I could in Los Angeles.

And I just stand there, looking at them. I'm not religious and never have been, despite my mom's best efforts, but at this moment staring at the stars out here and thinking *thank you, she's going to be okay, thank you so much* seems like the right thing to do.

After a while, I stop. I shake my head, then rub my face before I remember it's bruised and fucked up. I know I need to get back to the hotel, I need a shower, I need to check in with Gavin, update him on Darcy and talk to him about what's going to happen next, and I should probably eat something sometime.

But I keep thinking of her, asleep and fragile, and I can't stop wishing that it hadn't happened and I can't stop being grateful that this was *all* that happened. I stand in the hospital parking lot for a long time, staring up and trying to sort through everything, until someone else finally comes out of the hospital and walks to their car.

That shakes me loose, so I call a cab and head back to our hotel.

• • •

I hardly sleep. When I leave the hotel the next morning the desk attendant gives me a *holy shit what happened to you* look, and I just smile and shrug at her as I leave. To be honest, I've had my lip split so many times that I nearly forgot.

Stop number one is a car rental place, because I'm

gonna need wheels. Stop number two is a cutesy, homey cafe in downtown Tallwood that's got wood paneling on every wall and cross-stitched inspirational sayings everywhere. They also make damn good breakfast biscuits, so I grab one for me and one for Darcy.

Stop number three is the bookstore a block down from the cafe, because if I know Darcy she's already bored out of her mind.

Then the hospital again, quietly clenching my jaw and steeling myself as I walk through those big doors. That feeling of dread and nausea hits me full in the chest, all that shit flooding back, but I just keep walking.

The new nurses glance my way, but I guess they've been told, because no one tries to stop me from heading past their station and into Darcy's room, the morning sunlight flooding in through the window, making the bright hospital white even brighter.

I stop short. There's no Darcy. Just a messy bed with that pillow wedge on it.

My heart crashes into itself. This hospital's already got me tense and on edge, just waiting for something awful to happen, and I instantly think of the worst case scenario.

Her burns got infected, she had a concussion they didn't know about, when I tackled her it burst an aneurysm...

Jesus, I hate hospitals. Fucking *hate* them. I fight down the panic and take a deep breath, *knowing* I'm getting ahead of myself, and I step into the room.

"Darce?" I call.

"In here," she says, her voice echoing out of the bathroom.

See? You were worried about nothing.

"I brought breakfast."

"Come in, I'm not naked."

I toss the books and breakfast on the bed along with

my jacket, catching a glimpse of myself in the mirror as I walk for the hospital room's bathroom. I look like reheated hell. Not even fresh hell. Split lip, bruised face, a huge gash on one arm that I don't remember getting.

It's probably gonna scar and fuck up the tattoo of a dragon that's under it, but I'm okay with it since that tattoo was done after hours in the back room of a tattoo shop by some guy named Jesús, and Jesús was probably drunk and definitely high.

The tattoo isn't very good, is what I'm saying.

Darcy's standing at the bathroom mirror, both arms over her head and a pair of scissors in one hand. She's grimacing in pain and trying not to as she holds strands of hair up, examines them, and snips burned pieces off and lets them float to the floor, the bandages on her back stretching and wrinkling.

"The fuck are you doing?" I ask, standing in the doorway.

"Cutting off my burned hair," she says, her tone of voice suggesting *duh*.

I grab her wrist gently and remove the scissors from her hand. She puts up a token resistance but it's not much, and I deposit her arm at her side, gently.

She's not naked, but she's not what I'd call *clothed*. There's one hospital gown tied around her waist in a way that is *not* how hospital gowns work, and then her torso is wrapped in bandages, from her neck down, only a thin band of unharmed skin showing at the top of her hips.

It's everything I can do not to touch it because even now, even bruised, burnt, and bandaged, she's so beautiful I can't stand it.

Then I remind myself that *she's fucking hurt* and force myself not to get hard.

"You're fucking up your bandages is what you're doing," I say, letting her arm go. "You're getting tiny pieces of hair in them, and if your wounds get infected don't come crying — what are you smiling about?"

"You sound like someone's mom," she says, blue eyes lit up with a teasing smile.

A quick pang shoots through my heart. She didn't say *my mom*. She never says that.

"I don't want to have to visit you in the hospital any longer than I have to," I grumble.

"Can I please have the scissors back?"

"No."

"I promise not to run with them."

"Don't run anyway."

"So many *rules*," she says, still teasing. "Come on, my hair is gross. Please?"

I step forward and lightly take some strands in my fingers. Usually her hair is dark and wavy and soft and smells a little like vanilla — yeah, I know what my best friend's hair smells like, so fucking what? — but she's right, her hair is gross, frizzed and brittle, and there's a big chunk missing in the back. Probably because it was on fire.

"Which part do you want cut off?" I ask, running my fingers through it softly. They brush against her unburned shoulder.

My dick twitches the tiniest bit.

She is in the goddamn hospital, I order myself sternly. *Don't fucking do this.*

"The part that looks really bad," she says, reaching up to take a strand between her fingers. "Here."

She tries not to wince, but I can still read it on her face. I take the hair from her, snipping the end off.

"You approve?" I ask.

"Yeah, but don't quit your day job to become a hair stylist," she says.

"You haven't even seen the finished product yet," I say, lifting and snipping another strand. I try to toss the burned ends into the trash, but a lot of them don't make it. "I could be a master haircutter. You've got no idea."

Darcy just grins. I keep cutting.

"Call it women's intuition, then," she says. "I've got this *feeling* that you weren't a beauty school student by day and a bouncer by night."

"Maybe it's an innate talent, like in *Edward Scissorhands.*"

"He practiced."

"I've never actually seen it," I admit, combing my fingers through her hair, finding the burned parts, cutting them out. Trying to ignore how close I am to her or how my fingers brush her skin. "Just the porno version once. Low Valley Home Video liquidated and a buddy of mine got it on VHS."

"Edward Scissorcock?" Darcy guesses.

I stop for a moment and just look at her in the mirror.

"No, it's not *Edward Scissorcock*," I say, and Darcy laughs. "Who would watch that?"

"I swear I know this one," she says, leaning lightly against the sink. I go back to cutting her hair. "Edward Scissor... dick."

"That's the same thing as scissorcock."

She chews on her lip for a moment, eyes glazing over, deep in thought. I don't look at her, just cut off the fried ends of her hair and try to keep my thoughts to myself.

I don't think she knows what she *does* to me. Even now, even though we're in her hospital room, being this close to her is heady, overwhelming. I can't stop thinking about her bandages unraveling and falling off, revealing her perfect, soft breasts. I can't stop thinking about the way she *looks* at me sometimes, the way sometimes her lips move a little when she's thinking.

I can't stop thinking about her mouth on mine, her body underneath me, the way I bet she raises hell when she comes.

Great, *now* I'm fucking hard. Over my best friend.

39

Who's got unsexy second-degree burns down her neck and back, which I know better than to have erections about.

I cut off the last chunk of frazzled, scorched hair and toss it toward the trash. Darcy's still leaning on the sink, her eyes closed, one swollen and purple, one normal. I run my fingers through her hair one more time, just feeling the warmth of her body, the strands slipping through my fingers, and she opens her eyes and looks at me in the mirror.

"We're a fucking pair, huh?" she says. "We look like we got mugged in a dark alley."

"I wish we'd been mugged," I say, my voice low and confessional, just the two of us in this small bathroom. "It's easier to heal a stolen wallet than second-degree burns."

Darcy makes a face, then winces, then blows a strand of hair out of her face.

"Thanks for the haircut," she says, turning her head from side to side. Her jaw flexes in pain.

"It's the hot new style," I say, taking a reluctant step back.

"It's *something*," she teases. "Maybe I'll start getting written up in magazines like *Girly Rolling Stone* or whatever for my hot new riot grrl punk hairdo."

"Just tell them who your stylist is," I say as she steps past me and back into her hospital room, tiny pieces of hair swirling after her. "If this guitar thing falls through I've got a backup plan."

CHAPTER EIGHT
Darcy

Trent stays all day, even though I keep telling him he doesn't have to. I mean, when the hell am I supposed to read the copies of *The Hunger Games* that he brought if he never leaves me alone?

About an hour after visiting hours start, Gavin and Nigel, our manager, drop by. They've both got flowers, too, and Gavin whistles when he sees the Rose Parade float that Trent brought.

"Marisol also sends her love, and would like you to be careful," he tells me, shoving both hands into his pockets.

"For once, this wasn't my fault," I point out.

I'm not looking at Trent, but from the corner of my eyes I can see his face darken.

"I told her you'd say that, and she said to be careful anyway," he says, and I laugh.

He's also banged up, a couple minor bruises on his face. I wonder again what exactly happened last night, though I know I'll be able to get it out of Trent later.

"Tell her thanks," I say. "What's going on with the tour?"

"You're meant to be resting, not quizzing me about logistics already," Gavin says, crossing his arms and leaning against a wall.

"I'm *meant* to be playing in Boise tonight," I point out.

"When I got here she was cutting her own hair in the bathroom," Trent rumbles. "Good luck with talking sense into her."

"Is *that* what happened?" Gavin asks lightly, giving my head a glance-over.

"It actually looked worse before, believe it or not," I say.

"I believe it," Gavin says, and then swallows, looking out the window. "Listen, Darcy, I'm sorry. I ought to have insisted that they double-check the pyrotechnics or something. I knew those things were fucking dangerous and I just trusted a bunch of blokes I didn't know to take care of it."

I smile, and bite my lip to keep from laughing. The last time we went on tour Gavin spent it so strung out he could barely talk half the time, and now he's Mister Safety.

"It's not your fault," I say. "Don't blame yourself."

He sighs again.

"And tell me what the fucking plan is, already, come *on*."

"You don't let a thing ever go, do you?" he says, a smile tugging at his mouth.

"Nope."

"At least you're well enough to be a pain in my arse," Gavin says, and I just grin.

Nigel pulls out his phone and adjusts his glasses.

"We've cut three weeks from the tour and right now we're trying to tack it back onto the end," he starts.

"They said I'd probably be healed in two," I point out.

"We cut three," Gavin says.

Mentally, I roll my eyes.

"So that means that a few weeks from—" Nigel checks his watch — "Tomorrow, we'll be in Minneapolis for two nights, Chicago for two, Boston, New York, Philly…"

Nigel keeps listing cities, and though none of the three of us particularly need to hear where we're playing in a couple of weeks — all cities kind of blend together after a while — it's oddly soothing to hear his British accent just list them out, on and on. It makes it feel like this won't go on forever, that eventually I'll get out of this stupid hospital and my stupid back will be healed.

Gavin interrupts him, asks him something. The sun is on the foot of my bed, warming my feet through the covers as Trent joins in, pointing out something or other about a festival we've agreed to that they can't reschedule. Suddenly I'm *super* tired, warm, safe, slightly drugged, and I've been informed that the tour's still happening and they're not going on without me.

"Hey! Darcy."

The voice snaps me awake. The room's empty.

"I don't remember if you like chocolate, but..."

Eddie's voice bears down on me, and I half-sit up on the bed as he rounds the corner into my hospital room, talking at top volume about the box he's holding. Gavin, Trent and Nigel are all gone, the sun no longer shining into the window.

He stops, looking stricken.

"Oh, shit, were you asleep?"

I blink once, trying to get my bearings. I'm not normally a napper, and I don't usually wake up in a hospital.

"No?" I ask, still trying to wake up.

"Oh, cool," he says. "Right, so, you like chocolate, yeah? I got you this box, but if you don't, let me know and I'll like get you a stuffed animal or whatever."

"Chocolate is perfect," I tell him. "Thanks, Eddie."

He beams, proud that he's done something right, and hands me the red, heart-shaped box which I'm *positive* was the first one he saw in the gift shop. Then he shoves his hands into the pockets of his cargo shorts and looks around the room.

"Man, you got a ton of flowers," he says. "Do you even know this many people?"

"I know lots of people," I say, doing my best not to let Eddie try my patience.

Eddie is a perfectly nice person who doesn't always think through the consequences of his actions. Or his statements. Or... anything else he does, really, though he always means well.

Have I ever ranted to Trent about what a dipshit he can be? Yes.

But is Eddie a good drummer and a good person who's just kind of a space cadet, and who has to live under the shadow of our former drummer Liam? Also, yes.

"I guess," he says, sounding surprised.

There are a *lot* of flowers. Besides the normal bouquets from Gavin and Nigel, there's a bunch the size of a chair from the concert organizers, one from the record label, a few from roadies and tech guys on our tour, a few from various media outlets, one from Gavin's girlfriend Marisol, one from my friend Rosa who's taking care of my cat, and a few more I haven't even gotten to read yet.

"That big one's from Trent, I assume," he says, sounding bored.

I raise one eyebrow.

"What's that mean?"

Eddie shrugs, still looking around.

"Of course he gave you the big one," he says.

Then he starts laughing at himself.

"That's what she said, right?" Eddie says, winking at me.

My face goes as hot as my back.

"I think he just grabbed the first thing he saw," I say, suddenly grumpy.

"Oh, come on, man, I'm just joshin'," Eddie says. "I mean, everyone knows—"

He glances at me and *stops*. Possibly because my heart has seized in my chest and I'm trying to murder him with my eyes.

"—that you and Trent are, like, BFFs," Eddie finishes, his voice suddenly careful and neutral.

"I really think it was the only flower thing left down there at midnight," I mutter.

"Probably," Eddie agrees without looking at me. "That's all I meant, just that, it's a bunch of flowers but it's also just, you know, a bunch of flowers."

It takes him about three more minutes to find an excuse to leave.

Then I'm alone in my hospital room for almost the first time all day, staring at this flower bouquet that probably required its own container truck.

Fucking goddamn. Everyone knows *what*? That after being friends and then good friends and then great friends and then *best* friends I'm left lying awake at night and thinking about the way the muscles in Trent's forearms flex and move when we're playing together? When he doesn't catch me looking, my mouth going a little dry?

Does everyone know that I've fucking memorized his tattoos from looking at them so much? That I know where he got each and every one of them, or do they all know that he's got a raven on one shoulder that I *fantasize* about licking? Do they know that I've thought a billion and one times about what his body would feel like wrapped in my legs?

45

That one's a popular jerk off fantasy of mine. So's the one where we're in my kitchen and he bends me over the counter, mouth on the back of my neck. Or the one where we're on the patio furniture in his back yard and I'm straddling him, or the one where we're in the studio and everyone has left and I'm on the mixer's chair, Trent on his knees, face between my thighs.

Okay, they're all popular fantasies. Point being, I think about fucking my best friend a whole goddamn lot for someone who *does not want to fuck her best friend*.

Besides, I think it's one-sided. It's not that I don't think Trent cares for me deeply — I'm not stupid — but I don't think it's *that* way. I think he considers me his honorary little sister, the sibling he *can* help.

Cutting my hair? Total little sister move.

As I'm sitting there, sleep still fading from my brain, worrying about whether people think I have a *thing* for Trent, I hear voices outside my hospital room.

"—how to change the dressing," the nurse is saying.

She gives a quick *not asking permission, just warning you that I'm coming in no matter what* knock, and then Trent follows her into my hospital room, hands in his pockets, face serious, split lip slightly less swollen.

I was totally not just thinking dirty thoughts about you.

"How are we feeling?" the nurse asks cheerily. I think I can hear the Dakotas in her voice. Somewhere Midwestern for sure.

"*We're* feeling much better," I say, the sarcasm slipping out.

Behind her, Trent looks away, and I can tell he's trying not to smirk.

"That's *great*," the nurse says, picking up the giant wedge pillow from the floor. "All right, if you're

46

rearrange yourself onto this wedge, I'm just going to show your young man how to change the bandages on your wound—"

"Him?" I ask.

"Of course."

"He doesn't need to do that," I say quickly.

I haven't gotten a good look at my back yet, it being my back and all, but I know it's pretty gross and I could do without Trent seeing me at my most disgusting.

"Someone's gotta know how to do it for when you're released," he says, shrugging.

"I can just come back here, it's fine," I say.

I've already decided that it's easier to stay here, in Tallwood, for the next three weeks rather than fly back to Los Angeles. Planes are bad enough when your entire back *isn't* a blister-covered fresh burn.

"Twice a day," Trent says. "You're gonna rent a car, drive here, wait, get them changed, drive back, then do it again?"

"I don't have anything else to do."

The nurse glances at her watch.

"Darcy, come on. This is way easier."

He's right and I know it, but I don't like it. Changing bandages is like changing a diaper, somehow. A gross thing that you do for someone because you *have* to.

"No. It's disgusting, it's all blistered and oozy and there's blood, and it's just... gross."

"I've seen worse."

"No, you haven't."

"I promise you I have."

The nurse clears her throat. I stare at Trent, trying to get him to look away, but he doesn't. He just stares back, ink-covered arms crossed in front of his chest.

Fuck. I think I'm losing this one.

"Fine," I mutter, swinging my legs over the edge of my hospital bed. "But when you have nightmares about slime monsters and shit, don't come crying to me."

"I think I can deal," he says softly, and for a second I feel bad. Trent *does* have nightmares, and the only people who knows about them are me and the therapist I finally talked him into seeing.

I mouth the word *sorry*, and he shrugs a little before I flop onto the wedge pillow that I am *not* calling the fuck wedge.

"All right," the nurse says cheerily. "Now, clearly, step one is to remove the old bandage, and you want to do that as quickly and carefully as you can, though it's still going to hurt a little..."

I squeeze my eyes shut. *Look away*, I think, even though I know he doesn't.

"Ew," Trent says when the bandages are off, but I don't have to look to know he's laughing.

I sigh into the fuck wedge.

CHAPTER NINE
Trent

It's gross, but it's a *mildly unpleasant* gross. Her back is bright red from her left hip to her right shoulder, dotted with yellow button-sized blisters. It's shining wetly, and it sure doesn't look *fun*, but I've seen grosser.

Bone sticking out of a guy's arm? Check. Welts on my brother's back so swollen and infected they looked like he was smuggling giant slugs underneath his skin? Check.

The right side of my mom's face so black and blue I barely recognized her? Also check.

Like I said, Darcy's burn is *mildly unpleasant* to look at. Like taking a shower after everyone else in your family, so the water only heats up to lukewarm.

"She's doing well enough that we're giving her a new type of dressing," the nurse says, handing me latex gloves. I pull them on and they stretch like balloons on my hands.

"We'll get you some extra-large ones," the nurse says, adjusting hers. "First, we spray the wound with this anti-bacterial spray. Very important that you don't let anything touch the wound, since at this point our number one concern is infection..."

The whole process is pretty simple: take a bandage off, put new stuff on Darcy's back, put a new bandage on, tape it to her skin. The hardest part is the end, when we have to wrap her in bandages again, and she sits up, topless, with only a hospital gown hanging loosely around her neck as I hand her the roll, she wraps it around herself, and hands it back to me from the other side.

She's hurt, I keep telling myself. *She's hurt and you're helping, you goddamn pervert.*

"Very nice," the nurse says when we're finished, checking out my work. "Make sure you don't put these on too tightly, or they might irritate the wound. Now, you remember the first rule of burn care?"

Darcy and I look at each other.

"Don't... fuck it up?" she asks.

"Right, don't let *anything* that isn't sterile touch the burn," the nurse says, even though Darcy got it pretty wrong. "Let me get your vitals one more time, you can fill out some paperwork, and you're ready to go home."

• • •

A couple hours later, they let Darcy leave, or at least to the Snokamie River Inn where we're staying. She doesn't say anything the whole ride until I shut off the car and reach for the door handle.

Then: "Hey, Trent?"

She's staring straight ahead, like she's nervous about something. She's wearing a t-shirt of mine that I brought her along with a pair of workout shorts, the only thing I had that would even come close to fitting her, so she wouldn't have to wear a hospital gown out of the hospital.

The outfit she was wearing last night is... crispy.

"Yes, Darcy?" I answer, hand still on the door handle.

"You don't have to do this," she says, twirling one finger in the hem of the shirt she's wearing, eyes still dead ahead through the windshield. "I really don't mind going back in so they can change the bandages at the hospital, it's not like I've got anything better to do. Just in case you've had second thoughts or something, I mean, I know back at the hospital you didn't want to look like you were a bad friend or whatever in front of the nurses, but I can tell them that something came up in Los Angeles and you had to—"

I open the car door, cutting her off.

"For fuck's sake," I say mildly, and get out of the car. Darcy shoots me a frown as I leave, then slowly unbuckles herself as I walk around the car. I open her door before she finishes, offering her my hand.

She sighs, makes a face at it, but she takes it and I pull her up.

"Bring it up again and I'll carry you into the woods so you're eaten by bears," I tell her.

"That seems kind of extreme," she says, taking a deep breath, her face pale. I can tell that everything hurts, especially since the hospital didn't want her taking anything more serious than ibuprofen once she left. I grab a plastic bag with her stuff and shut the car door.

"Also, I can walk," she points out. "And I can walk away from bears just as well as you can, so your plan is dumb."

"Grizzly bears can sprint at up to forty miles per hour," I say.

"There aren't grizzly bears here, just the little kind."

"They've been reintroduced to the Pacific Northwest, and the *little kind* of bear can still fuck you up, so quit asking whether I really want to stay here and care for your disgusting back or not, because it's happening."

We walk through the lobby of the Snokamie River Lodge, which looks exactly like a lodge in Washington State should: made of enormous logs, supple leather furniture, vast stone fireplace with a mounted buffalo head on one side and an elk on the other.

"Thanks," she finally says when we reach the other side of the lobby, and I look down at her.

Darcy breaks my fucking heart sometimes, because as much as she acts like she's made of broken glass wrapped in barbed wire, I know her more than well enough to know better. And I hate that deep down, she thinks I only volunteered to help her so I'd look good to the nurses, or that I don't *really* want to be here with her.

My life was pretty fucked up for a pretty long time, but at least I know what being loved feels like. Sometimes it was toxic and sometimes it fucking hurt, but my mom really did love me. My little brother Eli really did love me, even if they were awful at showing it.

But Darcy? There's a reason she's got spikes a mile long.

"You're welcome," I finally say, even though it isn't one hundredth of what I want to say to her. We reach our rooms in more silence, then say goodnight to each other.

When I'm inside I don't turn the lights on, just toss my keycard onto a table and slump onto a couch, my face in my hands. I accidentally bump my split lip and remember again that I've got it.

That black hole deep inside me is still there. Punching the guy who fucked up the fireworks didn't make it go away. Knowing that Darcy is gonna be fine a couple of weeks didn't make it go away.

It's still there, small but heavy and sharp, gnawing at me. Saying things like *maybe he should get lit on*

52

fire, see how he likes it, and I know better than to listen to it but times like this, when I'm tired and it's dark and I can't stop thinking about the way Darcy clenches her jaw in pain every time she moves the wrong way, that it's the most tempting.

I take a deep breath. I clench my hands, unclench them, and don't punch anything, not even a pillow. I just go to bed.

CHAPTER TEN
Darcy

Twelve hours. I brush my teeth, fall into bed, and sleep for twelve damn hours.

When I wake up I'm on my stomach, diagonal across the giant king-sized bed, light filtering in from the curtain-covered window.

My first thought is, *I'm not at the hospital!*

My second thought is, *Are these curtains bear-patterned?*

I look around my room. Several things seem to be covered in bear-patterned fabric. When in Rome, I guess.

I get up. I pop a couple of ibuprofen, pull on shorts and a t-shirt, and find the coffee maker in my suite's tiny kitchenette and poke it a couple times.

That doesn't produce any damn coffee, so I slide my feet into flip-flops and head down to the lobby. The halls of this hotel, like pretty much every hotel in the world, have several huge mirrors in them. As I walk coffee-ward I can see my reflection even though I try not to look.

My hair's an unholy fucking mess. My face is still banged up, my black eye starting to turn from purple to yellow, though it's less swollen now. At least I can see out of it better.

God, even my boobs look weird, squashed beneath an ace bandage. I have no idea when I'll be able to wear a bra again, but thank Christ my tits are insignificant enough that I can get away without one for a while.

I can't fucking believe this. Two nights on tour, and I get *lit on goddamn fire* by accident. Now I'm out of commission for a couple of weeks. Everything's on hold again. I swear to God, Dirtshine is cursed.

But I round the corner into the lobby of the hotel, and once I'm in there I can't help but smile. One, there are three large tankards of coffee, ready and waiting for me.

Two, the whole place is straight out of *Rustic Grandeur* monthly. There's even chandeliers made of antlers. Who *does* that?

I grab a mug of coffee, drain it in short order, refill it, and wander outside. I'm pretty much done with sitting around.

The lodge is *beautiful*, by the way. Tallwood, Washington is a pretty small town and the lodge is a couple miles outside of it, tucked away in the forest and surrounded by massive evergreen trees and miles of hiking trails.

It's lovely. It's peaceful and nature-filled, and I'm pretty sure Gavin picked it on purpose because no one else from Grizzly Fest is staying here. I know he's nervous about staying clean on tour, because it would be easy to fall back into old patterns.

That, and I think he still hates doing this without Liam. Despite everything, Gavin still misses him. Fuck, we all miss him, but some messes are just too out of control to deal with.

I reach the woods and start down a wide, well-maintained path. I drink coffee, stroll slowly, and try not to think.

Because something's been nagging at me for the past day, something that sends a bolt of anxiety straight through my core despite the gorgeous, peaceful setting. And thinking about Liam just makes it worse.

They don't *need* me. I'm just the bass player, and we're just on tour. Anyone could learn to play these songs, and then they wouldn't have to cut a couple of weeks from the tour and do all this rescheduling.

Honestly, it's kind of a good idea.

And I fucking hate it. I hate everything about it. The thought of Dirtshine playing shows without me makes my stomach feel like I've got poisonous snakes nesting there.

What if they realize that the new bass player is a better musician than me? What if they just *like* the new guy better, so once I'm recuperated, they tell me not to come back?

We replaced Liam, didn't we? And he was there from the very beginning. He and Gavin were practically brothers, and we *still* booted him. I know it's a completely different situation, but that doesn't really make me feel better.

I breathe and stare at the bark on a pine tree, counting my breaths. In is one and out is two, three and four, until I'm a little calmer. It's a meditation thing. Yeah, I fucking meditate, what about it?

You have to stop doing this, I tell myself. *Freaking yourself out about something that you invented is totally worthless.*

I started doing it as a kid. I don't think I'm like this by nature, though fuck knows I've got nothing to compare myself to. But for as long as I can remember, shitty things have happened to me, again and again. My earliest memory is of a woman whose name I don't remember packing my things into a black garbage bag and then driving me for ages across the snow-covered expanse of Wisconsin. It was probably a twenty-minute drive, but I remember it seeming endless.

I was freezing, so cold my fingers hurt, and I clenched them into fists. I didn't tell her I was cold or ask her to turn the heat up. In my memory, I already knew better. I think I was three.

But I developed this habit, expecting the worst. Because when you expect the worst you can plan for it. It can't take you by surprise. So when shit kept happening, my things shoved into garbage bags again and again for transport, kids at school surrounding me on the playground and giving me a bloody nose, or finally the sound of my foster father sneaking into our bedroom and whispering *don't be scared* to my foster sister, the girl who had the bad luck to be on the bottom bunk, I had a fucking plan.

It wasn't usually a good plan, but it was always *a plan*.

But I don't need that now. It's been fucking ages since the worst happened. For fuck's sake, Gavin *told me* that they were putting the tour on hold. He and Trent — and Liam, it used to be, too — are my new family, and even if I haven't got the firmest grasp on that concept, they deserve better than dumb suspicion from me.

Also Eddie. We like Eddie.

My coffee mug's empty, so I turn around and stroll back down the path toward the lodge, wondering what time it is. I didn't even check. Maybe I should text Trent and see where he is so he can change my damn bandages.

And my stomach ties itself into a knot right as I emerge from the woods, thinking about Trent in rubber gloves, applying bandages and ointment to my fucking gross burn wound. If I were looking for evidence that he's not interested, there it is, because who volunteers to look repeatedly at weeping sores on someone they wanna fuck?

Christ, it's not even noon yet — at least, I don't think it's noon, it's still cool and foggy out — and I'd already like a drink. I cut by the pool on the way to the lobby, and there's no one swimming, but there's someone stretched out on a lounge chair, talking on the phone.

Wearing cargo shorts and flip flops. I wave, but Eddie's not looking at me, totally absorbed in his phone conversation as I walk toward him.

"I dunno, man," he's saying. "There's just like, so much *punching?* Like, come on, dude."

I wonder if he finally saw *Fight Club* or something. Eddie's a good drummer, but he's also the kind of guy who'd watch a movie called *Fight Club* and complain about the punching.

"Yeah," he says, as I pass behind his lounge chair on the way to the lobby. "I mean, I get it, I just feel really bad? But like, I can't just..."

His voice fades as I walk past, back into the lobby, where I refill my mug again and sit on a huge, plush, overstuffed leather chair and pick up a copy of *Modern Rustic Architecture*, because it's not like I've got somewhere to be right now.

And hot damn, this is the most soothing thing I've ever seen. It's mostly pictures of sharply angled, sparsely-furnished wooden houses built atop mountains emerging from the fog.

Given that every house I lived in until a year and a half ago housed at least seven people and was a cramped hell-hole, this is a peek into heaven. I'm so absorbed in the empty hallways and big, light-filled windows that I don't notice Eddie next to me until he says my name.

"Darce?"

I look up, blinking, because no one but Trent calls me that. Definitely not Eddie.

"What's up?" I ask.

He squirms a little in his overstuffed chair, looking at the buffalo head instead of me, and I feel bad. Eddie was *just* getting properly acquainted with the three of us last year when Gavin up and fucking punched the poor kid in the face.

Eddie *did* give Marisol, Gavin's girlfriend, pot-laced candy without telling her there was pot in it. And Marisol, who barely even drinks, *did* have a pretty awful time.

Still, there are a million goddamn ways to solve a problem without resorting to violence.

"You like," he starts. He squirms. I watch his face patiently. "You like, know lots of drummers, right?"

I get the weird feeling that he's trying to ask me something really strange and awkward. Like a kid who wants to know where babies come from but can't even formulate the right question.

"I guess?" I say. "I probably know about as many as you do, maybe slightly less?"

He nods, rubbing his hands on his cargo shorts.

"Why?" I ask.

"Oh, just, nothing, just wondering," he says, glancing nervously at the buffalo head. "I was thinking that I'm a drummer, and I know a lot of drummers, and then I was wondering if the rest of you also knew a lot of drummers, and...?"

I take a long sip of coffee, glancing around the lobby and wondering what the fuck Eddie is getting at right now.

Is he high? Is that why he wants to know how many drummers I know?

"I know lots of drummers," I confirm, hoping that my response soothes him.

"Cool. Great. Okay, cool," he says, standing. "Later?"

"Later!" I say, and he walks out of the lobby.

Musicians are a bunch of weirdo freaks, I think, and go back to looking at lovely, empty kitchens.

• • •

A while later, someone walks up behind me and puts his hands on the back of my chair. I'm curled up, drinking my fourth cup of coffee, carefully leaning back in a way that doesn't make my back hurt *too* much.

"There you are," Trent says.

"Was I hiding?" I ask, tilting my head back and looking at him.

Upside-down Trent lifts one eyebrow.

"Were you?" he asks. "You weren't answering your phone, I thought maybe you'd gone back to the hospital to keep me from doing your bandages."

"It did cross my mind," I admit.

"You're already an hour overdue."

I wrinkle my nose, but he *is* being very nice to me and he definitely doesn't have to be. I flop my magazine of soothing, peaceful interiors shut and toss it back on a coffee table fashioned from several logs.

"Your room or mine?" I ask.

"Supplies are in mine," he says.

Back in Trent's suite, I stand in the middle of his living room while he gathers the stuff he needs: size XL latex gloves, antiseptic burn spray, more giant bandages, tape, gauze, ointment, a whole medicine cabinet's worth of stuff.

He organizes it very neatly on his table, frowning. It's the careful organization of someone who's not totally comfortable with the task at hand, and who doesn't want to fuck it up.

"I don't think the package of bandages is quite parallel with the box of gloves," I point out.

"So fix it."

"I wouldn't wanna mess up your system."

"You mean the system of trying to make sure I don't put toothpaste on your burn by accident? Shirt off," he says, not waiting for an answer.

"Close your eyes," I say, looking over my shoulder at him. A slight smile lights up his face as he holds his hands away from his body, trying not to touch anything with the gloves on.

"You know I've seen you naked."

"We were drunk."

"*You* were drunk."

I make a face, because he's right. Trent doesn't really drink, aside from a single beer now and then. I don't blame him. If I'd grown up with his father I doubt I'd drink either.

"And high," I say. "Are you thinking of the time I tore off all my clothes because I thought they were turning into pancake batter, or the time I made you come skinny dipping because I was convinced that the ocean would give us super powers?"

I can't help but picture it again: moonlight, waves, everything silver and black. Trent calmly telling me not to try breathing underwater, and then when we finally went back to shore, the crisscrossed scars on his huge, muscled back. It was before I knew. I remember thinking they weren't real, but they are.

"I was thinking of the time we were in St. Louis and one of the girls from Candyboots dared you to go in the Mississippi River, so you tore off all your clothes and went in right then and there just to prove you'd do it."

Fuck, I'd totally forgotten about that. It was *not* a good decision. That part of the Mississippi isn't for swimming.

"You still have to close your eyes," I say.

Trent dutifully closes his eyes, still smirking. My heart's going about two hundred beats a minute and there's a tiny voice in the back of my head saying *so*

Trent wants to see you topless, isn't that interesting? I ignore it.

I pull my shirt over my head, leaving my arms in the sleeves so my back is exposed but my boobs are covered. I'm still pretty fucking naked, though, and it makes the squirming in my stomach start all over again.

"Okay," I say, my face hot and my eyes closed, arms clamped tightly over my boobs.

He doesn't say anything, but he steps in close behind me, his fingers on my side. You wouldn't think a guy who looks like Trent or who's got Trent's life story would be as gentle as he is, but I barely feel it as he releases the Ace bandage from around my back.

"Hold your arms out," he says. I hesitate for a split second, because *my boobs*, but just do it.

He circles his arms around me, handing the bandage to himself as he unwraps it from my body, and his chest brushes lightly against my back.

"Sorry," he murmurs.

"It's fine," I say, eyes squeezed shut, because here's another good reason that I should have just gone back to the hospital: having some nurse change my bandage wouldn't go directly into my spank bank, or whatever the fuck chicks are supposed to call it.

But I'm practically naked with my *very hot* best friend who's being *very sweet* right now, and in this moment, it doesn't matter that I fucking know better. It barely matters that he's about to witness me at my grossest, because rational thought has left the building.

Fuck, I want Trent to touch me. Grab my tits, kiss my neck, bite my earlobe, but he just keeps unwinding the bandage from around my body, brushing his thick arms against my torso, tattoos dancing and flexing in the low light.

And he's being a total fucking gentleman about it, because he always is. To me, anyway. God knows I've seen Trent do some ungentlemanly shit. For fuck's sake, right now he's got a split lip and won't tell me why.

Trent places the wrap bandage on the table next to him, and I hug my arms to my chest again. He brushes my hair away from my neck, his fingertips tickling me, then picks lightly at the tape holding the second bandage around the burn.

"This might hurt when I take it off," he says, his voice soft and low and quiet. I focus on an easy chair, patterned with a black bear and a couple of frolicking cubs.

"It's fine," I say.

He's right. It does hurt, and my eyes water, but I don't say anything as he gets it off crumples it up, and tosses it into the trash. The air is cool against my back, slightly damp from being covered and probably from gross burn blister leakage.

We don't say anything while he does the rest. I just stand there, head down to keep my hair off my back, half-naked. As much as I wish he weren't looking at blisters on my back, something about Trent's hands on me feels right, like he already knows his way around my body.

Quit it, I tell myself.

Once all the antiseptics and ointments and whatnot are on, he tapes a new bandage on, his fingers pressing carefully along the skin of my shoulder, the back of my neck, the side of my hip, and I shiver lightly at every single touch. Finally, I hold the ace bandage while he wraps it around me again, still without saying anything.

I pull my shirt back on, shake my hair out, and turn. "Thanks," I say.

Trent just smiles as he pulls his gloves off.

CHAPTER ELEVEN
Trent

I'm on the couch in my suite, feet up, slouched halfway down and staring at some TV show about mountain men who hunt deer with their bare hands or some shit. I'm not thinking about Darcy taking her shirt off earlier. I'm not thinking about her skin under my fingertips, about smelling her hair with my arms around her, or about how seeing her half-naked got me instantly hard as a rock, burn blisters or no burn blisters.

Nope. I'm just watching this television show, featuring a man whose snot has frozen into his mustache.

My phone rings. It's Nigel.

"Hey Nigel," I answer.

"Hello there Trent, it's Nigel," he says. It doesn't matter how I answer my phone, he still identifies himself to me every single time he calls.

"Right," I say. "Listen, so I went through that list of tour venues you asked me to look at, and—"

"I'm *so* sorry to interrupt, but that's actually not why I'm calling," he says.

Nigel sounds... weird. Nervous. Upset. And yes, the poor man usually sounds that way, but that's just his voice. This sounds for *real*.

"Is everything okay?" I ask, sitting forward and putting my feet on the floor. "I mean, you know, relatively?"

"Would you mind coming around to my suite in about fifteen minutes?" he asks, a strangely polite edge to his voice.

"What's going on?"

"Just come, please."

"Nigel, is something *wrong?*"

"See you there!" he says, and the call ends, his faux-cheery British tones still ringing in my ears.

I don't bother waiting the fifteen minutes.

• • •

When Nigel lets me into his suite, Eddie and Gavin are already there, and as I'm exchanging a *what the fuck is going on* look with the latter, Darcy knocks on the door and Nigel lets her in.

No one says anything, but she lifts her eyebrows at me.

I shrug.

Nigel sighs far more dramatically than you'd think a British man could, and then holds out one hand to his suite's dining table.

"Please sit," he says.

We obey, because we're way too confused to do anything else.

"Nigel, mate, is something wrong?" Gavin asks, leaning on his elbows across the table. "Whatever it is, we'll help."

Nigel just folds his hands, then looks pointedly at Eddie. Eddie's looking down at his hands.

For a long, long moment, no one says anything, and then Eddie takes a deep breath.

"I'm quitting the band," he says.

Dead fucking silence.

It's so unexpected that I'm just fucking *baffled* for a moment.

"What?" Gavin says, clearly having the same reaction I am.

"You can't," Darcy says, her voice already rising.

Still looking at his hands, Eddie nods.

"I think it's best for everyone if we—"

"Are you *fucking* serious?" Darcy says, her voice cutting through the room.

Eddie looks at her, eyes wide, and clears his throat.

"I've thought this decision through very carefully, and I think that my creative—"

"No you fucking didn't," she says. "You've never thought a thing through carefully in your entire goddamn life."

"We're *two shows* into a tour," Gavin adds in, still sounding more baffled than angry.

"You've got three weeks off now, I'm sure you'll find someone to fill in—"

"We don't want someone to fill in!" Darcy shouts. "We want someone to *be in our goddamned band*!"

"Eddie," Gavin says, jabbing one finger into the table, his voice nearly shaking with the strain of sounding reasonable. "Reconsider. You can't just leave now, we've got a massive tour all planned out and we *really do* need a drummer to complete it."

"You are *fucking us over*," Darcy says. "Did you think that through very carefully too? Or did you just think 'fuck these guys' and that was as far as you got?"

"Look, I'm sorry, but you've totally got time to—"

I stand up so fast my chair topples over, and everyone stops, turns, looks at me.

I walk away from the table and stalk ten feet away, seeing black because I think I could strangle Eddie right now.

That fucking *asshole*. Just when we get everything back on track, *just* when it seems like things might be going okay for once, he fucking up and quits the band.

In the middle of a goddamn tour, and then he acts like he's a fucking saint because we've got three weeks to find a replacement. Three fucking weeks.

It took us three *months* to find Eddie when we had to kick Liam out. Apparently, we should have taken longer.

What a shithead. Three weeks. Three *goddamn* weeks.

"No, I said you're a fucking inconsiderate prick, and you are," Darcy shouts. "Who the fuck joins a band, *starts a tour*, and then decides to fuck that band over?"

"The point wasn't to fuck you over—"

"*Please,* tell us the point then," Gavin says. "I sure fucking hope it's a good one."

"I'm going on tour with my side project. Stingraze."

I just turn and stare.

He's fucking going on tour with his *side project*. Leaving behind Dirtshine and arena shows and a platinum album for *his fucking side project*.

"Are you serious?" Darcy's voice is so vicious it's almost a snarl.

Silence.

"You fucking *cock*," Gavin mutters.

I feel fucking ugly right now, like I might throw shit, or like the shit I throw might be Eddie, because there's the rational, normal reaction to anger and then there's the reaction I've got sometimes, which is anything but.

"Are you fucking kidding me right now?" Eddie finally says.

"No, I'm not fucking kidding you, why would I be fucking kidding about how *bloody pissed* I am that you're leaving after two tour dates?" Gavin says, his voice rising.

"You *punched* me!" Eddie shouts.

"But you didn't fucking leave *then*, did you? You were happy to keep on sucking at the Dirtshine teat for another whole year!"

A chair scrapes back, then another.

"Guys," Darcy says.

"I should have left then!" Eddie shouts.

"Fucking right!"

"The three of you are total psychopaths," Eddie goes on, starting to really get worked up. "*You* fucking punched me, Trent fucking got medieval on that poor bastard the other night with the fireworks, *you're* a dismissive bitch who can barely be bothered to give me the time of day—"

FUCK no.

In half a second I'm back, both palms flat on the table, leaning toward Eddie.

"It's fuck you o'clock!" Darcy shouts. "How's that?"

"*What* did you just say?" I ask Eddie, my voice deadly calm, cutting through the racket.

"You *fucking drugged* my girlfriend!" Gavin shouts.

"Call Darcy a bitch again," I say.

Now the black is pounding through my veins with every heartbeat. Eddie can say whatever he wants about me, but Darcy?

No. Fuck no.

"Fucking ass-clown shithead cocktool dickface idiot mouthbreathing drummer," Darcy says. "*Fuck* you."

"You gonna get upset about her calling me *that*?" Eddie says, almost hysterical, talking to me and pointing at Darcy. "Or do you not want to fuck me, so it doesn't matter?"

"You don't know *shit*," I growl, and start for him around the table.

Eddie's eyes go wide, but Darcy grabs my arm, her strong fingers digging in, her eyes flashing.

"Don't," she says. "It's fine."

Gavin glares at Eddie, then the two of us, and turns to leave. The door slams behind him.

"Just fucking go," Darcy says through her teeth. "Don't make this worse."

I swallow. I know she's right, but what he said just keeps ringing through my ears, pounding through my veins as she pulls at my arm.

"Seriously," she says, and her voice is still brittle and angry but now there's a softer, pleading note in it and that's what finally makes the black fade a little. I clear my throat.

"Liam was miles better than you," I tell Eddie. "Even blitzed out of his mind."

It feels like all the air sucks out of the room. I turn and walk for the door.

"Buy some fucking pants!" Darcy says, following me. "Shorts are for children."

I head through the door, into the hallway, Darcy right behind me. Poor Nigel is still sitting at the table in the same room as Eddie, though I have a feeling he knew how that was going to go.

Darcy turns and storms down the hallway. I don't follow her. There's a window at the other end and I walk to that, shoving my hands in my pockets, and stare out at the forest, still shaking with rage.

Dismissive bitch, I think, and it feels like poison trickling through my veins.

Fuck him. Fuck Eddie and his easy insults.

Fuck him because he was supposed to be our friend, because he was supposed to be our *bandmate*, only to say *that* to her. The same thing that assholes everywhere keep saying about her, the same shit lowbrow music critics and neckbearded jackoffs who live in their moms' basements say about her.

I could tear Eddie's goddamn head off right now.

I don't do anything. I'm shaking with anger but all I do is lean my forehead against the cool glass of the window. It would be so fucking satisfying, but I can do better. I didn't the other night, but I can right now.

I've seen what'll happen if I *don't* do better. I lived with it for eighteen years, and I've got no intention of making anyone else's life that kind of hell.

It takes a long time, but the blackness eventually recedes. The rage subsides. My hands stop itching to strangle someone, so I stand up straight, open my eyes, and take a deep breath.

Then I go downstairs and head outside, because I desperately need to clear my head.

CHAPTER TWELVE
Darcy

I'm crying from sheer rage by the time I get back to my room. I fucking *hate* that I cry when I'm angry, but I do it every single time and it makes me crazy.

Sad? A few tears.

Furious? Full-blown snot-fest red-faced meltdown, complete with sobbing and hiccups. It's the fucking worst.

I'd throw myself dramatically on the bed, but my back's too fucked up so I lean my elbows on the counter in my tiny suite kitchen and gulp air, trying to make myself calm down.

But Eddie's leaving. He's leaving us for another band, right in the middle of our tour. And it's not even a good band, it's some crappy jam band that no one's ever heard of.

It has to be because he doesn't like us. What other explanation is there?

I thought we were okay, I think. *I thought we'd fought and made up, like bands do.*

Like friends do.

I fucking guess not, because he sure seems okay with leaving. And he sure as *fuck* seems okay with being a complete and total dick about leaving.

He's been with us for a year. No, it wasn't the smoothest year, but there aren't a lot of smooth years when you're a professional rock musician.

And he was part of us. We worked out songs together, we fucked around in the studio, we played music until it sounded right, we hung out trying new things until four in the morning and then we got breakfast burritos as the sun rose.

Eddie wasn't just *some drummer*. He was one of us. He wasn't Liam, and we all knew that, but we fucking tried. We weren't there yet but we *wanted* him to be one of us, part of our little made up family.

And fuck, I thought it *was* working.

Guess I thought wrong.

• • •

A couple hours later, I wake up face down on the bed, pants, socks, and shoes all still on. My spine feels weird, probably from falling asleep in the worst position possible, so I take a deep breath and push myself up slowly until I'm sitting.

The burn on my back protests, and my mouth tastes kind of like the comforter. Guess I'm still exhausted from the last couple of days, because I barely even remember getting on the bed before I passed out.

I splash my splotchy, red, one-black-eye, puffy-from sleeping-weird face off in the bathroom, then head down to the lobby. I've got a dim memory that the lodge has a free happy hour every afternoon from five to seven, and that's now.

I'm not really supposed to drink, since alcohol isn't *great* for healing wounds, but good advice can go fuck itself. Eddie's leaving the band just when I thought everything was okay again, and I want a goddamn glass of wine.

No one I know is in the lobby, which is just as well. Eddie's probably not showing his face right now — good, because I don't want to *see* his face — poor Nigel is probably dealing with Eddie's shit, Gavin's stone cold sober and has been for a year, and Trent barely drinks and is probably off in the woods wrestling a bear or howling at the sun or whatever's going to make him feel better.

The other people at the lodge are older, mostly dressed in casual-but-obviously-expensive cardigans and shit, all laugh very politely, and are almost 100% white. My ratty haircut, black eye, and torn jeans don't exactly fit in.

I grab a glass of red wine anyway. The bartender tells me what winery and vintage it is. I nod politely, like I give a shit, then start looking for the exit.

There's a printed sign on it, the font loopy and adorable: *no alcohol outside, please*.

I push it open and walk out. It's warmer than it was this morning, the late afternoon shadows stretching from the forest to the lodge, the scent of pine on a slight breeze wafting across the patio and the pool.

It's lovely. It's idyllic. And Eddie fucking left Dirtshine, so all the lovely idyllic places in the world can go fuck themselves. I walk along the patio, past the pool, and around the side of the lodge where I this morning, I saw a fire escape with the bottom ladder extended. It goes past a few windows and to the roof, which is only two stories up.

Climbing a ladder with a glass of wine in one hand and a fucked-up back isn't easy and it's sure as shit not smart, but it's only about ten feet before the metal stairs start and I take those all the way up. From the top platform, the roof is waist-high and sloped, so I set my wine glass on it very carefully and hoist myself up.

And nearly fall off. Fucking *Christ* that hurts, and I almost slip off and tumble back to the fire escape. At the last second, I kick and scoot myself forward, t-shirt catching on the roof tiles, facedown, back screaming in pain.

Jesus, that was dumb. I lie there for a long moment, forcing myself to breathe deep, willing the pain away until it finally subsides. Slowly, I manage to crawl onto the roof until I'm seated, feet planted, elbows on knees. My back still hurts but it's not as bad now.

And hey: I didn't spill my wine. Small victories, right?

I sit there. I stare at the woods beyond the lodge and think about every single time I've been mean to Eddie when he probably didn't deserve it. I wonder if this is my fault. If I didn't make him feel enough like part of us. If I brought up Liam once too often, if I should have gone out of my way to be nicer to Eddie.

I watch the shadows get longer while I sip my wine. After a while I try not to think even though it feels like everything is cracking apart.

CHAPTER THIRTEEN
Trent

I stay outside for longer than I mean to, but you know what? It fucking helps. I've always found nature relaxing. Even in Low Valley, as a kid, I loved exploring the shitty desert dirt lots that were around my parents' single-wide, the dirt cracked by the sun, the mountains looming off in the distance.

When I was six or so, my mom somehow got us a set of nature-themed encyclopedias. I have no idea where she got them or how she managed to use money for something useful before my dad spent it on beer, but I *loved* those things. I used to take them into the room I shared with Eli, my little brother, and pour over them until the ink started fading from the pages, since they weren't particularly high-quality.

I remember the first time I saw a big tree. It's probably a weird thing to remember, but I was ten and we were visiting my mom's sister who lived in some shitty town in the foothills of the Sierras, a couple hours north of Low Valley, and I just remember that the trees there were gigantic, towering all the way to the sky.

Of course, my mom and my aunt got into a huge fight about something, probably my dad, and we never went back. I always hoped we would, though.

I don't have a map or anything, and when I come out of the woods, I'm not at the trailhead where I entered. For a moment I pause, hoping that I'm at least back at the right lodge — I was pretty pissed when I left, and I wasn't really paying attention to where I was going.

There's someone on the roof. I walk closer.

It's someone who looks a lot like Darcy, and she's got a glass of wine in her hand, so I walk up to the building.

"Are you supposed to be up there?" I call, crossing my arms over my chest.

She flips me off.

"Are you supposed to be *drinking* up there?"

She tries to flip me off with her other hand as well, but she's got a wine glass in that one and it doesn't work very well.

I almost don't go up. I think of Eddie telling Gavin and Nigel and her that everyone knows I want to fuck her, and I think *prove him wrong, just go back to your own room. Watch shitty TV. Start calling all the drummers you know.*

But then I look back at her, middle fingers down, shoulders slumped forward, elbows on knees, and I think: *who fucking cares what Eddie says?*

A minute later I hop onto the roof from the fire escape and sit next to Darcy, leaning back on my hands. She swirls the wine around her glass, then takes a sip.

"Edward Penishands," she says after a moment, her voice thoughtful and distant.

"It was clearly a man with two dildos strapped to his fists," I say, looking out at the woods. "It looked like he was crotch-punching the actress."

Darcy snort-laughs.

"I'm sure someone's into that," she says.

"I dunno who," I say. "I was sixteen when we stole it from the back room of the video store, and I couldn't even jerk off to it *then*."

Darcy doesn't look at me, just takes another sip of her wine. I think she turns faintly pink, the color flushing over her cheeks, past the purple and yellow of her eye.

"There wasn't even one redeeming scene?" she asks, looking at me. "You watched a whole porno as a teenager with zero jerkoffs?"

"There was one," I admit grudgingly. "At the end, he gets cured of his dick-hand problem, and the big climax is him banging the girl with his normal dick. That wasn't too bad."

She's slightly pinker, looking out over the forest, and I wonder if she's thinking about the movie or if she's thinking about *me*.

"Did he have to get an erection to do anything with his hands?" she asks, looking over at me.

The movie, I guess.

"I don't remember," I tell her. "I wasn't particularly focused on the world-building aspects of the movie."

"Sounds like a real handicap," she muses. "Ever touched something that's been in the oven with your regular hand? Now imagine it's dick instead."

"I'd rather not."

"And you'd need to be *constantly* aroused to get anything done," she says, then tilts her head back and drains the last of her wine glass. "Otherwise, your hands are just... floppy, pointless noodles."

"Pointless. Thanks," I deadpan, and Darcy laughs.

"Did he pee from his hands?" she says.

"You're really asking for a deep dive into a porno I watch once ten years ago," I say. "I probably couldn't have told you the plot points right after I finished watching."

"Well, we've got three weeks and nothing to do," she says, and there's a long pause. "Except find a new drummer, I guess."

That's why she's up here. I had a feeling. We don't say anything for a long moment, because I'm not any better at this feelings shit than she is.

"Remember when Liam left?" she finally says, her voice quiet and distant.

"You mean when we kicked him out?"

Darcy blows air out of one side of her mouth, and a strand of dark hair flies up.

"Yeah," she says, her voice quiet and distant. "I *really* thought Dirtshine was done."

"I thought it was done the night we found them," I say.

"Then too," she agrees.

We sit there in silence for another moment as the sun lowers in the sky, and I try not to think about it again.

It's fucking seared in my memory forever, the second-worst night of my life: Darcy and I in the hall outside their hotel room, the four of us supposed to be on stage an hour and a half before, Liam and Gavin not answering the door.

Darcy and I pacing back and forth, arguing about where the fuck they could possibly *be* if they weren't in Liam's room. I was so *fucking* pissed at Gavin and Liam. For pulling this shit yet again and for being a couple of goddamn useless junkies who I had to babysit for the whole fucking tour.

And then, a memory in slow motion: a groan from inside the room, loud enough that even out in the hallway, we both heard it and stopped cold.

A bad, painful, familiar-as-fuck groan, and Darcy and I looking at each other, wide-eyed, her face white with sudden fear.

I don't remember deciding to kick the door in. I only remember my foot connecting with the solid wood, and I remember that it took a couple blows before the lock cracked the frame and the door flew open.

There were three of them. Gavin, Liam, and Allen, one of the roadies who'd been hanging out with them. Gavin and Liam still breathing but unconscious.

Darcy checked Allen's pulse. She had to find out he didn't have one. I still wish it had been me.

I remember standing in the hotel hallway, people swarming around, Darcy and I holding hands as tears slid down her face. Even though I felt like I'd been fucking gutted myself, I remember that I *hated*, fucking *hated* seeing Darcy like that.

I slept in her room that night, in the giant king bed. We didn't even touch, but neither of us wanted to be alone. I don't think either of us really slept, neither of us said anything, either, and even though it's been a year and a half, I still think about that night all the time. About how fucking awful it was and, despite *everything*, how in the morning I didn't want to leave.

How I just wanted to stay there, with her in that silence, a little longer.

"This isn't that," I finally say.

"I know," she says. "But I thought... I don't know. I thought we were better now. It finally felt like Eddie was really one of us, you know?"

I think of Eddie's voice saying *dismissive bitch* again, and my throat tightens in anger.

"Apparently, he didn't feel that way," I say.

"I wish I'd known," she goes on. "I would have been nicer or something to that dipshit."

"It wasn't you," I tell her. "But I did like 'it's fuck you o'clock.'"

Darcy laughs and leans her face against her hand. "I can't believe I said that."

"I can believe it. Have you *met* you?"

"It felt really clever at the time."

"I wish I could remember the rest of that insult."

"I think 'ass clown' was in there."

Darcy moves her wine glass to her other hand, stretches, and shifts so she's sitting cross-legged on the roof. I try not to watch the way her lithe body moves under her shirt, and I try not to think about how she's not wearing a bra.

"Twatwaffle? Did I use that one? It's pretty good," she says.

"I don't think you did."

"Damn."

We sit there for another long moment, the afternoon calm and peaceful, both of us lost in thought. I think again of Eddie shouting at everyone that I want to fuck Darcy, and I'm quietly thankful that we're just ignoring it.

"You think this glass would break if I threw it onto the grass?" Darcy asks.

"We're two stories up."

"But grass is *soft*."

"It's not that soft."

"We used to throw things into snowbanks and they wouldn't break," she says, peering over the edge.

She's arguing with me just to argue with me.

"This isn't snowbanks and beer steins," I say. "This is the ground and a wine glass."

"Beer steins? That's racist," Darcy teases, and I laugh.

"You *were* in Wisconsin," I point out.

"That's why it's racist."

"Well, throw it if you're gonna," I say. "Otherwise, it's bandage time."

Darcy sighs and makes a face, but she lets me help her off the roof. I hold the wine glass as we go down the fire escape, and drop it off in the lobby on the way to my room.

This time she just walks to the table and gets her shirt off, over her head, while I pull on gloves, then tries to undo the ace bandage herself, both hands behind her back.

I grab her wrists, gently pulling them away.

"Quit it," I say.

"I'm just trying to help."

"Well, fucking stop," I say.

That gets a laugh, and in a moment, I've got the hooks undone on the bandage and I'm unwrapping it around her. She's naked, nearly naked, inches away from me, and I don't give two shits if her back is covered in blisters, I *want* her.

I want her lips against mine. I want to kiss her neck and feel her heartbeat. I want to pinch her pink nipples and watch her arch her back with pleasure as she grabs onto me.

I want to sink myself into her and feel her come, want to hear her moan and *shout* because I know Darcy and I've got a feeling it'll be pretty fucking loud. I want to hear my name in her mouth and on her lips and I want to kiss her afterward and not let her go.

I unwind the last layer, my body vibrating. I'm hard as *fuck* and I can tell already that these three weeks are going to drive me completely fucking crazy.

But I also know there's no way I could be anywhere else.

"This might hurt," I say, pulling gently at the edges of the tape holding the second bandage on.

"I know," Darcy says.

I tug it off quickly, clean the burn, put all the stuff on, give her a new bandage. The whole time she stands there, head forward, the rounded vertebrae of her neck evident through her skin, a path for my lips.

I let myself slide one finger up it, like I'm moving her hair, and I could swear it raises goosebumps on her but I'm sure I'm seeing things.

"It looks better," I finally offer, taping her back up.

"Is it still gross?"

"Yeah, it's a real horror show back here," I deadpan. "Worst thing I've ever seen."

"Smartass," she mutters.

I smooth tape over her side, her hip, and then we re-do the ace bandage over everything and she pulls her shirt back on. Darcy turns and looks at me, her face somehow different than normal. Beautiful and vulnerable, soft in a way I almost never see her.

I swear to God I think she's going to kiss me, the way she studies my face for long moment, the way her perfect, plush lips just barely move.

I hold my breath, not speaking. I'm rooted to the floor, because right now this vulnerable, wounded girl has me fucking *powerless*.

"Okay," Darcy finally says. "You got dinner plans?"

I clear my throat, willing my voice back.

"No," I say, shoving my hands into my pockets. "You?"

"What do you think about ordering in Chinese and watching a dumb movie?"

"I think it sounds fucking perfect," I say, and the spell's broken.

Darcy pulls out her phone, starts searching, walks past me toward the couch. I pick up the TV remote to see if there's anything good on, and then we're talking about kung pao and fried rice and reruns.

And I think to myself, *I'm not gonna last.*

CHAPTER FOURTEEN
Darcy

The next day, Gavin and Nigel head back to Los Angeles. I guess Eddie leaves, too, though I don't really give a shit about where he goes.

We decide that, rather than try to find a *real* replacement drummer in two weeks, all we need for now is someone to finish out the tour. That'll be about a million times easier, and I don't think Gavin wants the responsibility of finding *a new drummer*, but he can handle finding a temporary drummer.

I think he wishes Trent and I were going with him, but plane travel sounds like a nightmare right now, and Trent's made it pretty fucking clear that he's staying with me. He's really dead set on seeing my gross back as much as possible, and I've given up arguing.

The two of us settle into a routine in the next few days, a cute little domestic-as-shit adorable routine. In the morning, whoever wakes up first hangs out in the lobby and drinks coffee until the other one shows up. We go change my bandages. We make breakfast in the tiny kitchenette, usually some variation on scrambled eggs. We play some music, we have a video chat with Trent about the drummer situation, we play some more music.

Once my back feels good enough for car rides, sometimes we go out in the afternoon: to downtown Tallwood, which is quaint as hell and very proud of its past as a major logging town; to Snokamie falls; to a lake that's not too far away.

Then I hit up the lodge's happy hour. We make dinner in the little kitchenette, because eating take-out gets old pretty fast. Then we pick a dumb movie and watch together, even though we usually end up talking over it.

He does my bandages again, and I go back to my room to go to bed.

I like it so much goddamn more than I should. Even though Trent and I have been friends for a while and *really close* for the past year, we've never spent this much time together. It's never even been close, but I like it, really *like* it in a way I wish I didn't.

Because it's really not healthy for me to want what I can't have.

· · ·

"You didn't have to come," I say, kicking my feet.

Trent crosses his arms over his chest, leans back in the chair, and keeps on scowling.

"I'm fine," he says.

I roll my eyes, leaning forward on the exam table, the paper under me crinkling.

"You're glaring the bejeezus out of every nurse who looks at you sideways," I say.

"Darce, I'm fucking fine," he says again.

"You can stay in the waiting room if you want," I offer. "Or the car. I could have driven here myself."

"You're not on the rental agreement, and I'm here so I can change your damn bandages correctly so stop

84

telling me to go be somewhere else, I'm already here and I'm staying," he says.

I shove my hair out of my face — I finally got it cut, so I look normal now, not like a five-year-old did it in my sleep — and grab a pamphlet off the wall titled DIABETES AND YOU. I tried to talk Trent out of coming, because I know he fucking hates doctors and hospitals and I knew he'd be grumpy this whole time, but he wouldn't take no for an answer.

I *could* kick him out, sure, but that would be pretty pointless, given that he's right. So I read about high blood sugar problems and the role of obesity in insulin resistance until there's a knock on the door and it opens, a women with graying hair and a lab coat breezing through.

"Hi, I'm Doctor Kowalski," she says, holding out one hand. "Darcy?"

We shake hands, and I introduce Trent. He *does* at least stand and try to be presentable, even though I can tell he's still in a dark, medical-facility-induced mood.

After a quick look at my vitals, all normal, Dr. Kowalski has me stand and undoes the ties down the back of my cloth gown as I hold the front tightly over my chest.

"You're healing nicely," she says as she peels away the bandage still stuck to me. "The blisters have really gone down. Hard to say how much scarring there might be, but it probably won't be too significant."

Scarring. I hadn't really even considered that yet, I'd just been worried about being able to move and *do* stuff again.

"I've got a good nurse," I say, nodding toward Trent.

"I can see that," the doctor says. "Any numbness or tingling? Any fever or joint pain?"

"Nothing," I say.

She cleans the wound off carefully and wraps me up again. Now Trent's leaning forward in his chair, elbows on his knees, paying close attention to what she's doing, asking her a few questions.

Finally, she turns me around and touches my bruised eye gently with two fingers, prodding it slightly like she's testing it.

"No impaired vision?" she asks.

I shake my head, and she looks over at Trent, who's still sitting in the chair.

"Would you mind giving us a moment alone?" the doctor asks.

Trent frowns slightly, but he gets up. I nod at him that it's fine, and he opens the door.

"I'll be in the waiting area," he says, and shuts it behind him.

"He doesn't like hospitals or doctors," I say. "Bad memories."

She nods.

"One of the things I'm trained to screen for is intimate partner violence," she says softly. "Particularly with injuries like yours, so do you mind if I ask how you got these?"

I almost laugh, and I almost tell her that Trent's not my *intimate partner*, just my friend, but I don't do either, because I don't mind some people thinking Trent's my boyfriend, even when they're asking if he hits me.

"I got lit on fire by a stray firework," I tell her, and explain the whole story. I know that it *must* be in my chart somewhere, and she *must* know about the bass player who was on fire, but I definitely made the Tallwood news.

But I think she wants confirmation from me, so I tell the story again. I do it clinically, trying to sound detached.

Like I don't remember that Trent saved my life, or that he held my hand in those seconds before help was there. Like I don't sometimes fall asleep thinking about Trent staying with me like that, being there for me in one of the worst moments of my life.

"There's video of it," I finish, and pause. "It wasn't Trent. He's never touched me."

The doctor just nods. I still don't tell her he's not my boyfriend, because it's oddly thrilling that someone thinks he is.

"Double-checking is part of my job," she says. "Better safe than sorry."

"Thanks," I say.

"Just so you know, it was the nature of your injuries, not the impression I got from you two," she says, sticking a pen through her bun. "Abusers don't tend to be quite so genuinely concerned. They're usually faking it."

I just nod. I feel horrible for Trent right now, probably sitting in the waiting room feeling miserable that he's here at all, not to mention the doctor just asked if he's been smacking me around.

"I see," I say.

We shake hands again. She lets herself out, I put my clothes back on over the new bandage, and leave the doctor's office. Trent's sitting in the waiting room and we walk out into the parking lot in silence. I almost say *they all think you're my boyfriend, isn't that funny*, but at the last second I decide to keep it to myself and keep pretending.

"It wasn't because of you," I finally say when we're in the car and he's driving out of the parking lot. "It's because I've got a black eye."

Trent checks traffic, waits for a car to pass, and pulls out.

"I know what it looks like," he says. "Believe me. She did the right thing, asking me to leave."

There's a long, long pause, as we drive down a curvy, tree-lined drive, Trent staring straight ahead.

Of course he knows what it looks like, I think.

"Thanks for coming with me," I finally say.

The corner of his mouth ticks up at last, and for the first time since we left for the doctor's office, I feel better because he's smiling.

"Of course," he says, then taps the steering wheel. He glances over at me, like he's thinking, then back at the road. "You wanna go get pie?"

"*Fuck* yes I wanna go get pie," I say.

• • •

We only found Aunt Sadie's House of Pies two days ago, but this is at least our fourth time here. Don't judge us. Pie's fucking delicious. We each order slices — I get apple with cheddar cheese on it, Trent gets cherry — and eat them in one of the old-fashioned wooden booths in the back.

"You know cheese on a pie is still wrong, right?" he asks, forking a pile of cherry into his mouth.

"Am I judging *your* pie choices right now?"

"Someone needed to tell you," he says, shrugging.

"I watched you put chili powder on watermelon the other day and I didn't say a damn thing," I point out.

"That's delicious."

"So is this!"

"I tried it. It's not."

I take another huge bite of cheese-topped apple pie and shrug at him.

"More for me," I say.

"You can have it."

"I will."

Trent swallows pie, then opens his mouth to say something. Instead he frowns and pulls his phone out of his pocket. He looks at it, then at me.

"It's Gavin, do I answer or pretend I'm in the shower?"

We've already talked to Gavin twice today, and I *almost* tell Trent not to answer, but the poor guy is scouting drummers all alone.

"Be nice, answer it," I say.

Trent makes a face, but pushes the green button, and Gavin's face pops up. He's in our recording studio, chin in hand, looking tired.

"Are you two eating pie again?" he asks.

I stab the final bite of mine and shove it into my mouth.

"No," I say, flaky bits of crust spraying out of my mouth.

"You were also eating pie the last time I called," Gavin says.

"That was this morning," I say, and swallow. "We weren't eating pie this morning."

"You've definitely eaten quite a lot of pie."

"Were you calling us to check on our diets?" Trent interrupts.

Gavin leans back, sighs, covers his face with his hands, and spins around in his chair. It's *very* dramatic.

"I still haven't got a drummer," he says. "I've found at least three who could do *some* of the tour but not all of it since everyone's got bands and tours and recording of their own, and finding an unattached drummer who I'd trust with this is..."

Trent and I just nod, in unison, in the pie shop.

"I'm still only partway through the list we brainstormed," he says. "I've got meetings tomorrow with another six bloody drummers, and God knows that at least one of them is going to show up here and say *tour? Oh I thought the advert said 'snore' and this was for a napathon* so I've got that to look forward to as well."

"Let us know if we can make any calls," I volunteer. I feel guilty just sitting up here eating pie and not helping, but there's also not that much I can *do* from here. One of the nice things about being a successful, famous musician is hiring people to do the messy work for you.

Gavin waves one hand.

"Nigel's done all the calling," he says. "Practically won't even let me near the phone, something about charging in and having no tact? I don't know what he's on about."

"Me either," I lie.

We all know the truth, and none of us is saying it out loud: until this time last year, Gavin was way more concerned about where his next fix was coming from than the logistics of a tour. There are plenty of people who wouldn't bother answering his calls.

"How's your back?" Gavin asks.

We chat for a few more minutes, giving Gavin the updates and the good news, even though there isn't a whole lot to talk about. Trent and I have started watching those dumb ghost hunter-type reality shows, but that's not the sort of thing you brag about.

That's the sort of thing that you keep secret with your best friend, because you know it's kind of a stupid thing to do.

"I ought to get home," Gavin finally says. "Since I'm unexpectedly in Los Angeles, I've been roped into some sort of corporate law firm event with Marisol and I think I've got to wear a suit and everything."

"Do you *own* a suit?" I ask.

I've sure never seen him in it. Gavin's good looking, I'd remember him in a suit.

"I'll have you know I own *two* suits," Gavin says, grinning.

Trent looks at me.

"We've lost him," he says, very seriously.

"First it's suits, then he'll be wanting to put synthesizer in all our songs," I say. "Maybe we should also just quit the band while we're ahead."

Gavin points at the camera.

"That's not bloody funny," he says, and the three of us laugh.

When we hang up, Trent leans back in the booth opposite me, hands on his head.

I look at my pie plate, smashing the crumbs between the tines of my fork, and try not to notice how it pulls his shirt tight against his chest, or how I can see *every* muscle in both his thick arms when he does this.

I notice nothing. *Nothing.*

"I gotta pee, then you ready to head back?" he asks, sliding out of the booth.

"Sure," I say. It's not like I had big plans in Tallwood today or something.

He saunters off to the men's room, and I do *not* crane my neck a little to watch him leave.

When Trent informed me that he was sticking around to take care of me and there was nothing I could do about it, a big part of me thought that maybe, *maybe*, being around him so much would cure me of my dumb crush on him, but it's done the goddamn opposite.

Now, every time he looks at me, I wonder what he's thinking. Whether he's thinking the same thing as me. If we accidentally touch hands, I wonder what would happen if I held on. I wonder what would happen if I leaned against him while we watched terrible made-for-TV movies at night.

Part of me desperately, *desperately* wants to try it, but what if he leaned away?

And what if he *didn't*? What if we fumbled through some make-outs, maybe even had sex a couple of times, only to find out that we just didn't click that way? Then what?

I can't give Trent up. I can't. And if keeping *this* means never getting to kiss him, never getting to straddle him on the couch while a stupid movie plays and—

His phone buzzes, jolting me out of my quick fantasy. It's still on the table, and he's still in the bathroom, so I pick it up.

The caller ID says COLLECT, and my stomach forms a tight ball. I'm pretty sure I know who's calling.

Fuck. *Fuck.*

Phone in hand, I slide out of the booth and stand, peering toward the men's bathroom. It buzzes again, but no sign of Trent.

Shit. I don't know what to do. I know he wouldn't want to miss this call, but it feels *really weird* to just answer his phone.

Another buzz. It'll go to voicemail next, and Trent can't possibly be more than another thirty seconds in the bathroom, so I think *fuck it*, hit the green button, and clear my throat.

"Hello?"

"Hello," says an automated voice. "This is a collect call from the North Delano State Correctional Facility. Please press 1 if you're willing to accept the charges."

I swallow hard, glance at the bathroom door, and wait a second. Still no Trent. I hit 1 on the keypad, palms sweaty.

"Thank you!" the voice says, sounding *way* too happy about this. "You will now be connected."

I wait. I stare at an old-fashioned sign on the wall of Aunt Sadie's — *Farm Fresh Milk, only 5¢!* — and I wait. Finally, there's a click on the other end of the line, and a man's voice.

"Hey, Trent," says a voice that sounds a *lot* like Trent.

I scrunch my toes in my shoes.

"This is Eli, right?" I ask, suddenly nervous.

"Yeah," he says, and pauses. "Who's this?"

"This is Trent's bandmate Darcy," I explain, still looking at the wall. "He'll be back in a second."

"You answered his phone?"

I blink at the wall.

"Yes, obviously," I say.

"Damn, girl," Eli says. "Damn."

There's a long pause, because I don't have a response for that. I'm not even sure what that *means*.

"So, is he gonna be back soon, or should I call later...?"

The men's bathroom door opens, and Trent steps out. I wave at him like a madwoman.

"Here he is!" I practically shout into the phone.

CHAPTER FIFTEEN
Trent

Darcy's waving at me like her car's broken down on the side of the road and I'm the first motorist she's seen in an hour. She's on the phone with someone, and after a second, I realize she's on *my* phone with someone.

"Here he is!" she chirps as soon as I'm close, and doesn't wait for a response from the other end before holding it out to me, eyes wide.

"IT'S YOUR BROTHER," she stage-whispers so loud that everyone in Aunt Sadie's hears.

Oh, fuck.

I take the phone as the cherry pie in my stomach turns to lead, every muscle in my body tensing. Eli and I talk the second Monday of every month, and I've never gotten a good call from him on any other day.

"Eli," I say, trying to sound casual. "What's up?"

"They moved me up the valley," my little brother says, his voice flat and affectless. Even though he's sounded like this for three years now, ever since he got to prison, it's still *deeply* weird.

94

"Up the valley to where?" I ask, even though I'm pretty sure I already know the answer.

"North D."

I turn and walk out of Aunt Sadie's, Darcy still wide-eyed behind me, the bells on the door clanging as they smack against the door.

"The fuck did you get moved to supermax for?" I ask, my voice rising.

"North D ain't supermax, it's regular max," Eli says. Still flat, like he's explaining how to pour concrete.

"Answer the question."

"These assholes came after me," he starts. "I don't know, man, I wasn't doing nothing and out of nowhere these three fuckin' cholos—"

I shut my eyes, because prison hasn't exactly made my idiot brother *less* racist.

"—Come up and, you know, they start talking some shit like *hey gringo, you know I like white ass-pussy—*"

"Spare me the soap opera and tell me what fucking happened."

There's a pause. I can practically hear the wheels turning in Eli's head.

"They came for me but I had a shiv because this other guy's been making noise about how he don't like me, and I gotta protect myself—"

"You stabbed someone?"

Silence.

"He still alive?" I ask.

Now I'm standing on the curb, facing into the street, watching the cars go by. I feel oddly detached, because it doesn't exactly *surprise* me that Eli's gone and stabbed someone.

Fuck, I wish it did. But I don't think anything he does can surprise me anymore.

"It was self-defense, man, they was comin' at me and what was I supposed to do?"

"Did you fucking kill someone else or not?"

"Nah, that fuckin' asshole is still alive, and his fuckin' friends are all probably laughing their asses off right now, about how they started some shit and I'm the one who got caught? Fuckin' *sneaky* sons of bitches, that's the thing, in here all the Mexicans stick together and all the Blacks always stick together but the second us white men start sticking together, it's—"

"Are you getting charged?" I ask, cutting off his next racially-themed rant. "Is that why you're calling me, so I can pay for your lawyer some more?"

"It was fuckin' self-defense, man, and they're trying for assault with a deadly weapon and a couple other things, and you *know* all that is bullshit," Eli says. "I got a right to defend myself. Even in here I got that. They came at *me*."

Just like that, anger *flares* through me, hot and black and poisonous. I have to take the phone away from my ear for a second, and I swear to God I almost pitch it into the street as hard as I fucking can.

Nothing's ever been Eli's fault. Not according to him. None of the shit he did as a teenager, stealing cars to joyride or smashing up store windows just because he could, usually fucking high or drunk or both.

When he got busted for assault and did eighteen months inside? Not his fault. He was totally being framed, according to him, because the police were out to get him. Nevermind that there was fucking security video footage.

There was video footage during the robbery, too, the one where he held up a liquor store with his idiot buddy, probably out of their minds on meth, and Eli beat the owner with a tire iron. He died later. Eli swore the tape was tampered with somehow, and now Eli's in prison for twenty-three more years.

But it's not his fault. It's just that everyone's out to get him. It's always been that way.

"Does Mom know?"

Now I'm pacing back and forth, *anything* to get the anger and frustration out of my system. The bells on the door jingle and Darcy comes out, arms folded across her chest, and looks at me questioningly.

I look away.

"I ain't told her yet. What's the point?"

"She should know where to visit you."

"She's not gonna know the difference."

"You should still fucking tell her."

Eli snorts.

"Yeah, sure," he says. "I gotta go. North Delano. My cigarette money's low, too, if you don't mind."

"You have to be *fucking* kidd—"

"Bye," he says, and there's a heavy click on the other end of the line. I'm left standing on the sidewalk, staring at the words CALL ENDED, my knuckles white from gripping my phone so hard.

I'm shaking, I'm so fucking mad. The only thing that keeps me from throwing my phone into the brick wall or into traffic is the fact that Darcy's standing right there, watching me, and she looks nervous.

So I shut my phone off. I put it into my pocket, and I don't even punch this fucking wall though I want to. I don't pick up the weathered wooden bench and throw it into the street, like I want to.

"How's Eli?" she finally asks.

I just shake my head and start pacing back and forth again, because I have to do *something*.

"That bad?"

"I fucking can't," I say, cracking all the knuckles on my right hand. "That fucking goddamn asshole, he calls me and then he acts like—"

I pass by Darcy again, still pacing, and she grabs my forearm, and any other time it would be like a lightning rod to my dick but I'm so *fucking* pissed at my brother that I just stop and glare at her.

"You're shouting," she says.

"Good, everyone can know what a shitshow my—"

Darcy puts a hand over my mouth. I'm so surprised that I stop shouting, I stop pacing, and we just look at each other. Her hand is small but strong, her fingertips calloused.

"You're gonna get us banned from Aunt Sadie's," she says, in a perfectly reasonable tone of voice. "Can you hang on one more minute, and I'll be right back?"

She takes her hand off my mouth without waiting for an answer, and a prickle of disappointment travels through me, even as my brother's dumb voice echoes through my head.

"Yeah," I say, and Darcy turns and disappears into Aunt Sadie's.

I get back to pacing. People on the sidewalk look at me weird, not that I give a shit. I don't even know why I'm so pissed, because what the fuck do a few more years in prison mean for Eli? He'll be forty-five when he gets out already, his twenties and thirties lost to orange jumpsuits, solitary confinement, stupid grudges against other prisoners and making toilet wine.

I just wanted something else for him, I guess. I wanted *him* to want better.

Darcy reappears a few minutes later, and I'm still pacing and fuming. She's got a whole pie in an aluminum tin, plastic lid, two plastic forks.

"Come on," she says, walking past me, and I just follow her. I don't know what the fuck else to do.

When we get to the car I unlock it. She puts the pie in the back seat and turns to me.

Then she grabs the keys out of my hand.

"Get in," she says, pointing at the passenger seat.

"You're not driving."

"Yes, I am. Get in."

"You're not on the rental agreement, you can't fucking—"

"I don't give a shit, Trent, and you're not driving like this so *get in the fucking car*."

I hold out one hand for the keys. She crosses her arms over her chest, keys tight in one hand, and glares at me.

"You're not driving like this."

"Like what?"

"Pissed about your brother."

"Darcy for *fuck's* sake I don't need you to fucking nanny me right now, I just need to fucking drive back to the fucking hotel, and—"

She opens the driver's side door, gets in, buckles her seat belt, and looks up at me, both eyebrows raised in her *so what are you gonna do about this* face.

"Motherfucker," I mutter, and walk around the car. Darcy's stubborn as a mule and she can be *impossible* to argue with sometimes, and besides, I haven't fucking got it in me right now.

Anyone else? Fuck 'em. But she's my weak spot and I lose every argument we have.

She starts the car and drives out of downtown Tallwood in silence. After about five minutes we're deep in the woods, on some winding two-lane road, the thick blue-green-gray pine forest surrounding us, the sound of wind whispering through the trees, and I feel myself start to unwind.

"Are we going back?" I finally ask.

"Nope."

"Where are we going?"

"You'll see."

I hate secrets and surprises, but I let her have this one. No harm in it, right?

We drive for a few more minutes, and there's nothing but forest and road, the occasional driveway to a house deep in the woods. It's astonishing how easy it is to get away from civilization here, how little time it takes before there's no other sign of human life.

I take a deep breath, because I'm still fucking angry but I don't feel so *dangerous* any more. I don't feel like I might just see white and hit something, then realize thirty seconds later that I've done something awful.

I'm not afraid of much, but I'm afraid of myself.

"He stabbed a guy and got moved to a maximum-security prison up the valley," I finally tell Darcy.

She steps on the brakes and looks over at me quickly, her blue eyes worried.

"Oh, shit," she says softly.

I tell her everything. She already knows the backstory, of course, but she just listens as she turns off the main road and onto a gravel one, the rental car bumping over ruts. After half a mile or so the gravel ends, and she pulls into a wide spot, then kills the engine.

"Come on," she says, getting out of the car, still moving a little gingerly.

I don't argue. I gave up arguing with Darcy, and I just follow her out.

The sound of the wind is even louder here, and it takes me a few moments to realize that it's not wind, it's rushing water.

Right at the edge of the little parking area is a huge, steep cliff, a river below about sixty feet down. There's no fence, no warning signs, *nothing.* There are a few spindly trees, but nothing strong enough to stop a car from going over.

Darcy points at a rock. It's about the size of my head.

"Throw it in," she says.

I look at her. She looks at me.

"Come on. Throw the rock into the river."

I almost protest. I'm still in a bad fucking mood, and I'm tempted to tell her that I don't want to throw fucking rocks into fucking rivers, I just want to go back to the hotel, but I'm already here.

"You'll feel better," she offers.

I don't think it's true, but I pick up the rock anyway.

"Over your head," Darcy says. "Really *launch* that bad boy. Maybe yell while you do it."

I heft it once. It's heavy, and I walk until I'm about a foot away from the edge, then lift the rock over my head.

This is fucking stupid, I think.

And I hurl it downward, straight into the river, where it makes a deep, satisfying *kerfloop* noise. Darcy looks over at me, a smile around her eyes, eyebrows raised.

"This is dumb," I tell her, and bend to pick up another rock. This one's even bigger. I throw it into the river even harder.

The splash is even more satisfying.

"*So* dumb," Darcy says, crouching to pick up a rock as well. I watch her cautiously from the corner of my eye as she lifts it over her head and chucks it downward, but she's fine.

We both watch as it splashes into the river, and without speaking, she bends and picks up another one.

"Try yelling," she suggests.

She doesn't have to suggest it twice, and I *shout* at the top of my lungs as I propel the next rock down, watching it tumble end over end until it hits the water. *Fuck* this feels good.

"Aahhhh!" Darcy shouts, picking up one more and holding it over her head. "Aaaaauuughhhhh!"

She launches it down. It falls in the river. We're both breathing heavily, but this might be one of the most satisfying things I've ever done.

"You feel any better?" Darcy asks, pushing her hair out of her face.

I pick up yet another rock.

"I'm getting there," I say, then shout as loud as I can and chuck it on down.

101

CHAPTER SIXTEEN
Darcy

If you search "things to do in Tallwood, WA" on the internet, this comes up on a message board. I have no idea if we're on someone's land right now, or if we're about to get chased off by the cops, but I don't particularly care. Judging by the beer cans strewn around, we're not the first people to come to this place.

We throw rocks into the river for a long time, shouting and screaming and grunting, and no one ever comes to ask what the fuck exactly we're doing, so I guess it's fine.

After a while, I can't even lift little rocks over my head any more. My arms are shaking and sore, and I'm barely doing more than dropping them into the gorge. Trent's still going, but I can tell he's starting to get tired. There's a half-circle of sweat ringing the top of his t-shirt, it's dripping down his face, and he's breathing hard.

And I can't stop staring at him. In a *completely* pervy way, and I know it's wrong and weird to do it because I'm watching him work out some kind of psychic pain about his brother, but I can't stop. I'm completely powerless.

Because it's fucking hot, and we're alone here. There's something raw and primal and *animal* about watching him just *go* for it, tossing these massive rocks into the river like they're nothing. I mean, he's sexy and ripped and he's lifting heavy things. What's *not* to like?

Finally, he stops. He runs one hand through his sweaty hair and leans against a thick pine tree. His shirt's sticking to him as he breathes hard, the muscles in his chest and abs flexing and bowing as he closes his eyes for a moment.

I.

Fucking.

Stare.

I finally have to close my eyes so I *stop* staring, because this whole rock-throwing episode feels like it's shaken loose the last part of me that can fucking behave herself and I'm just thinking about running my hands down his slick chest, his thick arms, unbuttoning his jeans while he kisses me hard, his fingers curling through my hair—

"That felt *good*," Trent rumbles, his eyes still closed.

It doesn't help the pervy thoughts, not one fucking iota.

"You feel better?" I ask, my eyes lingering on the spot where his shirt is sticking to his abs, *right* above the button on his jeans.

"A little," he admits.

"Even though it was stupid?"

He opens his eyes and one side of his mouth hitches upward in a smile.

"Stupid things can help," he says, and pushes himself off the tree. "Though that was a pretty good stupid thing."

"I got a stupid pie, too," I offer.

I grab the pie from the car, definitely not thinking dirty thoughts. I didn't get it cut or anything, so it's just that: a whole pie. In a pie tin. With two forks.

We sit on the hood of the rental car. The sun is lowering in the sky, the woods around us turning golden and blue, the river still loud static below us.

"No plates?" Trent teases. "How uncivilized."

I just laugh.

"Two thirds of my meals today are pie," I say, and stab my fork into the middle, pulling out a big, gloppy bite of apple-rhubarb. "No one's calling me Martha Stewart."

We eat for a little while in silence. I've got a thousand questions about his brother, about what the hell really *happened*, but I know that Trent doesn't know the answers either. If he did he probably wouldn't be here, shouting at the river and throwing things and eating pie straight from the tin like a barbarian.

I know it's not perfect. I know that shouting and throwing things and eating comfort food doesn't really *help*, but I know less about how to have a brother than I know about astrophysics. Rocks and pie is what I've got.

"He wanted to be a cop when he was a little kid," Trent suddenly volunteers.

I pause, fork halfway to my mouth. A glop of apple falls off.

"Eli did?"

Trent nods, fork in mouth. He's staring straight ahead, not looking at me, and I look at him from the corner of my eye as I chew and swallow. Something about this ties my heart into a knot, tugs at both ends and doesn't let go.

"Yeah. He even went as one for Halloween once. My mom used to have a picture somewhere. No idea where it is now."

"I wanted to be a social worker when I was really

104

young," I say.

"I thought you *hated* them."

"I did, later," I say, twirling the fork in my hand. "Eli turned out to hate cops, right?"

He stabs the pie, shoveling out a forkful.

"Point taken," he says.

"Before I really learned how the system worked, I thought the social workers were the ones in charge of where we all went. So I wanted to be in charge of where I got to live."

"And then you learned about middle management and your dreams died a horrible death?" he deadpans, his voice low.

"Basically," I say. "But if cops were the only people your dad was ever afraid of, I get why your brother might want to be one when he grew up."

"And instead he fucking stabbed someone in prison," Trent says, but he doesn't sound angry any more. He sounds exhausted and resigned.

"Dreams don't always work out," I say.

We put our forks back on the pie, and Trent sticks it on top of the car before leaning back against the windshield, both arms behind his head. I lean back, too, and he watches me carefully.

"Your back okay like this?"

"I'm fine," I say. "The cool glass is kind of nice, actually. You good?"

"I ate too much pie."

"No such thing."

Trent doesn't respond for a long moment, and the two of us just stare up at the sky, reclining together on the hood and windshield of the car, and it's nice. It's *really* nice, much nicer than this terrible-hey-your-brother-almost-killed-someone moment should be.

And God help me, but I like it. I like being alone with him. I like sharing these moments with him that I *know* no one else shares with him. I like the quiet between us right now, the intimate silence that happens because neither of us needs to say anything.

"I always wonder what I did wrong," he finally says, quietly.

"You didn't," I say, turning to face him.

He looks over at me, and his eyes roam my face for a moment before he looks back at the darkening purple sky.

"What if I did?" he asks, his voice soft. "What if the old man started again after I left? What if Eli tried to fight back too, only it didn't go so well?"

"You'd know."

"Would I?"

He swallows, takes a deep breath.

"He never talks about it. And my mom — I mean, Mom barely talks. If something happened I'd never know."

There it is again, the feeling like my heart's being squeezed to bursting. Like I want to rain destruction on everyone in Trent's life for making him — the best person I know, my closest friend, the guy who stayed in Tallwood to take care of me, who fucking *saved my life* — feel bad that he left a war zone the second he turned eighteen.

"Sometimes I feel like I took all the luck," he says. He's not looking at me, he's looking up at the stars, his voice coming from somewhere far away. "Like I took all the good stuff before he could get to it, and now he's stuck."

God, I know exactly — fucking *exactly* — how he feels. I prop myself on one elbow and look at him. My back doesn't like it, but that's just too bad.

"Trent," I say.

He turns his head and looks at me, his warm brown eyes meeting mine. The knot in my heart tightens again.

"For the last fucking time, it's not your damn fault," I say, and one side of his mouth hitches up into a half-smile. "You survived how you could, and that's what matters, because if you *hadn't* where the fuck would Eli be now?"

"Supermax instead of regular max security prison?" Trent says dryly.

"Damn straight," I say. "He's got you to *thank* for not being in that *Silence of the Lambs* getup with the plexiglass room and the face mask."

There's another long pause.

"You do know Eli didn't cannibalize anyone."

I stop short, frowning, and just look at Trent. He lifts his eyebrows.

"That was why he had the face mask."

"Who?"

"The guy in *Silence of the Lambs*."

"That was there so he wouldn't eat people?"

Trent's eyes crinkle around the corners, a sure sign that he's about to laugh at me.

"I haven't actually seen the movie," I say quickly.

"Really?" he says, just a hint of sarcasm in his voice.

I flip him off, and he laughs. I settle back against the windshield, the glass cool through my shirt and bandages.

"It wasn't you, Trent," I finally say. "You didn't make Eli do any of this and you don't have the power to save him."

There's a long pause, silence stretching out warm and familiar between us before he finally speaks again.

"I know," he says quietly. "I just wish you were wrong."

We sit there, on the hood of the rental car, for a long time, just being together in this silence, listening to the water below, watching night fall over the sky above.

I don't know what this is. I don't know the word for what Trent and I are, because *friends* doesn't quite seem right, but we're not lovers. He knows everything about me, knows me better than any other human on Earth, but we've never even kissed.

After a while, Trent points at a line of stars in the sky, barely visible.

"Is that Orion's belt?" he asks.

I tilt my head and draw my knees in until my feet are flat on the hood.

"I think that's the big dipper," I say.

"It's definitely not," Trent says.

"Ursula?"

"What the hell is Ursula?"

"It's a constellation," I say, like it's obvious.

"You're bullshitting me."

"Prove it."

I tilt my head over at Trent. He's still looking up but the telltale crinkles are there around his eyes, the ones that mean he's laughing at me, and I smile.

I don't know how long we're there for. We talk stars and trees and rivers and rocks; cars and old blues songs and autotune.

We talk places we went as kids, places we wish we could remember better. We talk about the first albums we ever really *loved*, something we've talked about a million times before, and I make him defend Nirvana yet again, because he loves them to pieces and I think they're only okay.

And then, at last, we go quiet again. The moon's moved and the shadows are different than when it first got dark. The air's gone chilly, and even though there are goosebumps up and down my arms, I don't want to leave. I want to stay here, in this secret place where we're alone and there's pie, just a little longer.

"We should head back," Trent says after a while, though he doesn't move.

I stretch my arms over my head, careful of the way my back moves against the glass of the windshield.

"I guess," I say.

"We've got another phone meeting with Gavin at nine," Trent points out.

I make a face.

"Do all people who get sober get annoying, or just him?"

"You *do* know that people do things at nine in the morning all the time, right?"

"Not people who routinely get off work when the sun's coming up," I point out.

He slides off the car, walks around the front, and holds out one hand. I look at it skeptically — it's just the hood of the car, I'm fine — but I take it anyway, strong and warm and dry, and hop down.

"Jesus, Darce, you're an ice cube," he says. "Why didn't you say something?"

He folds his hand around mine, practically engulfing it.

"I'm not that cold," I protest, even as I shiver in the cool air. I didn't realize how cold I was until I touched him.

"Bullshit," he mutters.

Trent slides his hands up my arms to my shoulders, then pulls my body softly against his. The man's practically a furnace, heat blasting through his shirt. I shiver again, despite myself, because now that my front half is warm I'm realizing how cold I actually *am*.

"If anything else happens to you, Gavin might murder me," he says, his voice rumbling through my frame, rubbing my upper arms like he's trying to create friction.

It's nothing, I tell myself. *You're cold and he's nice. It's nothing.*

But God, it feels like something, and it's terrifying. It feels like I can't stop, standing here against him. I want this but I don't; I want to hang out with Trent on cars in the wilderness and I don't want more because the thought of changing what we already have, of leaving it behind, fucking terrifies me.

"So you're warming me up to save your own skin," I tease.

"If that's what I say, will it work?"

"It's in the sixties out here at least," I point out. "I'm not gonna get hypothermia."

I'm protesting, but I lean my head against him, nestling myself in the hollow of his throat despite the voice in my head saying *don't, don't, don't.*

Trent doesn't answer. He just holds me by the shoulders while I lean against him, careful of my back. Slowly, I put my arms around him, because otherwise they're just hanging at my sides.

His chin's resting on the top of my head. I can feel his stubble through my hair, and his hands keep moving like he wants to put his arms around me, but he doesn't want to hurt my back.

"Thanks for this," he finally murmurs.

"I wish I knew how to really help," I say.

"You did."

I finally pull back, looking up at him, my arms still around his waist.

"I thought this was dumb," I tease.

"Throwing rocks as anger management is pretty dumb," he says. "It's also exactly what I needed."

I pull back slightly and Trent looks down at me, an expression in his warm, deep brown eyes that I can't quite read, though it makes my heart beat faster. He's got one big hand cupping my shoulder, the other drifting down my side to my hip, careful of my bandages.

I'm still pressed against him, still warm and safe as I've ever been even though I feel like I'm in the very center of a tornado. The eye of a hurricane. Like it's calm with deadly weather rushing around us, inescapable, the hum always moving closer.

Slowly, Trent slides his fingers along my shoulder, then my neck, his calloused fingertips sending shivers over my skin.

I think my heart might explode, a combination of terror and excitement coursing through my veins, but

I close my eyes. Now his fingers are in my hair, his thumb dragging along my cheekbone.

This isn't what friends do.

It's something else, and it's fucking dangerous.

It feels like my nerves are catching fire and popping out of my skin, my whole body wild and alive like I've never felt it before as Trent bends down so slowly that it almost feels like time has stopped.

"Darcy," he whispers.

His face is an inch from mine. Maybe less, his thumb still stroking my cheekbone, my eyes closed and head tilted back.

I want this. I might want this more than I've ever wanted anything.

I want it and I'm fucking terrified that I want it, a warning siren screeching through my brain that *this is it, this is how you change everything and lose him.*

I take a deep, shaky breath and Trent tilts his head, pausing, his lips a centimeter from mine.

"Don't," I whisper.

CHAPTER SEVENTEEN

Trent

I stop.

It feels like time's stopped, the earth has ceased spinning. Like I've turned to stone, the hardest thing I've ever done, hard like stopping a runaway truck barreling downhill, but I do it.

Darcy's trembling. I don't know if it's the cold or if it's me or if it's everything, but she doesn't pull away. She doesn't move at all, her eyes still closed and her face tilted up, lips slightly parted. Everything about her right now screams *kiss me* but she said *don't*.

And I could, but I don't.

Instead I lean my forehead against hers, disappointment washing through me like a tidal wave. The cold tip of her nose touches mine, and neither of us moves for a long moment.

Then Darcy slides one hand up my arm, puts it over my hand, laces her fingers through mine.

"I'm sorry," she says.

"Don't be," I whisper.

I pull back and kiss her on the forehead, her skin beneath my lips. I linger for a few seconds too long, heart hammering, mind racing.

This doesn't make any sense. I know that. I know that if you looked up *mixed signals* in the dictionary you'd find a picture of this moment, of Darcy telling me not to kiss her while she holds my hand and apologizes and I tell her it's okay.

But it strangely doesn't feel *wrong.* It feels disappointing, it feels tangled, it feels messy and sharp like walking barefoot through badlands.

I feel like a pool float that's deflating, sinking through the water toward the bottom, looking up at the strange, bright, distorted sky through the water.

But it doesn't feel wrong.

"We should head back," she finally says, and takes her hand out of mine.

When she steps away, she doesn't quite look me in the eye. On the drive back to the lodge, we don't speak, and then I'm alone in my hotel suite again, in the dark.

I put half a pie into the mini fridge, then slump on the couch and stare out the window at the moonlit night, and I try to think about all this but I can't.

• • •

At eight forty-five the next morning, I knock on Darcy's door with my elbow, a cup of coffee in either hand, and she answers looking like she literally rolled out of bed when she heard me knock.

"Hey," I say.

Darcy looks at the coffee in my hand, but not me.

"Thanks," she says, her voice flat and toneless. She's still not looking at me.

I hand her a coffee. She swings the door wide, and neither of us says anything. She's looking at the floor, the walls, the coffee, everywhere but at me.

I fucking ruined it, I realize.

113

All I had to do was stay the course. Be her friend, not something else.

And I fucking ruined it.

It's ten times worse than last night when she said *don't,* like sandpaper grating against my insides.

I should have just kissed her.

It would still be ruined but I'd have kissed her.

We sit at the kitchen table, drinking coffee, staring at the paintings on the walls and saying nothing. At 8:56, Gavin rings with a video chat. I've never been happier for him to be early.

"Morning, you two," he says, sounding chipper as *fuck*, practically grinning from ear to ear. Of course he is, he's back in Los Angeles with Marisol and probably got some morning nookie or something.

"Hi," I say.

"Hey, Gavin," Darcy says, taking a long swig of coffee.

Gavin's eyes on the screen narrow slightly, though maybe I'm imagining it. The screen's not very big.

"I've got news," he says. "Actually, I've got fantastic news."

"Yeah?"

"What is it?" I ask.

We're not nearly as excited as Gavin thinks we should be, that's fucking obvious. Now his eyes *definitely* narrow, and he leans down toward his phone camera.

"What's happened?" he asks.

We glance at each other, the first time we've made eye contact that morning.

"Darcy, you're all right?"

"Fine!" Darcy says, *way* too fast.

"Have you punched someone?" he asks me.

"It's early," I say gruffly, because I want him to stop fucking prying via videochat. "What's the great news?"

Gavin leans back, almost going out of frame, and grins.

"We've got a drummer for the tour!" he announces.

"That's great," Darcy says, her tone not reflecting *great* in the least.

"Who?" I ask.

"You're familiar with Girl Bomb, yeah?"

Now Darcy sits up a little straighter, suddenly interested.

"I love Girl Bomb," she says. "Girl Bomb is fucking *great*."

I just nod in agreement.

"Well, they're taking a break right now, so Joan Leonard's agreed to fill in for Eddie for the rest of our tour."

Darcy gasps, one hand flying to her mouth.

Gavin reaches out and turns the phone. Sitting next to him is a woman wearing a black tank top with a white skull and crossbones, her curly brown hair shot through with gray, one hand curled around a mug.

"Hi, I'm Joan," she says, waving.

"Hi," Darcy breathes.

"I asked her if she could come by yesterday and give some of our songs a go in the studio," Gavin says, adjusting the phone again so we can see them both. "And it really went beautifully, and she's available, so as long as the two of you approve, here she is."

"That's fine!" Darcy says, still gawping at the screen.

It's obvious that she thinks this is *way* better than fine.

"She's obviously not ours permanently," Gavin goes on. "Girl Bomb's set to start recording — when was it?"

"Some time this winter," Joan tells him.

"But we've bought ourselves quite a lot of time to find another replacement," Gavin goes on.

"I don't envy you," Joan says.

"I don't envy us either," I say, half-joking. "We thought it had worked out the last time."

"It's almost like musicians are temperamental or something," Joan says dryly.

"Yeah, they can be pretty crazy," Darcy pipes up, leaning in toward my phone. *Clearly* still starstruck.

"We'll be there Friday next so we can start rehearsing," Gavin says. "So, Nigel found a few places up near Tallwood that might be suitable as a rehearsal space but obviously neither of us has been able to check them out..."

Gavin, Darcy and I talk business for a while. Darcy reassures Gavin about twenty times that her back is healing properly, even though her eyes keep darting to Joan, who's sitting next to Gavin, piping up every so often with thoughts and advice.

Darcy's the bass player for one of the biggest bands on the planet. She's played in front of fifty thousand people, in huge arenas. She's met Bono and Mick Jagger. The four of us — her, me, Gavin, and Liam — once got high with Snoop Dogg.

Once, when the bass player for Green Day sprained his hand doing something dumb, they asked her to fill in for a show.

But right now, she's so star struck that she's practically silent, just nodding along wide-eyed. Girl Bomb has never been a particularly huge band — successful, sure, but not wildly so — but they've been around forever, and Darcy's loved them for as long as I've known her.

Fuck, the first time I ever watched Gavin and Liam shoot up together we were listening to Girl Bomb. We were all sharing a dressing room as some shitty club in San Francisco, and Darcy and I were sitting on a couch, sharing her iPod headphones and trying not to watch the other two stick needles into their arms.

I'm forever going to associate the lyric *hold my heart, break it if you want* with that moment: Darcy so earnest and unguarded, one of the first times I saw her with her spikes down as the other two nodded out. Half wonderful and half terrible.

I don't share that particular memory with Joan.

When we end the call half an hour later, Darcy still hasn't said much, and she still doesn't make eye contact as she drains her coffee mug, the phone screen black. I lean back, putting my phone into my pocket again, and just look at her.

Finally, she looks at me across the table, her bright blue eyes a shock against her nearly-black hair, still wild and mussed from sleep. And she's fucking beautiful. She's always fucking beautiful, even now when she looks down and takes a deep breath and chews the inside of her lip and looks into her paper coffee cup like there's going to be something written on the inside of it.

"Do you want more coffee?" she finally asks. "I figured out the coffee pot."

"Sure," I say, because there's nothing else to say. She scrapes her chair back, grabs my mug, and heads across the room into her tiny kitchenette. She's wearing short shorts and a t-shirt, the wrinkles of her bandages visible through it as she leans over the sink, rinsing mugs out.

Silence as she pours water and measures coffee grounds. Silence as the coffee brews and she stands on one leg, her other foot perched against her knee like a flamingo, gazing out the window. Silence as she puts sugar in hers and leaves mine black, then brings them back to the table.

"Let me change your bandages before I get out of here," I say, blowing on the hot black liquid to cool it.

She swallows.

"You don't ha—"

"I thought we were fucking done with that?" I say. It's too sharp and she looks at me, her light eyes hard, but then she looks down again.

"Thanks," Darcy says, her voice soft but distant, just in case I didn't already fucking feel like a monster.

We finish the coffee. We walk to the bathroom, where her burn supplies live, and I wait with my back turned while she takes off her shirt and covers her front. I still brush her hair from her neck as I unwind the ace bandage. I'm still gentle as I pull the tape off, always careful not to hurt her.

The burn doesn't have blisters any more. It's faded to a bright, ugly pink, the skin puffy and shiny, and for the thousandth time I fight the urge to kiss the top border where it overlaps her shoulder. For the thousandth time, I touch her and watch the goosebumps travel up her neck and down her arms, down her sides, past the dimples in her back right above her jeans.

I tape on another bandage, the process considerably less involved now that it's halfway to healed, and I let my fingers drift over the vertebrae in her neck, the notch of her waist, and I try not to think about the way her thighs would feel against my face.

It doesn't work. They'd feel fucking fantastic, not to mention the way I know she'd *moan*. Grab my hair in one fist.

Fuck. I'm hard, but I turn away, pretending I'm not. Darcy wraps the bandage back around herself, pulls her shirt over her head. I think about all the different kinds of dog breeds that exist — Corgis and Dachshunds and Great Danes and Dalmatians — until my hard-on has faded.

We leave the bathroom, still not having said a word.

"I'll be back again this evening," I say, shoving one hand through my hair. It's the first time we've scheduled this, because normally we're already together. But I have a feeling we'll be spending today apart.

Darcy bites her lip. She swallows, her hands in her pockets.

"There's supposed to be a *There's a Ghost in My Beach House* marathon on right now," she says.

I shift my weight to my other foot.

"I was watching the previews of it last night and once of them's a dog ghost," she goes on. "Want to hang out for a couple of episodes?"

I do. Despite fucking everything, despite the fact that I should be going back to my suite and jerking off, or hell, going to wherever single people hang out in Tallwood at ten in the morning and finding someone to fuck, I do want to watch stupid TV with her.

Goddamn it.

"What kind of dog?" I ask.

"Great Dane."

I shrug, trying to look nonchalant and not like there's nowhere else I'd rather be.

"Sure," I say.

Darcy half-smiles, the first one I've seen from her all day.

We sit on the couch, Darcy leaning back gingerly. There's an enormous 18th-century mansion on the Connecticut coast on the TV.

"How do you think the dog died?" she says, her body an inch from mine. "And why's it haunting the house?"

I consider this for a moment as the camera swoops in through the front door of the house, panning up a huge staircase.

"Hunting accident," I say. "And because it knows where the bones are buried."

Darcy snorts at my dumb joke, but she's smiling, and I let the first glimmer of hope stick in my chest.

It's not what I want, but maybe it's not fucked. Not completely.

CHAPTER EIGHTEEN
Darcy

"Gavin, Joan, and Nigel landed in Seattle," Trent says, looking at his phone. It's the first thing either of us has said in ten minutes.

"Okay," I say. I don't know what other response, exactly, that statement warrants.

We're standing next to a huge corrugated metal building, in the middle of a field in the middle of a forest, and it's raining. There's an overhang, so we're not getting wet, but everything is damp, my shoes are kind of soggy, and I'm cold.

Secretly, I was kind of hoping that the rest of Dirtshine would get delayed or something, because I am not in the fucking mood to deal with Gavin's post-heroin drive and organization, nor do I really feel like meeting one of my idols while I'm still half-gimpy from my back and I'm in a grumpy fucking mood.

"What time is that girl supposed to be here?" Trent asks. He's standing a couple of feet away, arms crossed over his chest, feet apart, staring out at the rain like he's going to ask to see its ID before letting it into an exclusive club.

"Ten minutes ago."

"Did you call her?"

"I don't have service."

"Are you sure it was three-thirty we were supposed to be here?"

I turn my head away from Trent and roll my eyes. For two nights now — ever since we almost kissed — I've been sleeping shittily, trying not to think about what almost happened, failing *miserably* at said attempt, and then trying to convince myself I don't regret it.

Combine that with us finding a practice space for the band at the last *possible* second, and we've been dicks to each other for most of today.

"Maybe she meant three-thirty a.m., not p.m.," I smart-ass.

"I'm just asking," he rumbles.

I almost say *you weren't just asking, you were asking like an asshole and you know it*, but just then a white SUV pulls into the parking lot, its windshield wipers going full-force, its headlights off. Trent and I stare sullenly, and wait.

And wait.

Just as I think it's just someone who's lost, the door swings open and a hot pink umbrella pops out, unfurls, and is quickly followed by a pair of legs in flip flops. When the car door shuts, it reveals a young redhead in cutoff shorts and a tank top who waves at us.

She's cute. She's kinda hot, she's showing plenty of skin, and she almost certainly doesn't have burn blisters all down her back, so I'm already annoyed with her.

And it really doesn't help that, as she walks toward us, she's *blatantly* checking out Trent.

"Hi!" she says. "Sorry I'm late, my roommate got locked out of our apartment and so I had to call her boyfriend and go give *him* a spare key, but then he wasn't answering his phone so I had to call my roommate back and get *his* roommate's phone number and then I woke the roommate up at like two-thirty in the afternoon and I had to explain the whole situation to *him*, so that all took *forever*."

She laughs, the sound bubbling out of her. I can't help but notice that even in one thousand percent humidity, her hair looks *great*.

"So you're Darcy?" she says to Trent, holding her hand out.

"*I'm* Darcy," I say.

"Oh! Hi, I'm Allison, the summer coordinator," she says as we shake hands.

"Trent," Trent says, then lapses back into silence.

Allison blinks and looks from him to me and back, then shrugs, holding up a keychain that has far more doodads than keys on it.

"All right, well, let me show you the practice spaces we've got," she says, opening the door. Trent holds it for me and I walk through, following Allison's bouncy hair and bubble butt into a high-ceilinged concrete hallway with what look like small metal houses on either side. I recognize them as sound-proofed rooms.

"Since it's summer you've basically got your pick of whatever you want," she says, her voice echoing. "There'll be a couple students from the community college around, but like, it shouldn't be too bad or anything. You want to just see the nice one first?"

She looks at Trent.

"Sure," Trent says.

"It's over here," Allison goes on, her plastic flip-flops echoing through the hallway between two tiny rooms, each barely big enough for a piano. Trent glances back to make sure I'm behind them, then follows Allison. "You know, someone was telling me one time that this place used to be an airplane hangar during World War Two or something? And then sold it to the community college for like a dollar because they didn't have anything else to do with it and the college needed the space..."

Allison keeps talking. Trent keeps grunting in response, not that she seems to notice his lack of enthusiasm, because she just keeps going and going, and my mood gets blacker and blacker.

I don't know why. I've seen girls flirt with Trent before. I'm pretty sure that I've seen him pick girls up before, though actually, the last time I remember that happening was over a year ago, back before Gavin, Liam, and Allen overdosed.

You don't have a claim on him, I remind myself. *You turned that down, remember? And now everything that happens that you don't like is your own fault.*

"Okay," she says, unlocking the door to a much bigger room than all the rest, then putting her back to it and smiling coyly at Trent. "You ready?"

"Sure," he says, both hands still stuffed in his pockets.

She pushes it open, flicks on the lights, and shouts, "Ta-da!"

It's a rehearsal room. It's nothing special: about twenty feet by twenty feet, some chairs, some music stands, a piano in one corner, soundproofing panels lining the walls. It's fluorescent-lit, tile-floored, and pretty much unremarkable in every way.

Trent and I look around while Allison holds both her arms out, smiling radiantly.

"What do you think?" she asks Trent.

"It's nice," he says, his voice still placid and neutral, his hands still in his pockets.

"Yeah," I say, mostly to remind her that I'm also there.

"This is the newest one," she says. "The soundproofing is only a couple of years old, it's really well-insulated, everything. I have some friends in a ska band and sometimes when no one's using this one I give them the keys, and this is their very favorite place to practice!"

That's because it's obviously better than someone's garage, I think.

"It's a good space," Trent says, his hands still in his pockets. I can tell he's just talking to fill space between Allison's words, and he wanders over to an upright piano in the corner of the room and opens it, playing a chord.

It's a little out of tune, and I make a face. Trent looks at me, tries another chord, his brow wrinkling slightly because that one's also off.

"Sounds good otherwise," I tell him, walking toward the back of the room.

He plays something else, still out of tune, and I turn to the back wall and listen.

"Like I said, the ska band really likes it, the lead singer was telling me that the sound in here is really crisp and..."

I ignore Allison, walking further around the room while Trent goes through some chord progressions. He's not a pianist, and he's not *good* at it, but if you're a professional musician you're eventually going to learn to play the piano a little, like it or not.

It sounds mushy up against the walls and the corners have an odd, unpleasant ringing effect that I'm not crazy about, but it's a practice space, not Carnegie Hall. It's good enough.

"...Was complaining a little bit about the trumpets, I guess, because cellos can be hard to hear or something? But then the bassist told me that *actually* the guy was just complaining because he left the door to his practice room open so he could get the breeze in or something, and so really it was his own fault if he could hear the horns!"

"We'll take it," I tell her.

"Oh! That was fast."

124

I almost roll my eyes and tell her it's fast because it's pretty much the only suitable space in all of Tallwood and we can't afford to be fucking picky, but I swallow those words and smile instead, because I don't need to be known as *that bitchy girl from Dirtshine*.

"It's nice," I say, and I don't sound convincing to myself but Allison beams.

"Awesome!" she bubbles. "You guys like it?"

Trent flips the cover over the piano keys and straightens up, crossing his arms over his chest again. Even that simple gesture makes all the lines and muscles stand out, makes his shirt hug his biceps. I can tell Allison notices, too, and I just about glare a hole in the side of her head.

"It's exactly what we're looking for," he says, his voice slow, placid, and calm. The usual Trent.

"Cool!" she says, swirling her tchotchke-filled keychain around one finger. If it hit someone I think it might take them out. "Let me go to the front office to grab the paperwork? I know you said your manager was gonna be the one filling it out because he's got all the info, but I figure it can't hurt you two to see it beforehand? You can hang out here, I'll be right back."

She looks at me, smiles at Trent, and then flip-flops her way out of the room, her butt twitching back and forth in her small shorts.

"It's a good space," I say to him, just to say *something*.

"It's good enough for a ska band, I guess it's good enough for us," he deadpans.

"I hope Joan works out."

"Well, she pretty much has to."

I just snort.

"You know that's not true," I say. "She could have ten side projects who she likes working with better than us."

"Joan's not Eddie, Darce."

125

I sit down in a metal folding chair and then look over at the wall, suddenly feeling like I might cry. I didn't think I was all that attached to Eddie — yeah, I liked the kid, but we weren't particularly friends or anything — but his departure left a bigger hole in me than I'd have expected.

"I just don't want to get attached and then she leaves," I say quietly.

Trent just *looks* at me. He doesn't say anything, but I can feel his eyes searching my face, practically dismantling it, for a long time before I turn and make eye contact.

"She's going to," he says. "That's the whole idea."

"I know," I sigh.

"Things change, Darce," he goes on, his voice suddenly soft and low. "People change. The world moves on. Life's not static."

My heart catches in my throat. I hold my breath. All my nerves seize up but I look at Trent anyway, into his deep brown eyes as he stands there like a monument under the ugly fluorescent lights, and I know we're not talking about Eddie and Liam and Joan any more.

"It doesn't have to be a disaster," he finishes.

I slam my mouth shut and look away again, because I'm not good with words and I'm not good with emotions and holy fuck am I not good when I'm supposed to be doing both at once, especially when my stomach is some turbulent mix of regret and nerves combined with the insane impulse to jump out of this chair and just kiss the hell out of him, see what *that* does.

But I don't. I'm a fucking statue made of inertia, stubbornness, and the disinclination to launch myself from a cliff, so I turn my head and study the pinpricks on a soundproofing tile.

He turns away, hands in pockets, strides to the other wall and pretends to examine that soundproofing, and somehow, my stomach drops even lower than I thought it could.

I've fucked this up, I think. *I don't even understand how but I did.*

And I wish that I'd at least kissed him before I fucked it up.

A moment later, there's a smacking noise at the door and Allison walks back in, flip flops loud at fuck, waving some papers around, her massive keychain jingling obnoxiously as she beams at us but particularly at Trent.

"Okay! I got the papers," she says, *much* too enthusiastically about paperwork. "So, some of this stuff I think your manager's gonna have to fill out, but if you two have the dates and stuff already then we can start... is everything okay? Is something broken in here?"

Trent and I both just shake our heads, and Allison goes back to telling us about the facility schedule.

CHAPTER NINETEEN

Trent

Gavin's guitar cuts out in a jumble of sound, and for a moment he tilts his head back, eyes closed like he's counting to five. He probably is.

"It's D-flat, E-flat, F," he says. "Just a regular fucking F chord, mate."

I look down at my fingers on the neck of my guitar. I'm not sure what the hell they're doing, but it's not a F chord, so I rearrange them into one and strum.

"Got it," I say, my voice tight even to my own ears.

"You sure? Do you want it written down or something?"

"I said I've got it."

"Because you haven't got it the last several attempts we've made."

I take a deep breath and clench my jaw, counting to five myself. It's nearly six in the evening and we got here at eight-thirty this morning, and aside from fifteen minutes to scarf down lunch we've been playing nonstop, just the four of us in this room. We've played

Alleyway Saint about twenty times in a row. I can practically see everyone's nerves fraying.

Ten feet away, Darcy is sitting in a metal folding chair, left hand silently forming chords on the neck of her bass, not looking up at Gavin and I bickering. We've said about five words to each other all day. She's barely made eye contact with me, and even worse than Gavin being kind of a prick right now, *that's* like sandpaper under my skin.

"I'm fine, just start at the chorus," I snap.

Gavin glances back at Joan, who nods, then counts off, and we start playing again.

Normally I know this song by heart. We've been playing it for years, and every note *should* be practically ingrained in my fingers. Usually they are, but today's a fucking unusual day.

We finish the chorus, loop back into the second verse. I'm staring at the wall, making myself concentrate on the task at hand. *Not* on Darcy, who's wearing a dress with Doc Martens and no bra.

Not on the night by the river, with rocks and pie. Not on how I half hate myself for thinking it might work and half still think that it might, because the desire hasn't gone away. If anything, it's gotten worse.

The band heads into the bridge. D-flat, E-flat, F, and then I look over at her just as she glances at me.

And her finger slips, the note going bad, then the next one's off the beat.

Gavin stops playing and throws his hands in the air, then rests them on his head, turning in a circle, the cable on his guitar dragging behind him.

"Jesus Holy *Christ*," he says, shouting at the soundproofed wall. "I could have sworn we were a band who'd played this song a million fucking times, not some buskers come in from off the street who—"

"Gavin," Joan says, and we all turn to look at her. She's sitting perfectly upright on her stool, drumsticks in one hand, her hair pulled back, reading glasses on.

The three of us are silent for a moment, like we're suddenly aware that we're having a family fight in front of a stranger. Which we kind of *are*.

"We've been practicing all day," she says, her voice calm and reasonable. "You and I just got in late last night, why don't we call it for now and come at this fresh tomorrow?"

Gavin shoves hand through his hair, heaves a sigh, then crosses his arms. He's obviously stressed about this, and I think the slavedriver part of his personality — the one that was a surprise when he finally kicked the heroin — would rather we stay here until we either all get it right or kill each other.

"I think Joan's right," Darcy volunteers. "We'll all be less grumpy if we sleep on this."

"I'm not grumpy, I just want to fucking—"

Darcy rolls her eyes.

"Are you fucking kidding me right now?"

"Trying to get something right isn't being grumpy, it's—"

"—Yeah, I'm just inspired as *shit* right now to get this right and you getting in my face about it is really helping, Gavin—"

"—Apparently rather than consider practicing, the two of you have spent the past weeks fucking around!"

"I couldn't fucking lean back in a chair for a week! I *still* can't play standing because the strap rubs against my back!"

Gavin paces back and forth for a moment, clenching and unclenching his hands, shaking them out because he's been playing for eight hours straight. There's silence in the room. Darcy closes her eyes, takes a deep breath.

"I just don't want us to embarrass ourselves when we go out there again," Gavin finally says, forcing his voice calm.

"Gavin, you used to—"

"I think Joan is right and we should all head back to the lodge, get some rest," I cut in. Darcy glares at me, but I'm pretty sure she was about to bring up the fact that back in his heroin days, Gavin nodded out on stage more than once, and that's not a fight we need to have right now.

"Works wonders, I swear," Joan says, pushing her glasses up her nose with one drumstick.

Gavin covers his face with his hands, then runs them both through his hair.

"Fine, you're fucking right," Gavin mutters, pulling his guitar over his head. "Everyone go take a fucking nap, we'll get back at it tomorrow morning. Bright and early, yeah?"

He practically throws the guitar into a case, grabs his own jacket, and in about thirty seconds he's fuming out of the practice studio, leaving the door open behind him.

Darcy and I look at each other again, then we both look at Joan.

"Sometimes I miss the heroin," Darcy says. "It did calm him down."

"He's a real dickhead sometimes," I add.

Joan just chuckles, standing and cracking her back.

"Girlbomb goes to therapy twice a month," she says. "All three of us together. Don't worry, I've seen some band fights."

Darcy stands from her chair, puts her bass down, and stretches. Her dress rides up her thighs by a few inches, the top going tight around her breasts, and my mouth goes dry.

"But you're still together," Darcy points out, and Joan laughs.

"Ava once tried to set Nadine on fire," she says, heading for the door. "They didn't speak for a year. Trust me, you all aren't doing so badly. At least when you got set on fire, Trent here put you out instead of literally fanning the flames."

"He's still an asshole," I say, putting my guitar down on a stand. "And he can be a real high and mighty motherfucker sometimes, like he's never fucked anything up."

Joan just looks entertained as she opens the door.

"You should try meditating," she says. "It'll help with some of the anger. See you guys tomorrow morning."

And with that, she's gone, leaving me in a swirl of desire and irritation and sleeplessness that makes me feel like someone's going at my brain stem with a cheese grater.

I can't play these songs right, I can't talk to Gavin without getting into a fight, I can't even fucking look at Darcy without popping a boner, and she can barely look at me.

The two of us walk out of the room in silence, shutting the door and turning off the lights. We walk to the outside door of the old airplane hangar in silence, Darcy a step ahead of me as I try not to watch her legs in that dress.

It's a long fucking walk, or at least it feels that way, and every step is worse. Fucking excruciating.

This can't go on. It can't. She pushes open the door to the outside — it's raining lightly — and as the cool air hits my face, I think: *I can't undo this but maybe I can fix it*.

"Hey," I say, and Darcy turns. She just looks at me, doesn't say anything. "Can you catch a ride back with Gavin or Joan?"

"Sure," she says. "Why?"

I have an idea of how to fix this. It might be a stupid idea, more stupid than throwing rocks into the river and yelling, but it's something and I need to goddamn *try*.

"I'm gonna take a walk. Clear my head. You know."

She opens her mouth, like she's about to ask something else, but she just nods instead, then walks toward the parking lot, waving one arm at Joan.

I watch her walk away for a moment, then duck back inside.

CHAPTER TWENTY
Darcy

I'm already in bed when someone knocks on the door. I'm playing a dumb game on my phone, though I've got my book next to me. I *meant* to read it, but what I really need is colors and lights flashing in front of my eyes and distracting me, not something that might let me *think*.

I pause when I hear it. On my phone, a stack of jewels crashes down and shatters, but I'm hoping that whoever it is will go away and just leave me alone.

But no. They knock again, and I sigh, because I'm pretty sure I know who's at my door. There's about a five percent chance it's Gavin or Nigel and maybe a one percent chance that it's Joan, which leaves an eighty-nine percent chance it's Trent, if my math is right.

And I don't know what to say to him. I don't know what to do around him, how to hold my hands or where to look or what face to make, because I still wish I'd said *yes* instead of *no* and despite everything, I don't feel like I can reverse it.

He knocks *again*, and I roll out of bed, wearing old boxer shorts and a t-shirt, and shout "I'm *coming*!" as I head through the bedroom and the living room, both dark.

I yank the door open, already afraid he's left.

"Did I wake you up?" Trent says, looking over my shoulder into my dark suite.

"I was reading in bed," I say.

There's a long pause. He's got a brown paper bag in one hand, and it crinkles when he shifts.

Is he drinking?

"What's up?" I finally remember to ask.

"Can I come in?"

I step back and hit a light, my eyes still on the bag as he closes the door behind him.

"I can't stand this," he rumbles.

"Can't stand what?" I ask, like I don't fucking know.

"So I came here to fix it," he says, looking toward the window where the moonlight is on the trees. "You were right. I got carried away at the river, I was in a bad place, I was just being..."

He drifts off for a moment, my stomach clenching, his face suddenly distant, closed off because *fuck* I don't want to hear this. I don't know what I fucking want to hear, but *I only tried to kiss you because I was really upset* isn't it.

"Reckless," he finally says. "And it was stupid, and I'm sorry, and I came here to make things normal again."

I almost say *you showed up at my hotel room at eleven at night, after I was in bed, to make things normal again?* But it's not like we've ever quite had a normal friendship, so I don't.

Instead I swallow and nod, not sure what to say, feeling like broken chunks of something I can't identify are floating around my heart.

"I'd like that," I say.

135

Trent walks to the dining table, plops the paper bag on it, and starts pulling things out: two headlamps, a flashlight, a length of rope, a meat thermometer, and a canister of baby powder.

I find myself uncharacteristically speechless for a long moment, and Trent just looks at me, arms crossed, the shadow of a smile on his face.

"Caving?" I hazard, because I have *no* idea how this is going to make things normal again.

"Nope," he says.

I cross my arms in front of myself, because I'm not wearing anything under this very old, very *thin* t-shirt, and Trent doesn't need to know my nipples' opinion of him right now.

It's a positive opinion. Despite myself.

"Coal mining?"

"Still no," he says, reaching into the bag again. He pulls out a long-sleeved black t-shirt that's *way* too small for him, so it's probably for me.

"Mime school."

"Closer."

"Is it?"

The smile's still flickering on his face.

"No."

"I give up."

He crumples the paper bag in his massive hands and tosses it into a trash can.

"There's a haunted mansion about twenty minutes outside town," he says. "And after watching every episode of *I Think My Cabana Has Ghosts* or whatever it was, I figure we're ghost experts."

"Right now?" I ask, even though I already know the answer. Yes, *right now*.

"Unless you'd rather go to bed."

I can't help but smile, because given the options of *go ghost hunting with Trent* or *sleep,* it's not even a choice.

"I'd rather find some ghosts."

"I thought so."

Trent tosses me the black shirt, the smile still playing across his face.

"Go put that on, I can't have you giving us away," he says as I catch it.

"I would never," I protest. "Tell me about the ghost while I get changed."

I leave the bedroom door open and step behind it so I can hear Trent as he talks, standing by the table, not facing the door.

And I think about it. Fuck yes I do. I think about stripping naked except for my bandages and walking out and saying something like *try kissing me again,* but this feels like it might finally be normal again, like we might have gotten over the madness that happened two nights ago and back to baseline.

Baseline, where I think about Trent more than I wish I did and got jealous of a college student in short shorts earlier today. *Someday that has to stop*, I think.

"This place was built by a lumber baron, Woodford Beechcourt, in the late 1800s on the side of a mountain. He apparently put it there so he could oversee all his workers from his front porch while he drank fine wine and counted his money."

I slide a tank top over my head, since I still can't wear a bra, and grin at my bedroom.

"And he was murdered by the men he overworked and fed into a woodchipper," I call.

"Better," Trent says.

"Better than murder by woodchipper?"

"He was having an affair with a local woman, and his wife found out," Trent goes on. "But when she went to confront the other woman, the two of *them* fell madly in love, so they conspired to murder the husband, collect his insurance, and then travel the world together as lovers. They used arsenic or something that was untraceable back then."

"And then they woodchippered him."

"There's no woodchipper, and remind me never to do something behind your back," he says, his voice low and laconic.

I sigh dramatically, the knot of nerves that's been in my chest for days slowly unwinding.

"Anyway, the plan worked," Trent says. "The wife was properly shocked, blamed heart troubles or something. She waited an appropriate amount of time after the funeral, then just took off one day with the mistress. Sold the house and no one ever saw the two of them again. The next owners turned it into a bed and breakfast."

I come out of the bedroom, practically skipping I'm so excited. I swear Trent glances at my chest for one second, but then it's eyes on my face again as he leans back against the table, arms crossed in front of himself.

"A few years later, the east wing was nearly burnt down in a terrible fire, rendering the whole place pretty much unusable. Rumor has it," Trent says, a slight smile on his lips, one eyebrow raised. "That an *unwed* couple shared a room, and the very conservative Woodford's ghost was so enraged that he set fire to the place."

"He had an affair and got mad about an unwed couple?"

"I guess ghosts can be hypocrites too," Trent deadpans, and I laugh.

Then I stop.

"Did anyone die in the fire?"

The burn on my back tingles slightly at the thought, but Trent shakes his head.

"Everyone got out and the fire was contained," he says. "The rest of the mansion is virtually pristine."

I grab a headlamp and a flashlight from the table and shove them into my pockets. Trent does the same, I put on my jacket and shoes, and we're out the door.

Even if I've got a vague premonition that I shouldn't be going places alone in the dark with Trent.

Even if I know what happened the last time we did, even if it's a miracle that things aren't more strained between us right now.

I don't even know that I'll say *no* twice. I don't know if I can. That one word, *don't*, felt like pushing a boulder out of my mouth. Maybe the hardest fucking thing I've ever said, because even though I knew it was a bad idea, I *wanted* to kiss him.

Dear God, did I want to. Maybe more than I've ever wanted anything, or at least it felt that way, but I *know* better, and I know that people who kiss each other break up and I can't, I just fucking can't.

And now here we are, *again*, and I'm dumb as a box of rocks — ten boxes of rocks, if that's dumber than one — to be doing this, but I'm all out of self-control.

"Do I really have to wear this?" I ask as we walk outside, pulling the headlamp from my pocket and putting it on.

"You do now," he tells me.

I flip him off. He grins. Something warm and *nice* percolates through me, from my toes to my belly to the top of my head.

This is exactly what I can't lose, I think. *Don't fuck it up.*

CHAPTER TWENTY-ONE

Trent

"Why'd a lumber baron make his house out of stone?" Darcy asks, her voice quiet in the low light of Beechcourt Mansion's enormous entryway.

"Maybe he got tired of looking at wood," I say.

Darcy grins.

"*The Lumber Baron* would be a great nickname for a porn star," she says.

I just raise my eyebrows at her.

"He's got a lot of wood?" she says, and grins at me. I roll my eyes, but I'm smiling. "Think of the porn setups a lumber baron could have. Hey there, can you inspect my wood? I've got too much wood, can you take some off my hands? Wood for sale, long, hard and..."

She trails off, thinking and staring up at the ceiling of the mansion. There's a hole in it, the stars shining through.

"Splintery? Maybe don't use that one."

"Because the others were solid gold," I tease, walking toward the sweeping stone staircase on one side of the huge foyer. This place feels like an old hunting lodge crossed with a medieval castle or something, empty and made of stone, our voices echoing through it.

I check out some of the stone work, little carved patterns along the railing, but I'm wondering if she watches porn. I'm wondering what kind she watches, whether she watches it at night, after I leave, and I can't help but picture her.

Screen glowing, Darcy in one of the chairs with the ugly bear-patterned fabric. One hand down her pants, moving quickly, the way her eyes might drift shut when she gets close, her other hand clutching the armrest, her lips parting.

God *damn* it, I'm doing this again.

Since she turned me down I feel like this is *all* I do. She'll say something dirty, or even just salacious, or I'll see a sliver of skin or a glance I'm maybe not supposed to see and I can't stop thinking about her, Darcy, what if she'd said yes.

I'm fighting the urge to kiss her neck when she stands in front of me, the urge to slide my hand into her jeans from behind when I tend to her burn, see if she's as wet as I'm hard. Fuck, I watch her ass every time she walks away and think about the way it would bounce while she rode my cock in reverse cowgirl.

The more time I spend with her, even *after* getting turned down, the worse I want her. The more I think about all the ways I could make her come and how fucking spectacular it would be when I did.

I shake off the thoughts, yet again, and slowly circle the room we're in. It's on the first floor of the mansion, big stone blocks forming the floor, a sweeping staircase going to the floor above and then the floor above that. Walls made of cut stone blocks, doorways lined with smaller stone.

It's like we're in a medieval castle, only we're two hours outside Seattle. I think Woodford might have been slightly insane.

"All right," Darcy says, suddenly behind me as I stare into a doorway, half thinking about Woodford and half thinking about how I want to pull her hair and watch her eyelids flutter. "Which part is supposed to be haunted?"

"The whole thing, as far as I know," I say.

She looks around, the pupils in her blue eyes wide and black in the darkness.

"So we've gotta explore the whole place?"

"I guess."

"And what time is sunrise?"

I smile at her, just slightly.

"You think you'll last that long?" I ask.

"What, you think there's gonna be a weird shadow and I'm gonna run screaming?"

"No, I think you might get tired and bored when there's no ghost," I say.

Neither of us actually believes in ghosts. Or, at least, I don't. Darcy says that she's agnostic on the topic of ghosts, but has never seen any compelling evidence in favor of them. We've debated this about a billion times while watching trashy ghost-hunting reality shows.

"If there's no ghost it's your fault," she says. "You found this place."

"My options were limited," I point out. "Let's see if you can find me a more-haunted mansion in this small town on short notice."

She takes a step closer, smirking, as a gentle breeze blows through the broken windows and past us.

Somehow, I manage to meet her gaze instead of looking to see whether her nipples stiffen in the cold. She's stopped wearing the Ace bandages around her wound — doctor's orders — and the tank top she's wearing instead of a bra doesn't do a whole lot to hide when she's cold or excited.

It's another nail in my coffin, sheer goddamn torture. Two days ago, when we were drinking on the roof again, talking about the tour coming up, there was a lull in the conversation and I caught her looking at me?

Excited.

Happy hour yesterday, when she drank two glasses of wine, I drank one, and she teased me for ten full minutes about the middle-aged woman who recognized me and *might* have been flirting?

Also excited.

"I think that's Woodford right now," I say, the breeze still moving her hair slightly. "He's angry that we're questioning him."

Darcy just laughs, her eyes flicking to my face in a way I don't quite understand, and she twirls one finger in the air.

"Turn around and let me get our ghost-hunting equipment out of the backpack," she orders.

Minutes later, we're walking through a wide stone doorway and into another room, this one with a massive fireplace. Darcy's got the meat thermometer in one hand, held out like a sword or something, and I've got the can of baby powder.

The thermometer is for finding cold spots, which apparently indicate ghosts. The baby powder is... I'm not exactly sure. I just know that reality TV ghost hunters are always throwing powder everywhere, so I bought some.

"This is stupid," Darcy whispers.

"It really is," I whisper back.

She hits the button on the thermometer, then peers at the tiny LCD screen. I sprung for the instant-read kind, because I'm fancy.

"Sixty-six point six," she says. "Satan's temperature."

"That's a good lead for sure," I say.

"I don't think these are really designed to take air temperatures, by the way."

"I'm gonna tell you what I told you before," I say, slowly looking around the room. "I'd like to see you do better."

She grins and flips me off before walking through that room and into the next, then the next, and I follow.

Soon, we're not really ghost hunting any more. We're just exploring this crazy mansion. There's not much left in it, hardly any furniture, but there are a few random knickknacks here and there. She finds a letter opener in a corner, and I find an old spoon lying under a sink that clearly hasn't been used in a long, long time.

And beer cans. There are plenty of beer cans, not to mention weeds growing through the cracks in the stone floor, giving the whole place a half-wild feel, like we're adventurers discovering a lost city in the Amazon.

We talk about whether the roof's going to cave in. We speculate about why Woodford would want to haunt this place and not somewhere else, maybe somewhere with more people to be haunted.

We move through the entire first floor of the house this way, slowly. Darcy sticks the meat thermometer into her back pocket and forgets about it. I toss the baby powder back into the backpack I'm carrying, because we're obviously not using it.

"I think he haunted this place because he really hated premarital sex," I say.

"The guy with the porno name hated premarital sex?" she says, a smile tugging at her lips.

"You know it's not a very good porno name, right?" I tease, ducking my head slightly through a doorway. "It takes a little too much thinking to get the joke."

"And people were doing it here?" she asks, looking away. We're walking back through some of the first-floor rooms toward the foyer where we entered, our feet brushing softly against the grass that's grown between the cracks, encouraged by the sunlight through the broken windows.

"Doing what?"

"Premarital sex."

"That's what the legend says. That they were doing sex," I say, repeating her phrase just to tease her.

"Maybe he's just jealous that he's not getting any, being a ghost and all," Darcy says.

"Married couples didn't seem to have the same problem with the bed and breakfast burning down," I point out.

"Maybe they didn't have sex while they were here."

"But it's a romantic getaway."

Darcy walks through doorway and back into the foyer, then looks around at the staircase sweeping upward, the partially-gone ceiling above.

"Is it?"

"What, you don't think so?"

Darcy looks at me with an expression I can't decipher, and I wish I could hit delete on *that* sentence.

"Well, it's either that or a serial killer's lair," she says. "Middle of nowhere, totally secluded, no one can hear you scream regardless of *why* you're screaming."

"I promise not to serial kill you," I say, half-laughing, the words out of my mouth before I can think them through.

"Thanks, but I wasn't worried," Darcy says. "If you haven't serial killed me yet, then I'm—"

THUMP.

Darcy stops, mid-sentence, her mouth still open, and my blood chills.

Scuff creak scuff...

145

Footsteps. That's footsteps. Darcy's mouth snaps shut as she looks at me, eyes sparking, reaching for the thermometer in her back pocket.

"It's probably a squirrel," I whisper, half trying to convince myself.

I don't think it's a squirrel. Not unless it's a squirrel carcass dropped from a hundred feet, the only way a squirrel could conceivably be loud enough to make that *thump*.

I'm thinking bear. I'm thinking vagrant, squatter, someone who's made their home here and is probably not happy that we've shown up all of a sudden.

"Sounds like Woodford is angry," Darcy murmurs, the hint of a smile playing around her mouth. "And we haven't even—"

She stops. We look at each other, the first time since that morning over coffee that we've come close to talking about what didn't happen. Sort of, kind of, and in that second, I read her face, surprised like she just slammed on the brakes.

Darcy closes her mouth. She clears her throat, looks away, her back straightens and I think she turns pink though it's hard to tell in the dark, her self-defense spikes out in full force.

"Let's go find him," she says, takes the thermometer out of her back pocket, and darts up the stairs.

"Darce, wait," I say, but she doesn't listen to me. "Darcy. Fucking seriously, Darcy!"

CHAPTER TWENTY-TWO
Darcy

I don't stop, I just bolt up the stairs feeling like an idiot because I think I'd way fucking rather face an angry bear or a vengeful spirit right now than keep talking to Trent about how we're *not* fucking, about whether this is romantic, or even be in the same room with him.

"Darcy, for *fuck's* sake you have no idea what that noise was—"

"I'm fine," I say, stopping on the second-floor landing. "It was probably just a branch or something.'

"Branches don't *walk*," he says. "And for Chrissake, you're still hurt, you're armed with a *meat thermometer*, you shouldn't just go running off in old houses because fucking *anything* could be up here—"

I start laughing.

"Dammit, I'm serious," he says, but now Trent's grinning too.

"I've got you," I say. "What could I *possibly* be afraid of?"

"Squatters with guns and a temper," he says. "Bears, rattlesnakes, drugged up vagrants, serial killers—"

"I actually wasn't looking for a list," I say, and brandish my meat thermometer at him. Trent makes a face and grabs the end of it, and I hit the button.

"Ninety-six point three. You're cold," I say.

"Extremities are always colder," he points out.

"Maybe you're a ghost."

"Maybe I've been a ghost this whole time," he says dryly, raising his eyebrows. "Maybe I'm secretly Woodford himself."

I reach out and grab Trent's forearm. Warm and solid.

"I'm a stealth ghost," he says, his voice moving lower.

"Is that a thing?" I ask, my voice matching his.

"Sure," he says, and I can see a smile creasing around his eyes, even in the dark. I know Trent so well that I don't even have to see him to know what he looks like, what he's doing.

My hand is still on his arm. I should take it off. I don't.

"What's a stealth ghost *do*?" I ask. "Besides be ninety-six point three degrees?"

"Ghost stuff, but *stealthy*. Boo."

"Walk through a wall or get the fuck out," I tease him.

Trent tilts his head and eyes the wall behind me, his eyes raking over the cracked plaster, wooden slats visible here and there. The interior walls on this floor aren't stone, just the exterior.

"I think I could run through that wall," he says.

We're both still holding onto this meat thermometer that's supposed to be finding ghosts but has only managed to find that I *still* want my best friend, because my hand's still on his arm.

"*Could* and *should* are different things," I point out.

148

"You know you're talking to the Low Valley Leveler, don't you?"

"You ever leveled a wall?"

"Just people so far," he says, and I scrunch my nose. He chuckles. "They knew what they were getting into, don't make that face."

I turn and look at the wall. I'm about ninety-nine percent sure that Trent's got no *real* intention of running through it, but it does *kinda* look like he could.

"You're not gonna get through that undamaged, and I think Nigel might have a stroke," I say. "Literally, Trent. You could kill a man. And then Gavin would come after me for letting you do this."

Trent chuckles. We're still holding onto both ends of the thermometer, and even though it's a really dumb substitute for holding hands, I don't want to let go.

"I won't," he says. "I'd need about ten beers and probably a couple of bumps first, and I haven't done that shit in years."

It's true. Trent hasn't exactly always been the sober one, but he's always been the soberest. Meaning he's saved my ass more than a few times, like the time I went skinny dipping in the Mississippi or the time I wandered into a corn field, somewhere in Iowa, out of my mind on shrooms, convinced that I was in a maze with a chocolate fountain at the center.

I hardly remember that, but apparently, I *really fucking wanted* that chocolate fountain.

"What I *should* do is just throw baby powder on you to find out for sure," I say. "Though I'm still not really sure—"

CRASHthump.

I whirl around, my breath stuck in my throat at the same time as Trent grabs my arm and shoves his way between me and the door. I stumble a little but I'm fine.

Scratch scratch. Thump.

"Stay here," Trent tells me.

149

He glances at the meat thermometer still in my hand, looking unimpressed. Then he bends down, grabs a wooden bannister railing, and pulls it off with one jerk.

Even though my heart is hammering at about a thousand beats per minute, I still notice the way his forearm muscles bunch beneath his tattoos. And I *like* it.

He turns and walks through the doorway, ducking his head just slightly as he moves into the dark. I ignore his order to stay there — like *fuck* I'm staying behind, where the serial killer's serial killing friend can just come grab me? No thanks — and walk softly behind him.

It's nothing, I tell myself. *It's a squirrel, or a bird, or maybe an owl or a chipmunk or—*

I frown, trying to think of more woodland creatures. I grew up in the suburbs and then the city, and none of my parents were ever exactly the *take the kids on a nature walk* type. My education there is mostly limited to the animals who helped Disney princesses clean their houses, as seen on very blurry VHS cassettes.

Tap tap tap tap THUNK slide tap scratch.

I freeze. The room we're in now is big, shelves lining each wall. Probably used to be a study or something, broken windows framing the spindly, spiny arms of evergreen trees outside. The windows up here aren't as broken, meaning that these still have plenty of solid panes left.

Also left in this room, unlike downstairs: furniture. Or *something*, huddled in a mass in the center of the room, covered in a huge white sheet. Even though I know, logically, that it's probably a bookshelf and a desk and a chair or something, it looks spooky as *hell*.

The wind blows. The trees move. The pale shadows left by the moon move.

And under the sheet, something *also* moves.

I gasp, grab Trent's arm, and smash my face into his shoulder blade, the least-brave ghost hunter who's ever existed. I'm good right up until something might actually happen, apparently.

He chuckles.

"Shut up," I whisper, bravely peeking out around his arm.

"I'm pretty sure it's a raccoon," he murmurs, his voice low and steady. "And I'm pretty sure it's more nervous about us than we are about it."

"They're rabid sometimes," I offer, like it excuses my abject cowardice.

"And they're also known to kill humans for fun sometimes," he says.

I squeeze his arm tighter, despite myself.

"You're fucking with me."

"Yeah," he admits, a grin in his voice. "But you thought about it."

"Well, it can have this room," I say. "This is the raccoon's house now."

"I thought you wanted to hunt for ghosts," Trent says, his voice still low and teasing. "You charged up that staircase a couple minutes ago like you were Queen Fuck Everything of I'm The Shit Mountain."

I'm still holding onto him, my body still pressed tightly against his, and it's not because I'm really frightened anymore — the sheet over the furniture keeps wiggling, but I'm pretty sure he's right that it's a raccoon — but because I like it.

I fucking like it and I fucking want this and I want him. Like this, in the dark, in an old romantic getaway that's full of ghosts and wildlife, where he rips railings from bannisters to defend us from cute little woodland critters.

I keep thinking this feeling will go away but it hasn't. It's only built, for *years* now, from the night we met and I thought *hey, he's cute* to sitting together in dressing rooms, listening to music while Gavin and

Liam got high. To telling him all my bad, dark shit, about being a foster kid and running away at fifteen, and instead of backing away like everyone else he told me about his own bad, dark shit about a drunk dad and a mom who wouldn't leave.

Cracking each other up at three in the morning, driving our van from college town bar to college town bar, the other two asleep in the back. Eating breakfast from rest area vending machines as the sun came up. Discovering a shared love of absolutely stupid television and a fascination with weird museums in small towns.

Trent staying here, in Tallwood, to take care of me when he didn't have to.

So I hold onto him, thinking all this and trying not to think at all. Thinking so rarely gets me anything *good*.

Trent crouches down, his arm slipping from my fingers, and he grabs a small chunk of plaster from the floor. Then he stands and tosses it at the sheet-covered furniture.

There's an angry squeak, followed by a scrabbling sound.

"Yeah, I think we're serial killer free," Trent says, crouches for another chunk of plaster, and does it again.

This time a small, pointy, gray face peeks out. It's got that unmistakable bandit mask around the eyes, and is *super* fucking cute.

"Go on, get," Trent says, tossing more plaster at it, small pieces that are only big enough to annoy it, not hurt it.

The raccoon scurries toward the wall where windows are missing. More plaster tossing. More scurrying. Every couple of steps it looks back at us, and I swear it looks way more annoyed than afraid.

Actually, given that I'm still half-standing behind Trent, I think this raccoon might be *judging* me. Fucking wildlife.

"Jesus, this one's an asshole," Trent mutters, pitching one more plaster chunk at it while the thing looks at us disdainfully from the window sill.

"It can have the house, I already said that."

"Go *away*," Trent says, and lobs a final piece. It hits the raccoon square on the side and bounces off harmlessly, clattering to the floor.

The raccoon rolls its eyes. I swear it does. Then it finally leaves, disappearing out the window with the rustle of tree branches.

Trent looks over his shoulder and down at me.

"You can come out now," he murmurs.

"I'm not afraid of raccoons," I say, still half-hiding behind Trent. From the raccoon.

"Sure."

"I just... they have diseases, you know?"

"So you wanted to use me as a human shield."

He's teasing, and I know he's teasing, but something in the way he says it hits me right in the gut. Like I've been using him or something, which is the very last thing I want him to think.

"That's not what I meant," I say softly.

Trent turns to me, and now we're facing each other. The breeze stirs the trees outside and, ever so slightly, the sheets over the furniture.

Suddenly I can't breathe and I can't look him in the eye. This is everything I want and nothing, goddamn *nothing* that I deserve. I charged up here like an asshole and Trent came to save me, and this after two weeks of being my fucking nursemaid.

He didn't know it was a raccoon. He knew it could be something *actually dangerous* and he came anyway without thinking twice.

"Darce, I was just kidding," he says. "I know."

I make myself smile, still looking down because I can't look at him. I can think about a million things I want to say right now, because for some reason this dumb episode with the raccoon has made all of them surface and I don't know *why*.

But I don't say any of them. Instead I whip out the meat thermometer, into the six-inch space between our bodies, and hit the button, the LCD screen lighting up.

"Sixty-five-point-four," I say. "Is that ghostier or less ghosty than downstairs?"

"Less ghosty?" he hazards.

"Or it's an angry ghost."

"Or an angry raccoon."

"That raccoon was annoyed at best," I say. "And why would Woodford be angry?"

I very nearly say *we're not doing any unmarried fucking* but Trent is so close to me that I can feel his body heat and I'm not backing away. *Unmarried fucking* is just about the last thing I'm currently brave enough to say.

"I've got the feeling he's not the most reasonable of ghosts," Trent murmurs.

He's closer. How the fuck did he get closer? I'm still staring at this thermometer like a mix of idiot and asshole, my heart slamming into my ribs with every beat.

"Seems like anything could set him off if he set fire to his own house because someone got it on," I say.

Silence. I turn the thermometer off and put it back into my pocket.

"I guess we should leave before we upset him," I offer, still looking away. At the walls, at the windows, anywhere but at *him* because I'm terrified that he'll be able to see every single thought I've had in the last hour on my face.

"Are we going to upset him?" Trent asks, his voice so low and gravelly that I swear I can feel it in the floorboards.

Look at him, fucking look at him, what's wrong with you?

I squeeze my hands into fists and finally, slowly, raise my eyes to look at Trent. Every nerve in my body is exploding.

"I lied when I said I didn't want this," I whisper, the words coming out in a rush, like someone's yanking them from my mouth.

"You never said that."

"I told you not to kiss me."

"But you never said you didn't want me to."

I touch my fingers to the back of his hand, which twitches, but before he can take my hand in his I move it up his arm, over his patchwork of tattoos to his shoulder, until the back of my hand is resting against his collarbone, and I step in toward him.

Just like that, his arms are around me, warm and thick and familiar because we've hugged probably thousands of times. I know this so well but at the same time I don't.

I've got one hand on his shoulder. The other finds its way, somehow, around the back of his neck. My eyes close again and his hands trace my spine in a whisper, so gentle against my new scar that I can hardly feel them.

Then up, over my neck, and Trent's fingers are warm and solid in my hair. I'm on my tiptoes, eyes closed, and he strokes a thumb across my cheekbone, leaning his forehead against mine.

You can't uncross this bridge, I think. *You still haven't actually kissed him yet, you can back out and it'll be okay, probably—*

I kiss him.

I do it so gently that for an instant I'm not even sure I did or whether my nerves somehow got the better of me and I've started hallucinating, but after a fraction of a second his hand tightens in my hair and he presses his mouth harder against mine and he's warm and hard and soft all at once, everything that I always thought kissing Trent would be.

We kiss harder, his mouth moving against mine, somehow rough and reckless, and I can feel his fingers digging into the base of my spine, tugging me against his wildly before he pulls back, his lips leaving mine.

Trent pauses, just for a split second, like he needs a moment to collect himself. He's breathing hard, and he runs his thumb over my cheekbone again, like he's making sure of something.

And then his mouth is back on mine, harder than before, *needier*, like a dam's burst and he can't hold back. I kiss him fiercely, ferociously, opening my mouth and meeting his tongue with mine, my fingers tight on the back of his neck.

I bite Trent's lip. He groans quietly, pulling my body against his by the hips, his other hand still in my hair. He's hard as a rock, his erection against my lower belly and I move my hips against it, something wild and wanton unlocked inside me as he groans again.

Because Jesus, I fucking *like* that noise and more than anything I like that he's making it.

We pull back again and this time he catches my lower lip between his teeth and I gasp, his fingers digging into my hip, tightening in my hair as I do. Trent pulls my head back, just a little, and he kisses my jaw, his lips lingering there, my throat, the spot just below my ear. There's a noise like someone's whimpering and it takes me a moment to realize it's *me*.

I swallow hard, and wonder—

Through my closed eyelids, there's a flash of white light on the ceiling, and my eyes fly open just in time to see another one.

"Shit," I say out loud.

CHAPTER TWENTY-THREE
Trent

I stop dead in my tracks, lips on the soft, luscious skin of Darcy's neck. I can feel her heart beating a million miles a minute, her voice vibrating through me.

"What?" I ask, letting my mouth brush her, and it works. Her hands tighten on me, and I'm rewarded with a wave of goosebumps on her neck.

I lick it, slowly, and I'm rewarded with another wave. Jesus, I could do this all night.

"Cops," she whispers. "I think they're—"

Darcy's cut off by the unmistakable sound of a big wooden door opening and a man's voice saying something, mid-sentence.

"—kids again, just do this and we'll be back in a jiff," the voice says at a conversational level.

"They never learn, do they?" a woman's voice asks.

The man clears his throat loudly.

"ALL RIGHT, PLEASE COME OUT WITH YOUR HANDS RAISED, YOU'RE TRESPASSING ON PRIVATE PROPERTY WHICH IS AN

ARRESTABLE OFFENSE IN THE STATE OF WASHINGTON. THIS IS THE PONDEROSA COUNTY SHERIFF'S OFFICE."

"Oh fuck," Darcy breathes.

We're still tangled together, and even though I know that getting arrested would be an absolute fucking disaster for me and by extension the band, I almost don't care. I just want them to fucking turn around and leave, because this feels like goddamn heaven and because there's a part of me that's afraid Darcy will back out again.

"Trent, you can't get arrested," she whispers, telling me something I absolutely already know.

I don't move. I hardly breathe, keeping her wrapped tight in my arms, trying to figure a way out but just looping back again and again to Darcy's mouth on mine. The noise she made, her goosebumps under my lips.

"Shhh," I say, hoping that maybe if we stay perfectly silent right here, they'll decide it's nothing and just leave.

But Darcy shakes her head against my chest and pulls away, grabbing my hand. She glances over her shoulder at the door, and the sudden cool air against my front shakes me out of my reverie.

Dammit.

"Come on," she whispers, squeezing my hand in hers.

Down below I can hear the two cops talking to each other as they move around the first floor.

"They'll hear us," I point out.

"Trent, they'll find us if we stay here," she murmurs. "And you know exactly what's going to happen *then* and I'm not about to let Gavin murder me because I let you get your third strike for fucking *ghost hunting*."

The officers downstairs are still clearing rooms, their voices echoing dully. Darcy's eyes are steel, her voice sharp and protective and fierce and that's what finally shakes me out of my reverie and into reality.

And in reality, she's right: I can't get arrested. I don't even want these cops running my record, because they're not likely to let me go afterward.

"Be *quiet*. Walk as close to the walls as you can, the floorboards are usually sturdier there. Whatever happens, just keep moving," she says, her voice rushed and quiet as she pulls on my hand, leading me away from the staircase.

"We might draw more attention to ourselves by jumping out a window," I point out.

She's tiptoeing along, her back to a wall, and she looks at me like she's almost amused.

"We're taking the servants' stairs," she says.

We pass through a doorway, and while Darcy's somehow perfectly quiet, a floorboard squeaks under my foot and I freeze, afraid it'll happen again if I take another step. I can't hear the cops downstairs anymore, so I don't know if they've heard me, if they're coming up the main staircase now...

"Keep moving," Darcy orders me. "It's an old house. Everything is making noise, all the time."

She squeezes my hand again.

"Trust me," she says, looking over her shoulder and *almost* smiling.

And I do. I trust her because I trust *her*, and because even though sneaking through the dark is completely out of my wheelhouse, it's right in hers.

We both had our bad years. I spent mine in the dust and dirt of Low Valley where nothing I ever did was quiet or sneaky, where when I broke the law I did it good and hard and *loud*.

But Darcy's were spent quieter, surviving Wisconsin winters in abandoned buildings, stealing food and clothing, breaking into houses and crashing on the couches of families gone for the winter. And she mostly did it without getting caught.

So when she tells me how to sneak around somewhere without the police catching on, I do what she says.

We get through two more rooms. The floor boards creak below our feet and my heart hammers on, chanting *don't stop, don't stop*, and we keep moving until we're in a hallway with no windows at all, pitch-dark, the only light from a small hole in the ceiling.

We stop. I can hear Darcy breathing softly, and I press my back against the wall.

"Is this—"

Darcy whirls and claps her hand over my mouth, and in the almost-total dark I can just barely glimpse movement. I think she's shaking her head, and then she slides her hand around my face, steadies herself against my shoulder, lifts her lips to my ear as she pulls my head down.

"They're coming up the stairs," she says, her voice so quiet I can barely hear it. "The back stairs are at the end of the hall. Hold onto the bannister, walk next to the wall, and pray they haven't rotted through."

Darcy doesn't wait for an answer, just pulls me along in the dark, and I let her lead, groping along the wall until she finds the space and lets go of my hand.

The back staircase is narrow and dark, so dark I can barely see Darcy in front of me, moving silently downward. I'm less silent, less practiced in the ways of knowing where to step on stairs that haven't been used in a hundred years, and when we reach a landing I stumble a little, bumping into the wall.

"You okay?" her disembodied voice whispers.

"Fine," I answer, and we go down the second flight, the faint moonlight trickling in as we reach the first floor.

There's a door at the bottom. Thank Christ, there's a door at the bottom, because even though I can't identify *where* I can hear the two cops creaking along the floorboards somewhere upstairs, and it wouldn't take a genius to figure out where we went.

I reach a hand toward the knob, but Darcy grabs my wrist and stops me. I let her, and she turns the knob slowly herself, her eyes wide in the darkness, listening for a squeak.

There's nothing. She pulls the door open, but neither of us move.

On the other side, it's completely boarded up. The boards are old and dried-out, cracked and weak-looking. There's another creak upstairs, and Darcy's eyes dart after it, nervously, and she bites her lip.

I eye the boards over the door. They're not that strong. I can't see any nails sticking out, and I take a step back, getting ready.

Hit it on the edge, maybe pop the nails out. Wouldn't take more than a few blows, Darcy could get out pretty easy at least.

She grabs my arm like she can read my mind, which maybe she can. Even in the low light, even as she's nervous about the cops' footsteps along the floor above, she's giving me a *don't be an idiot* look.

I shrug.

She points to the next room, which has a row of shattered windows, and I swear she smirks at me before grabbing me hand again and leading me through this door into the room filled with light and the tiny, dull sparkles of old shattered glass.

In seconds, she finds the emptiest window frame. She walks up to it, old glass crunching underfoot, and inspects it like an expert. There are still glimmers of glass in the frame but it doesn't look freshly broken, it looks old and weathered but still sharp. Still dangerous.

"Darce," I murmur. "Don't get—"

Before I finish the sentence, she's whipped her long-sleeve shirt off and tossed it over the window frame, nothing but a black tank top underneath. As she

161

hops up onto the window frame, her shirt covering the glass, despite my entire *being* I can't stop myself from noticing the way the moonlight highlights her nipples through the tight fabric, the way her chest jiggles through the tight shirt—

She hops off the other side. I close my eyes and swallow, listen to the footsteps overhead, ever closer to the back stairs, remind myself that this is *no fucking time*.

Darcy's face appears again on the other side, eyebrows raised.

Come on, she mouths, so I follow suit, over the broken glass beneath her shirt, onto the grass below. Darcy pulls me against the wall to the left of the window and we stand there for a long moment, backs against the wall, breathing hard.

I don't watch her pant for breath. I don't watch the way her chest expands and falls underneath her tight tank top, I don't notice the way her nipples pucker in the cool night air or the way she leans her head against the stone wall as she breathes hard, her neck waiting and soft and perfect and even more tempting now that I know what it *tastes* like—

"Now's the risky part," she says.

I dart my eyes back to her face, and she's watching me, desaturated in the moonlight, her expression somewhere between nervous and mischievous.

"Now?" I murmur, because despite how *fucking* bad it would be for me if I got caught, how *fucking* bad that would be for all of Dirtshine, this doesn't feel risky. It at least feels familiar, like something I used to know but sort of forgot about.

But Darcy, saying *I lied when I said I didn't want this?*

That's fucking new, it's untouched, it's wilderness territory, a dreamscape, a land I've never visited before and can't fucking *wait* to get back to. In comparison, cops are old hat.

"We've gotta run across the yard for the gate and hope they don't see us," she says.

"Wall's closer."

"The wall is seven feet high."

"I can get you over."

Darcy gives me a long, slow, sidelong look.

"Can you get *you* over?"

"Of course," I say, hoping I sound confident because I'm not fucking sure. I've never climbed a mossy seven-foot high wall before, but I'm fucking *certain* I can get Darcy over and somehow, that's more important.

She shakes her head.

"The gate is better," she says. "If we get caught, you just make a run for it and I'll try to let you get away. My record's fine, all my juvenile shit is sealed, so—"

I walk for the wall, leaving Darcy mid-sentence because this was *my* idea and like hell I'm letting her take the fall if something goes bad. Yeah, I'll be fucked, but I'd rather that.

"*Trent*," she hisses, and I keep walking. The gate's on the other side of the house completely but the wall's not far from this side of the house, just around the corner from the window we got through. In ten steps I'm there, staring at this thing, starting to wonder what the fuck I was thinking.

Soft footsteps behind me and I turn. She's glaring, but behind her I see a flashlight beam through the window, bouncing off a wall in the house.

"Goddamn it," she whispers, and I crouch, lacing my fingers together in a foothold.

"Come on."

"You can't just fucking—"

"I'm not going over until you're over and we both know it," I murmur. "So hop on if you don't want me to spend the best years of my life behind bars, Darce."

"God fucking *damn* it," she mutters, but she puts one foot into my hands, steadying herself against the wall, her leg straight and I stand, practically launching her upward. In a second she's got her other leg over the top, stomach down on top of the wall, and then she takes a deep breath and disappears, a *thud* on the other side.

I'm not worried. I'm pretty sure Darcy knows how to jump off a wall like this without getting hurt.

But now I've got another problem, because lifting her was a fucking piece of cake and now I've got this wall to contend with. It's made of stone but all the rocks in it are smooth, rounded, half-covered with moss and lichen so they don't offer a single handhold or foothold.

I glance back at the house just as a flash of light washes across a still-intact window.

We left her shirt there, I realize. *They'll know we're out here.*

Fuck.

One of the cops walks into something, probably flashlight-blind, and I hear him curse. I hold my breath, desperately scanning the wall for something, because I'm afraid that if I try to just jump it my hands will slip, I'll fall, and *then* I'll be well and truly fucked.

"Hey," I hear the female cop say.

"Yeah?" the other answers her.

"There's fabric over this window frame."

And they've found it, and I'm fucked if I don't get over this wall *right fucking now*.

I'm out of options. I take a few steps back. Take a deep breath, flex my hands, and take a running leap at the thing.

CHAPTER TWENTY-FOUR
Darcy

I hold my breath, the rocks and fallen sticks on top of this wall digging into my ribs and my tits, scratching me where my tank top's ridden up. It's a ways down on the other side and so dark where the moonlight doesn't shine that I can barely see the ground at all.

This isn't even the worst you've done, I tell myself. *Don't be a fucking pussy.*

Before I can think about it, I slide my legs over the other side of the wall and then I'm dangling, torso on the foot-wide wall, absolutely *smashing* my tits as my fingers clutch the smooth rocks, trying to find some kind of purchase at all.

It doesn't work. I'm sliding. This was the stupidest possible way to go over this wall, and now all there is it to do is to let go.

I hope there's not a moat and I hope I don't fall onto broken glass, and I let myself drop.

It's just sticks and leaves below me, thank God, and it's uneven so I stumble a little and then fall to one side, but I'm fine. I'm bruised and scratched but fine, and instantly, I stand, looking for Trent.

No sign.

I should have helped, I think. Not that I know what the fuck was I going to do, since it's not like I can lift six-foot-something Trent over the wall my own damn self, but I could have done *something*.

"Trent?" I hiss.

Nothing.

My heart's racing. I'm still panting for breath and fucking *powerless* to do anything but stand here, watching the wall. I can't even get back over myself — there's no way to climb its smooth, slick surface that I can see and it's not like I've got the upper body arm strength to grab the top and pull myself over.

The fuck was his plan? I wonder. *The fuck was he thinking, he can't climb this, if he tries to grab something he'll slide off and Jesus I shouldn't have let him do this, I should have dragged him around to the gate, we'd already be gone by now and he wouldn't—*

Trent's head appears with a gasp, both hands grabbing at the slick rocks.

I run over, both hands covering my mouth so I don't yelp, but I don't know what the fuck I can *do*.

One of his hands slips and he crashes to his elbow with a grunt, but he finds purchase with the other and pushes himself up, listing to one side. I hold my breath, hoping that the cops can't see him, hoping that he doesn't crash to the ground on the other side because they will *definitely* see that.

Trent heaves one leg onto the top of the wall, then the other. I breathe again and he exhales loudly, his breath whistling onto the stone. Then he heaves himself over, feet first, and he lands better and more gracefully than I did.

And he grins at me.

"Told you," he says. "You okay?"

I just nod, silent. On the other side of the wall I can hear a wooden thumping, like the cops are stomping back through the house, but then it fades.

"They leaving?" I whisper.

Trent shrugs. He's still breathing hard, his shirt torn in one spot where something must have caught it.

"I'm on this side with you," he points out. "Let's get outta here."

I glance around, looking down the wall. This side is carpeted with sticks and leaves, all crunchy and loud as hell. We could run through the woods, but I've got no clue at all where we'd end up then — most of the area around Tallwood is forest, so we'd be as likely to die of exposure or something as to ever make it to the car.

So I stand quietly. I listen hard, and the night is dead quiet aside from the breeze rustling the trees, the sound of our own breathing, Trent softly clearing his throat as he crosses his arms in front of his chest, watching me. Waiting for the go-ahead, because sneaking out of a situation instead of punching my way through is my area of expertise, not his.

And I'm lost. I'm half thinking about how to get out of here without being seen, about whether the cops will hear us crunching through the forest or whether they'll catch us walking back down the long driveway to our car, but I'm half thinking that I should just kiss Trent again, right now, because fuck everything else, *that's* what I want.

I want *him*, because I've already lied to myself for years and this is where I snapped.

"Well?" he rumbles, a half-smile lifting his lips in the moonlight, and I exhale, shaking off thoughts of me against a wall, legs wrapped around him.

"I think we're okay," I whisper. "I didn't hear the car leave, but I think they're at least heading that way..."

I stop abruptly.

Voices.

Unmistakably *cop* voices, and in that second every muscle in my body tenses. I nearly tell Trent to go, *run*, but I bite my lip because I know it's stupid.

"Get down," I hiss instead, lurching forward and grabbing his arm. "Against the wall. Be *quiet*."

In a flash we're there, backs to the cool stone, sitting on the ground that's half-dirt, half leaves. I'm trying not to move, not to *breathe*, because I think we're out of options. If we run they find us and if we make noise they find us and if we do nothing at all, they *maybe* still find us.

Neither of us breathes a word, just look at each other. It's long and slow and searching and moonlit, and even though it's chilly out here it sparks something, and suddenly I'm nervous and I don't know why, other than the feeling that I'm about to jump off a waterfall.

He reaches out, slowly. He runs his thumb along the skin on my chest, just above the low-cut neck of my shirt, and I shiver, looking down. There's a long, ugly scratch, blood welling up in droplets. I hadn't noticed it before, but now he's looking at me, eyebrows up, the question obvious.

I shake my head.

It's nothing.

But I run my hand down his torso until I find the hole in his shirt. I poke one finger through, wiggling it.

He shakes his head, a smile around his eyes.

It's nothing.

I lift his shirt and find a bruised scratch underneath, and even in the moonlight I can tell it's already purpling. I lift my eyebrows at him, not sure of the game we're playing now, but knowing that it matters over the cold and over the stones sticking into my back and over the footsteps of the police officers slowly growing closer.

Really? I'm asking.

Trent grins and grabs my wrist, his hand somehow warm as a furnace despite the cold, and he pulls me until I'm facing him and my arm is around him, his face almost against mine.

"I'm fine," he rumbles, his voice barely audible even to me, an inch away.

"You sure?" I ask.

Trent smiles, and I feel it more than I see it, the faint motion of his face against mine.

He kisses me again, and again there's a slow rush, the feeling that my whole body sings one perfect harmonic note, the wave of disbelief and nervousness as I kiss him back, press my mouth even harder to his.

We move slowly, silently. His lips move against mine and I open my mouth against his, because even here, on the cold ground, in the dark, I want more because I've always wanted more.

Trent pulls back, barely, and ends the kiss silently.

"Yeah, I'm sure," he murmurs.

Then his hand is in my hair and we're kissing again even though I can hear the cops coming closer. They're talking about something inane, something to do with their sergeant's kid and how he won't eat anything but goldfish crackers and milk and I know they're *right there* but I don't care. I can't even try.

We pull back again. I'm breathing hard and trying to do it quietly, running one hand along Trent's jaw and down his neck, finding the muscles in his shoulders and digging my fingers in, half just to make sure that this is *happening*.

"—Ought to make it clear that he's not getting any dinner unless he eats what the family's eating," a female voice says, just close enough that I can hear.

Trent pulls me in again, his hand on my waist, my hip, his fingers pressing into the dip of my lower back. I kiss him again, pushing myself into his warm, solid body, feeling like I need this more than *air*.

"We tried that with my oldest and she was stubborn as a mule," the male voice says, getting closer.

He pulls me again, harder, and there's something urgent and insistent about it, like he needs this *now* so I throw one leg over his lap and now I'm straddling him, up against the wall. I'm trying to be silent but it's fucking *hard* because I'm so turned on and lit up that I feel electric, anything but *quiet*.

Trent grabs my hips and pulls me down, *hard*, and suddenly I'm pressed against something hard and thick and *big*. I gasp into Trent's mouth and he growls, quietly, his teeth on my lip.

"...just got to show them who's in charge," the woman says, and she's close. Close enough that I should stop, that *we* should stop if only for thirty seconds but I've already passed that point.

Instead I tighten my finger in Trent's hair and fight down a moan, rolling my hips against him, the heat between my legs sending sparks jittering through every inch of my body. I'm so far past *I shouldn't do this* that I can't even see it in the rear-view mirror.

Trent pulls my head back. He presses his lips to my jaw, my neck, the spot right under my ear and I grit my teeth together, forcing myself not to make a sound as I move my hips again, one hand flat against the cool stone of the wall.

Something snaps under my knee. It's *loud*, and the moment it happens we both freeze.

The murmured chatter from the other side of the wall stops instantly. I hold my breath, afraid *that's* enough sound to alert them, even as Trent softly takes his lips from my neck, and I lean my forehead against his, one hand on his face.

They have to come around, I think frantically. *They're not going to climb that wall, and while they do we can run for it, they've only got guns and a car...*

Maybe he'll get out of it. He's polite, he's not a teenager, maybe they'll let him off with a warning and won't check his record.

He kisses me again. So softly I barely feel it, but I kiss him back, my heart in my throat.

"Okay," says the man. "How should we do this?"

"This is your last chance to surrender yourselves," the woman says.

They pause. We don't make a single fucking sound.

"Right, thought so," she mutters. "I'll go around and you wait by the car, in case they make a run for it the other way? If they run through the woods they're liable to get eaten by bears."

She says the last part louder, like it's for our benefit. We don't move.

The man sighs.

"Right, let's get it over with," he says. "I'll—"

There's a sudden burst of static, and he curses.

"Jesus, how come radio silence is the loudest damn part?" he grouses. "Yep, Russell and Jones here."

I can't make out what the radio's saying, but I'm barely breathing. I think my hands are shaking, because I'm thinking frantically: *maybe if we run we can make it. Don't take the driveway, just head downhill through the woods...*

It's fucking stupid and probably dangerous, because careening downhill in the woods is how you do dumb shit like fall off boulders and cliffs, but that might be better than the alternative.

"We should go *now*," I murmur into Trent's ear. "I think we can—"

Trent grabs my wrist, holding me down.

"Wait," he whispers. "Listen."

I listen. I close my eyes and strain my ears but I can't make out a goddamn thing over the crackling of the radio and my own nerves, and I shake my head.

"I can't—"

"Did you get all that?" the man says.

171

"Is it that damn 7-11 again?"

"Allen and Main," the man says.

"Armed?"

"Yup."

She sighs.

"Let me guess, we're the closest because Kurzweil and LaCroix are out at some tweaker cabin in the mountains trying to talk someone down off a pile of meth."

"You said it, not me."

"At least it's a real crime," she says, sounding resigned.

Then she raises her voice and *unmistakably* shouts at the wall where we're sitting.

"Don't trespass!" she calls. "There's cameras everywhere, it's not worth your dumb ass spending a night in jail!"

The man chuckles. They walk away, their voices receding away until they're gone.

It must be a full minute until I can breathe again. Maybe longer. I wonder if it's some sort of elaborate trap to get us to fuck up and come out, but nothing else happens.

Except slowly, almost thoughtfully, Trent presses his lips to my neck again and my eyes slide closed despite myself. Slowly, his hand makes its way under my shirt, his thumb stroking my belly as I move my hips against his again because even here, like this, I can't help myself.

Finally, Trent stops me. He pulls me back, panting for breath, and looks at me through heavy-lidded eyes. I tilt my head to one side and swallow hard, suddenly afraid he's going to say *we should take it slow* or *this isn't what I want from you* or something equally bullshit.

Because I don't want to take it fucking *slow*, I want Trent here and now, cold and dirt be damned.

"Yes?" I finally ask.

"We should go," he murmurs.

I stop for a moment, not sure what he means.

"You're freezing and there's cameras," he points out. "But I've got a very warm hotel room."

CHAPTER TWENTY-FIVE
Trent

I don't want to leave. I want to stay here, like this, with Darcy on top of me, writhing and a little bit dirty but beautiful as *fuck*.

"I'm not that cold," she says, even though I can see the goosebumps on her arms in the moonlight.

I pull her in and kiss her again, just because I don't want the moment to end, not yet. I want her naked in the dirt, against the wall, on top of me. I want her wherever, it doesn't fucking matter. I just want *her*, like I always have, only now I'm impossibly close.

"I'm not waiting for them to come back," I murmur into her ear. "Once was enough, don't you think?"

Darcy sighs, and the sound turns to a gasp as I bite her earlobe, tugging it between my teeth.

But we have to go. The only consolation is the disappointed look on her face, confirmation that I didn't fucking imagine this, that I didn't somehow ruin the best thing I have.

We walk the stone wall and hold hands. There's no cop car, though we walk along the very edge of the driveway, like we can dive into the woods if one comes along. Darcy's hand is freezing in mine, and every time I look over at her I swear her nipples are puckered harder, just *begging* me to stop in the road and suck them into my mouth, one by one, just to hear the way she'd gasp.

I don't. The cop obviously wasn't lying about the cameras. They knew we were here somehow.

When we finally get to the car, there's an envelope stuffed under a windshield wiper. Darcy takes it off, looking amused, and when she flips it over she starts laughing.

"Guess how much," she says, her eyes dancing.

I sigh. No, I didn't fucking think this ghost-hunting trip through. I came up with it five hours ago because I was desperate to make things better with Darcy, because even though she was right there I fucking *missed* her.

It did work.

"Fifty bucks," I say, thinking that Tallwood is a pretty small town, so the parking tickets should be reasonable.

Darcy just snorts, then jerks one thumb upward as I unlock the car.

"A hundred."

"When was the last time you got a parking ticket for a hundred dollars?" she says as we get in and buckle up. I turn the car on and crank the heater, directing all the vents toward her. She makes a face and turns it down.

"I don't know the last time I got a parking ticket," I say.

Darcy rolls her eyes, but she knows I'm not lying. I'll circle a block for thirty minutes before I risk having to interact with a cop, even parking enforcement.

"It's not a hundred dollars."

"Two."

"Closer."

I turn on the headlights, splashing a bright pool in front of the car, tree trunks going ghostly in the sudden light.

"Two-fifty."

"Two sixty three."

And fucking worth it.

Even if they run my plates and catch me for trespassing, fucking worth it.

I look over at her, dark hair spilling in front of her face, flipping the ticket over in her hand.

"It's fucking highway robbery. Literally."

"Darce."

She looks up, tucks her hair behind an ear.

"C'mere," I say softly.

Darcy gives me a quick glance, up and down, like she's not sure what I want, like she's not sure that *I* want it, but she leans in and I kiss her again just because I can. Because deep down I'm afraid that between here and the lodge she'll realize again that this is a bad idea, that she'll want to turn back the clock because she's afraid of losing us the way we were.

But then her mouth is on mine. I lick her bottom lip and she lets me in, her hand in my hair, half-turned in her seat, and I've got one hand on her thigh and when we pull back she swallows, breathing hard, then bites my lip just for good measure.

I drive dangerously fast back to the lodge. The whole way we talk about nothing, just like we always do.

• • •

It's late when we get back, well past midnight. The moon has lowered again and the stars are out full force, though I hardly fucking notice.

I kiss Darcy again in the parking lot, before I get out of the car, my fingers wandering down her body. I think about climbing into the passenger seat, on top of her, and just taking her right there because it's late and no one's around and I feel like I'm coming out of my skin I want this so bad.

But I can see the window of my room from there. I can put this off for sixty seconds to avoid a public nudity charge.

We walk through the parking lot, my heart pounding, her hand in mine. This time when the breeze moves her hair off her neck and I can see the pink scar of her burn, I don't stop myself. I lean over and plant my lips right at the edge, where her back meets her neck, and I listen for the noise she makes deep in her throat even as all her muscles tense.

"C'mon," she laughs.

We're right in front of the heavy wooden door to the lodge, and I spin her around, push her against it. Gently, because of her back.

"C'mon what?"

Darcy grabs a fistful of my shirt and tugs, tilting her face up toward mine.

"C'mon, we're in public," she teases.

"And?"

"And *public*," she says.

"It's two o'clock in the morning," I say, resting one forearm on the door over her head. "No one's here. We could get up to *anything*."

I swear her breath catches a little at *anything*, her fist on my shirt tightens, and I push my hips against hers, the pressure delicious on my rock-hard cock. Darcy bites her lip and smiles, her eyes drifting closed.

"Who the fuck are you and what did you do with Trent?" she asks.

I chuckle and slide one hand under her shirt, up her side, her breathing fast and her skin soft under my fingertips.

"What makes you think I'm not Trent?"

"Because Trent is my sweet, quiet, broody, best friend who does a lot of glowering and acts like I'm his little sister," she says, but there's a smile in her voice.

"Are you sure he's not your broody best friend who glowers and thinks about this nearly every day?"

"Not anymore," she says.

I close the last two inches and kiss her hard, up against the door of the lodge. I move my hand up her torso, past her ribcage, as she opens her mouth into mine and her tongue darts into my mouth. I'm nearly shaking with desire, with the force of finally doing something I've thought about for *years*, and there's a part of me that wants to tear her clothes off right here, right now. Lift her against this door and take her hard until she fucking *screams*, her nails raking down my back.

But I don't. I run the pad of my thumb along the undercurve of one breast and she sighs, pressing her hips harder against mine so I keep going. I run my thumb along her nipple and feel it harden as I do.

Fuck it's satisfying. *Fuck* if the way she grabs my hip, pulls me harder against her isn't exactly what I've always dreamed of, so I do it again. She bites my lip, but she puts one hand on my chest. Pushes slightly.

"C'mon," I tease.

"You know there's cameras out here, right?" she murmurs, still smiling.

I sigh and lean my forehead against hers.

"Fucking police state."

"You know someone would pay for footage of us..."

She stops short, blue eyes wide and smiling in the dark.

"Don't stop there."

"Getting friendly."

"You weren't going to say *getting friendly*."

"Whatever I was going to say, someone would pay for it."

I push her harder against the door, my aching cock pressed between us, my hand still up her shirt, and I put my lips to her ear.

"You've got the filthiest mouth I know of and you were going to say *fucking*," I murmur, praying I'm right. "Dunno why you suddenly got shy. It's just me, Darce."

She swallows so hard I can hear the muscles in her throat move.

"Well, I know where there's no cameras."

Darcy slides her hand into mine.

"And?"

"And it's two hundred feet away."

"And?"

I close my teeth around her earlobe, just for fun. She inhales sharply.

"*And*, I propose we go there instead of staying here where your dick is going to end up in the National Enquirer."

I can't help but laugh, because *there* it is, the filthy Darcy I know. I don't answer her, just yank open the door next to the one she's up against and we step through, into the lobby, as Darcy pulls down her shirt and runs one hand through her hair.

Sitting in one of the overstuffed recliners by the fireplace, Gavin turns to look at us.

Darcy stops short. I nearly run into her, and for a long moment, we all just look at each other.

"Oi!" Gavin finally says.

"Hey!" Darcy says back, too bright and chirpy. "What are you still doing up?"

Gavin shrugs, standing.

"Couldn't sleep for shite," he says. "You had the same problem, I assume?"

He's giving us both a once over and obviously doesn't think we had the same problem, given that my shirt is torn and Darcy's arms are scratched up and we're both dirty, our pants muddy in spots.

"Something like that," I say.

Gavin leans against the back of a leather chair and crosses his arms, half looking at us and half glancing around the lodge's lobby.

"The heroin *did* help me sleep," he says reflectively. "Rather too much sometimes, but it was useful for that."

"It even helped you sleep on stage," Darcy points out, and Gavin just laughs.

"True," he says. "Listen, while it's just us three in the middle of the bleeding night, I may as well apologize for earlier today. I was being a right cock at practice, and I ought to know better."

Darcy sighs and folds her arms in front of her.

"Yeah," she agrees. "But there's been a whole lot of shit lately, between the delay and Eddie's bullshit and, you know, *everything* so it's okay. I get it."

I shove my hands into my pockets and just nod.

Gavin sighs and rubs his face in his hands.

"Thanks," he says. "I'm trying to be better about everything, but you know it's a bit... strange, doing it all like this."

"You mean not high?" Darcy says, to-the-point like usual.

"I mean not high, not drunk. Fully fucking present."

There's a pause. Darcy looks at Gavin and Gavin stares into space for a moment, then looks back at us. I can sense that this conversation is somehow important, that we're seeing a window into the new Gavin, the post-heroin, with-Marisol Gavin, and I should be treasuring this moment as the beginning of a new kind of friendship with an old friend.

But god*damn* it, I was in the middle of something.

"And to be honest, it's been a year now without Liam and I still fucking make mental notes of the things I ought to tell him sometimes," Gavin admits. "Christ, it feels like he's dead sometimes, doesn't it?"

Darcy doesn't answer, just steps forward, reaches out and pats Gavin on the shoulder. Somehow, she's much better at this than me, which is why she's the glue that holds us all together. Me, I'm broody and I glower too much. Without her, we'd all have scattered ages ago.

"If he were dead, someone would probably have told you by now," she says, and Gavin laughs.

"Cold comfort, that is."

"I'm not gonna blow sunshine up your ass."

"And thanks for that."

"Look, drink some tea or whatever and try going back to bed. You'll feel better in the morning," Darcy says, rubbing his shoulder lightly.

"Yeah, that always helps," I chime in, because I feel like during this heart-to-heart I should say *something*. Even if what I want to say is *can we please fucking talk about this in the morning.*

"You're right," Gavin says, and stands up straight. "Shall we?"

Shit. His room's right across the hall from mine.

"Let's go!" Darcy says too brightly, glancing quickly at me as the three of us leave the lobby.

CHAPTER TWENTY-SIX
Darcy

Even if I'm not exactly sure what's happening between Trent and me right now, I know one thing: *Gavin does not need to know about it.* For fuck's sake, I'd at least like to know about it before I go broadcasting it to my bandmate.

Who I imagine won't be thrilled. Who I imagine will just see it as another pitfall that Dirtshine could fall into, another hurdle to get over. We've never discussed intra-band relations before but I've got a feeling that Gavin — particularly new, *sober* Gavin — isn't going to be a fan.

"Yeah, it's late," Trent rumbles. "Better get some sleep before practice tomorrow."

"Sleep is really important," I add, sounding fucking stupid.

Gavin gives me a slight side-eye, and I imagine it's because it's dead late at night and I've obviously been up to something that wasn't sleeping. But then he kinda shrugs as we turn the corner into the hall where our rooms are, and I glance at Trent.

He glances back at me, the side of his mouth just barely hitching up and I know exactly what he's thinking: *sleep's not that important.*

I walk ahead. Gavin starts chatting about something else, but I'm not listening and I don't think Trent is, either. Instead my whole body is alive, humming, *waiting*. It's the feeling I get when we're out on stage, the lights down, seconds before we start a show. When the crowd is screaming and stomping and losing their minds, just before we start.

Like I'm swimming through pure anticipation, like swimming through cement toward our rooms. I don't think anything's ever gone slower, but at last Gavin stops and pulls his key from his pocket.

"This is me," he says. "See you all bright and early, yeah?"

"Heh," Trent says, pulling his own key out. Our rooms are all clustered together at the end of this hallway, so I grab my room key as well, figuring I may as well keep up the charade.

"Sure, bright and early," I lie, and stand there, my key hovering over the lock.

Gavin gives me a slightly weird look, but then he seems to shrug it off. He unlocks his door, the light flashes green, and he turns the knob.

"Goodnight then," he says, and disappears into the dark beyond.

Trent and I look at Gavin's door, like we're waiting for him to reappear, point at us, and say *I know what you're about to do.*

But he doesn't. Of course he doesn't. The door stays shut and after a long pause, we turn to each other and now my nerves are singing, fucking vibrating, strings wound so tight the notes could shatter glass.

And Trent grins.

In a second he's in front of me, pushing me against my door, his mouth on mine as he takes the key out of my hand and puts it into the lock while I grab the front of his belt and *pull* him against me because I've waited years for this and I don't fucking think I can wait any longer.

The door beeps. Trent bites my lip, growling, pulls the key out and reinserts it.

It beeps again, flashing red, and I start laughing.

"It's upside-down," I tell him.

"I hate these fucking things," he mutters, flipping it around.

This time it works, the door opens behind me, and I stumble backward into my hotel suite. The door swings shut by itself, Trent tosses my key somewhere, takes me by the hips and walks me backward until I'm pressed against the counter in my tiny kitchen.

He kisses me, hard, grinding me against the fake marble, his erection against my belly and his tongue in my mouth. I grab his shirt and pull as hard as I can, even though every inch of his body that can be is already touching mine, alive and electric.

There's a tearing sound, and Trent breaks the kiss, laughing.

"Did you just tear my fucking shirt?"

I look down, laughing, my fingers through the hole.

"I only made the rip bigger," I say, but he's grinning, his face above mine, a hungry, *ferocious* grin with a light in his eyes I swear I've seen a thousand times.

"You're so fucking eager for this you tore my shirt," he goes on, and slides both his hands under my tank top, his palms rough against my skin. Even though it's warm in here, I shiver as he pulls my shirt over my head and I'm half-naked in front of him.

It's not the first time, but it's the first time like *this*. The first time he grabs my breasts in both hands and pinches my nipples while he claims my mouth, then chuckles as I moan.

"I wish I'd known," he murmurs.

I yank on his shirt again. It tears more and I can feel his hard, warm skin underneath.

"You know now," I say, and shove the fabric up, tugging it over his head.

I've seen him shirtless before. We fucking toured in a van together, of course I've seen him shirtless before, but suddenly I get to *touch*. I get to *feel* him, every muscular ripple, every tattoo, every raised white scar. The dent in his collarbone where it got broken once, the three pale partial rings on the front of his shoulder from a hot stove.

They're covered with ink, some good and some shitty, and they're hard to see. But I know where they are because he's shown me, and I touch every single one. Trent just watches my face, his hands holding onto the counter on either side of me until at last, I grab the back of his neck again and pull his face down to mine and we're skin-to-skin, so close I can feel his heart beating.

His hands are everywhere on me, insistent and urgent, except he's careful of my back. Even as he rolls my nipples between his fingers and I gasp his name, my nails digging into his skin, he doesn't touch my back, because this is *Trent* and for all that he's broody and glowering and I know he's capable of serious damage, he's never hurt me and I know in my bones that he never will.

I yank on his belt, fumbling with it, my tongue in his mouth as he grinds into me, his hands everywhere. I finally get his belt undone and shove my hand into his jeans.

Shit, he's big. It's not like I didn't know — van, remember? — but I've never seen him hard and as much as I thought about this, being here with Trent growl-moaning as he bites my lip while I stroke him, it's kind of a surprise.

With my other hand, I frantically get the buttons on his jeans undone, jerk his fly open, and the whole thing springs out. Trent's breathing goes ragged, his hand locked in my hair, his face against mine.

"Fuck, that feels good," he whispers, so I bite my lip and stroke harder.

"Handjobs, huh?" I tease, and Trent smiles.

"I just like it when you touch my dick," he says, half-laughing, so I stroke him again, the bare tip of his cock against my belly.

He kisses me, grabbing the waistband of my jeans, and somehow with one yank he undoes them, slides the fly down, and then his hand is inside my underwear, between my legs.

"Seems like you like it too," he murmurs. I know I'm wet as hell, throbbing and *aching* as his fingers explore me.

He strokes my lips, just barely dipping one fingertip inside, and I grit my teeth, forcing myself not to shout, but as he finds my clit and rubs it slowly, I can't fucking help myself.

"Trent," I whisper.

He nuzzles my face and growls.

"Say it again."

I swallow.

"Trent?"

"Not like it's a question," he laughs, his fingers still moving. "Say it like you're half-naked, wet as hell, and I'm about to find out how loud you are when you come."

I grab the back of his head with the hand that's not on his cock and pull his face to mine, my eyes closed because he's fucking right about all of it.

"*Trent*," I say, and before I can say anything else his lips are on mine, hungry and desperate, his whole body pressed against mine as my legs start to weaken.

But he stops. His lips still on mine, he pulls his hand out. He yanks my jeans and panties down, lifts me by the hips, sits me on the counter. Pulls them the rest of the way off and shoves my knees apart, his body between them. I wrap my legs around him, still throbbing.

His lips land on mine, my neck, my throat, my collarbone. One by one he sucks each nipple into his mouth as I gasp, my head back against the cabinets, his hands still on my inner thighs as I reach back and grab a cabinet knob, just to grab *something*.

It's strange as hell, but it's *right*. I don't do this, let anyone see me this way, naked and vulnerable and *wanting*. I don't fucking spread my legs on my kitchen counter and gasp someone's name.

But this is anything but *usual*. Sex is *usually* infrequent and drunk, under the covers when the itch gets bad enough I need to scratch it.

Trent's mouth moves to the valley between my breasts, over my ribs. He dips his tongue into my bellybutton and I gasp.

"What are you doing?" I whisper.

He looks at me, eyes laughing, like I'm an idiot.

"I'm eating you out," he says. "The fuck did you think I was doing?"

He doesn't wait for a response, because then his face is between my thighs and he licks me with one long, slow swipe from my swollen lips to my slit and back. My whole body jerks. My toes curl. My hands tighten, one on the edge of the counter and one on the cabinet pull. I think I *grunt*.

"Okay," I whisper, and I swear to God he laughs but as long as he doesn't stop, I don't care.

He doesn't stop. His fingers dig into my thighs, my head back against the cabinets as his tongue swirls around and dear fucking God it feels good. I can't remember the last time something felt this good.

I'm sky-high in what feels like seconds. I'm squirming, gasping for air, trying not to kick Trent, and I do but he doesn't seem to care. I've got one hand in his hair and the other still on the damn cabinet pull.

"I think I'm gonna come," I whisper.

Trent licks me harder, faster. He sucks my clit into his mouth, flicking his tongue across and I think I fucking *shout*, just about to go over the edge.

Then he does it again, and I shout, "Oh, *fuck!*" and I fall. I come fucking hard and I'm fucking loud. My whole body jerks, my hand jerks, I open and slam the cabinet by accident. I definitely kick Trent but he doesn't stop, not until I feel like I've melted, tremors still running through me as I gasp for air, feeling like a blissed-out dying fish.

He kisses my inner thigh. Then he bites it and I laugh, head still back against the cabinets, pretty fucking sure I can't move.

"Try not to break any dishes," he murmurs, his face against mine. He's grinning and he smells like me, but I don't give a shit so I give him a long, slow kiss. "The answer is *loud*, by the way."

He pulls me forward, off the counter, and I stand on shaky legs and kiss him again. I reach into his jeans and stroke his cock again and this time he moans, shuddering, leaning into me.

"You might make me come like this," he growls, but he doesn't stop thrusting slowly into my hand, letting me stroke him.

"Don't," I say. "I'd be fucking pissed."

"Why?" he asks, teasing even as he's breathless.

I tighten my hand on his cock, stroke harder, slower.

"Say it," he growls.

"I'm in no mood to wait."

"You mean you'd be pissed if you couldn't fuck me now."

He tweaks one nipple, and my whole body jerks.

"Don't be fucking polite, Darcy. There's nothing fucking polite about this. It's pure *I fucking want you* and it's pure *you drive me out of my mind*."

"Trent."

He just growls.

"Go get in my fucking bed."
He grins, kisses me.
"There it is," he says.

CHAPTER TWENTY-SEVEN
Trent

I leave my shoes in her kitchen and my jeans somewhere outside her suite's bedroom door and I don't bother shutting it because Darcy's in front of me, gloriously fucking naked. I grab her by the waist and pull her back against me, my cock nestled against her ass and the small of her back, and for a second I just stand there with my arms around her and *breathe*.

Then Darcy arches and stands on her tiptoes and tilts her head back, lips open, and it's over. If I was thinking that this feels a little like the end of something between us, I don't fucking care because it's also the door to something new and beautiful.

I kiss her. I spin her around and walk her to the bed and lift her up and nearly throw her on it, laughing, but at the last second I remember her back and I put her down gently. Darcy wraps her legs around my waist and pulls me in, tangling us together.

Her bedroom's dark but her hair is fanned around her, stark against the white hotel sheets, and for a moment I just *look* at her while her eyes roam my face.

She runs one finger over the lump in my collarbone, the half-circles on my shoulder, the same look in her eyes as before.

"What?" I whisper.

"You drive me out of my mind," she whispers back.

Darcy reaches down and grabs my cock again, tightens her legs around me, lifts her hips until I'm at her entrance, and I slide inside.

She gasps. Her eyes go blurry and lose focus, her fingernails digging into my back and her thighs tightening on my hips, and inside her is tight and hot and right now I'm breathless, fucking wrapped in her so I can barely think, barely breathe.

Fucking drowning in her. Fucking melting.

I pull back and thrust again, and this time we both moan together, her head to one side, her eyes closed, breathless and beautiful. I've imagined this moment a thousand times — a million maybe — but this is better than all of them combined, the slow rhythm of our bodies moving and working together.

I fuck her harder, faster, and she *shouts* with her head thrown back, nails digging into my shoulder. I grab her knee and put it over my shoulder, the back of her thigh against my chest, and somehow I get even deeper.

Darcy gasps my name, shouts it, her hand slides off my shoulder and grabs the sheets in a fist as she clenches around me like she's about to come. Thank fuck, because I'm unraveling fast, my self-control unspooling with every second.

I put my hand over her fist, on the sheets, and she lets them go so I can lace my fingers through hers and I hold onto her tight, like she's my lifeline. Her eyes come open, and she's sweaty and undone and wild. She grabs my hair and looks me in the eyes.

"*Fuck*, Trent," she gasps.

And she comes. I can feel it as her whole body tenses, wrapped around me, and in seconds I'm following her over the edge, face buried in her neck as I shout some string of nonsense, coming so hard I think my vision goes blank.

Even when it's over, we don't move. I can feel her heartbeat, her chest move as she breathes, and I'm still wrapped in her.

Slowly, we unfurl. I flop over next to her, both of us diagonal on the enormous bed, and Darcy rolls over onto her stomach, hair around her face. I think she's smiling. I reach out and lightly run my knuckles along the lumpy, smooth-skinned new scar on her back.

"You okay?"

Darcy raises the one eyebrow I can see, like she thinks it's a funny question.

"I'm fine," she says.

"I mean your back."

"Yeah, I got that. These sheets have a thread count of a million or something, it was like fucking on a cloud," she teases me.

I just slide my knuckles carefully along her back. I feel like this situation should have weight, should have gravity, that I should say something meaningful to her right now that could tie what just happened to the years before of *us*, but I can't think of a damn thing.

It doesn't feel heavy. It feels weightless. I take her arm, tug, and she scoots toward me until her head's on my shoulder, her other hand drumming patterns on my chest. I stroke her hair, my mind blank.

"Trent," she says after a while.

"Darce."

"This wasn't a bad idea, was it?"

"This was a *great* idea."

She laughs, her fingers still playing patterns on my chest.

"Are you still gonna think that tomorrow?"

"I've got a good feeling about it."

More drumming. Something else occurs to me.

"Hey, Darce?"

"Yeah?"

"You're still on the pill, right?"

She rolls in, resting her chin on one hand, and looks at me like she's laughing.

"Don't you think the time to ask that was ten minutes ago?" she teases.

"Ten minutes ago I was barely thinking," I admit.

"I'm still on it," she says. "You're not barebacking groupies right and left, are you?"

I snort. Before tonight I hadn't been with anyone in months. Not that I couldn't have, but random hookups weren't what I wanted.

"Don't you think the time to ask that was ten minutes ago?" I tease right back.

"I was *hoping* you'd be a gentleman and wrap it up if you thought you might have super-syphilis," she says.

"I'm quite safe with my five-groupie-per-night habit," I say, and Darcy just rolls her eyes.

"Glad to hear it," she deadpans. "You get the other four out of the way before we went trespassing?"

"Something like that."

"I think we left the meat thermometer behind," she says, turning onto her back, her head still propped up on my chest. "And the baby powder, whatever that was for."

"Shit, that was a nice thermometer," I say. "I could've used it for steak or somthing."

She just laughs and tells me I can't cook for shit, and I say I can, and even though we're naked and we just had insane, explosive, world-ending sex this feels... the same. It feels like everything I liked about us, only with less clothes.

After a while, Darcy sighs, yawns, looks over at me.

"I should brush my teeth before I fall asleep," she says.

Until a couple years ago, when we all suddenly had money, Darcy's teeth were constantly giving her problems, because it's not like any of her foster parents were going to pay for dental work. It was the first thing she spent her Dirtshine money on, and she's *religious* about her teeth. Drunk, high, drunk and high, doesn't matter. She brushes.

"Are you kicking me out?" I ask, half-teasing.

She looks over at me, hair spilling onto my chest.

"You don't have to go," she says, her voice suddenly careful. "If you don't want to."

She pauses.

"I've got an extra toothbrush," she offers, and I laugh.

"My toothbrush is next door," I say. "I think I can make it."

We sit up. I kiss her, just one more time, then grab a towel, go to my room next door, and get my toothbrush. I bring it back and brush my teeth next to her, both stark naked in her hotel bathroom.

We get back into her giant bed, and even though there's enough space for us to both splay out like starfish, she curls against me and I put my arms around her. We fall asleep that way.

• • •

It's not nearly late enough when I wake up to a knock at the door. I've got the sense that it's been going on for a while, that someone's been knocking for ages, but I lie there and stare at the ceiling, feeling like my eyes had been glued shut.

Darcy's still lying on one of my arms. The knock sounds again, louder, and she suddenly wakes up with a snort.

"The fuck is that?" she asks, somewhere between baffled and furious.

"Door."

I'm still half in the strange dream I was having, where I was trying to chase an incredible number of iguanas from our recording studio, but I sit up, legs over the edge of the bed.

"I'll get it."

"It's my room," she says, plopping her face down onto her pillow. She sighs dramatically, then rolls over, sitting up as well. "I got it."

She grabs a robe from the bathroom, tugs it around herself. I flop backward onto the bed and listen to her walk to the front door. I wonder, briefly, if the bed is visible from the door, but I decide it's not.

"Hey," Darcy says, opening the door.

"Hi," says Gavin, who sounds far too fucking awake for — I check the clock — 9:30.

"Shit," Darcy mumbles. "Is it time for stuff already?"

"Did I wake you?" Gavin says, obviously teasing her. Dick.

"*Guess.*"

"Sorry," he says, and he sounds like he's trying not to smile. "I was actually just looking for Trent, I wanted to talk over a slight guitar modification I'm thinking of but he's not in his room or the lobby and he's not answering his phone. You've not seen him, have you?"

There's a long, long pause.

"Me?" she finally asks.

Listening in the bedroom, I put a hand over my mouth so I don't start laughing.

"Yes," Gavin says.

"Trent?"

"Yes."

"I haven't... uh, I don't know? He could be anywhere? Like sometimes he goes and walks around or something, maybe he didn't take his phone but I'm sure he'll be back soon. I haven't seen him, that's all just a guess."

"If you do see him, would you mind telling him I'm looking for him?"

"Sure," Darcy says, then yawns.

"Thanks," Gavin says. "Go back to bed, rehearsal's not 'til noon."

"Thank *fuck*," Darcy mutters, and the door closes.

She shuffles back in, already throwing the robe off, then crawls back into bed.

"Gavin's looking for you," she mumbles, her face already on the pillow.

"I heard."

Practically on cue, something buzzes *very* faintly in the other room of the suite.

"Bet that's him."

"We can talk later," I say, rolling over and carefully throwing an arm over her back. "Plenty of time."

CHAPTER TWENTY-EIGHT
Darcy

When Trent leaves later that morning, he kisses me goodbye, and it's electric and warm and familiar, all at once.

"See you in thirty," he rumbles, kissing my forehead. I'm in the robe again, still sleepy. "Oh, and Darce?"

I raise my eyebrows.

"If we're not going to tell Gavin and Joan about this, you might consider lying better," he teases.

"He just thought I was tired," I protest. "Also, shut up."

Trent laughs, then he's through the door. I turn, yawning, for the kitchen, and have to step over a pile of clothing.

And I stop. I look at the front door, then back at the clothes strewn everywhere.

And I realize that this morning, Trent's jeans were *exactly* in the line of sight from the door, clothes practically pointing a giant arrow to my bedroom.

I rub my eyes and sigh.

I could have had anyone in here, I tell myself. *Gavin has no reason to think it was Trent.*

Besides us coming in at two in the morning yesterday.

I pour some amount of ground coffee into a filter, pour water into the reservoir, and just watch the coffee drip into the carafe for several moments.

Whatever, he'll say something if he's going to get upset about it, I tell myself. *Nothing I can do now, so fuck it.*

• • •

Rehearsal goes way, way better that day. Trent stops fucking up songs he knows by heart, Gavin's in a better mood, and Joan seems like she's taking to us like a fish to water. I think we're all fucking relieved that yesterday's disaster doesn't get repeated.

Afterward, we all go out for dinner together at the sole Thai restaurant in Tallwood, where Gavin has zero beers, Trent has one, and Joan and I each have a couple. Thirty minutes later she's telling me a story about the time one of her bandmates got silly string in another's hair and they didn't speak for six months.

Gavin and Trent are laughing politely, Joan's laughing so hard she snorts, and I've got tears rolling down my face.

Fuck Eddie, I think. *We're still a band without him.*

• • •

Trent sleeps over again. I'm pretty tipsy, and even though he's not, we only make it as far as the dining table in my suite before I've gotten us both out of our clothes. Sober Darcy wants to fuck Trent, but drunk Darcy really *really* wants to fuck Trent.

It's even louder than the night before.

. . .

The next week is all pretty much like that, though without the part where I get drunk. We rehearse with Joan, we hang out afterward, Trent sleeps in my bed, we wake up in the morning and do it again.

The last day before we leave again, we end rehearsal early so I can have a last checkup at the hospital. Trent insists on coming with me, even though I'm *fine*, and even though I protest I don't mind.

Actually, when I'm sitting in the waiting room for forty-five minutes, I'm pretty glad he came.

They clear me to go back on tour, which is good, since I'm doing it no matter what my doctor says. My back still can't take the friction of the bass strap rubbing across it, so I have to sit, but otherwise, I'm good to go.

Afterward, we get delivery pizza, a bottle of wine, and hang out in Gavin's suite. When we show up, he's on the phone, so we put the pizza down on the coffee table and flop on the couch.

"I'm just saying, I don't know how many interpretations there are for that," he says, but he's grinning. "Seemed like quite a decided thing."

Marisol? I mouth at him, and he nods.

"Listen, Trent and Darcy have just shown up with pizza so I'm off," he says, then listens. "Sure, if they're amenable."

He turns to us.

"You willing to say hello to Marisol?"

I just hold my hand out for the phone.

"She says yes," Gavin says. "Love you. Talk tomorrow."

"How's L.A.?" I ask.

"Same as always," Marisol says, sounding chipper. "How's your back doing? Don't let Gavin talk you into doing shows if you can't yet."

I just laugh. Gavin's got a piece of pizza in his mouth and raises one eyebrow at me.

"I'm fine," I say. "I got the all-clear and everything. And we got a *throne* for me to use on stage."

"Ooh, tell me about the throne," she says.

Marisol and I chat for a few more minutes. Joan comes in, carrying a half-gallon of ice cream, and puts it in the freezer, then sits in an armchair and grabs a slice of pepperoni.

Trent talks to Marisol for a bit. I eat pizza, drink a glass of wine, and discuss Bigfoot theories with Gavin and Joan. Joan thinks it's all bullshit, and I think she's probably right, but Gavin won't quit winding her up.

We open another bottle of wine. Nigel shows up and practically chugs two glasses, then sits on the couch and actually seems to relax for once.

We finish off the pizza, the wine, and the ice cream. We stay up later than we should, since everything is packed and we're supposed to be on the road early tomorrow, but this is *nice*. It feels good, like we're a real band again and everything.

Of course, I thought that about Eddie sometimes. Maybe I wasn't wrong. Maybe the members can change sometimes and the band can stay. Things can take a lot of forms.

• • •

I wake up in the middle of the night to the sound of Trent's phone buzzing like crazy on his bedside table. He's already sitting up, blinking, staring at the screen like it's written in hieroglyphics.

"The fuck?" I mutter.

He just shakes his head.

"It's fucking four in the morning or something."

"Sorry," he says, unplugging his phone and swinging his legs over the side of the bed, his voice rough and grainy with sleep. "Trent Ryder," he answers it.

There's a long pause. He looks at me, then walks out of the bedroom, still stark naked, and pulls the door behind him, though he doesn't quite close it all the way.

"How the fuck are you *calling* me?" I can hear him ask, and *that* wakes me up.

It's a bad phone call. I can tell.

CHAPTER TWENTY-NINE
Trent

"I'm *definitely* not putting five thousand dollars into your account if you won't even tell me what the fuck for!" I say. I'm trying to keep my voice down, but it's not fucking working.

"I'm not asking for a handout, just an advance," Eli says in his flat, affectless voice, the one he's had since he went to prison.

"You realize that funding your commissary account *at all* is a fucking handout, don't you?"

No response.

"The fuck are you going to do with five thousand dollars? Buy ten thousand cigarettes?"

"It wouldn't buy that many."

"That's not my point, Eli," I say, shoving my hand through my hair. I'm pacing back and forth in the living room in Darcy's suite, and I'm trying to stay calm despite the rage and panic spiking through me.

"I'm just saying."

I take a deep breath and turn on my heel, stalking back toward her kitchen.

"You need to tell me why you're calling me in the dead middle of the night from prison and asking me for five thousand dollars," I say, trying to control my voice. "Fuck, Eli, you need to tell me *how* you're calling me at four in the morning, because I'm goddamn sure this call isn't state-approved—"

"The only thing I *need* is the money," he says, and suddenly there's a snarl in his dead, flat voice. "I don't owe you shit, Trent, and I don't have to *tell* you shit."

"And I don't have to *give* you shit."

"Are you really gonna do this to me?" he asks, the snarl quiet and dim, but still there.

In a strange way, it feels *good* to finally piss my brother off, because for years whenever he calls, whenever I've visited, it's felt like I'm talking to a brick wall.

"Yeah, I fucking am," I say.

There's a long pause on the other end of the line, so long I almost think he's hung up.

"You've always been like this," he says. "You get lucky and think you shit gold, and I get the short end of the stick and you won't even—"

"Don't even start, Eli."

"I don't know what else you call it. You get the nice fucking grandma judge and she gives you *fucking parole,* I get the hardass who tosses me into a prison upstate run by Mexican gangs."

I take the phone away from my ear and stalk back across the living room, because I'm seeing fucking *black.* Eli was there the day everything happened. He fucking knows *why* it did, and he fucking *knows* it's not the same.

"I didn't beat someone to death on camera," I say through clenched teeth, even though I know I shouldn't argue back. I should hang up and go back to bed, because fighting with Eli's never done a damn thing but piss me off.

"You still got off light," he says, voice back to flat. "And now you can't even help someone who didn't."

"I'm not having this conversation," I tell him. I should have told him that the moment I answered the phone. "Unless you're going to tell me what the money's for or how the *fuck* you're calling right now."

Silence. There's a shuffling noise in the background.

"Bye, Trent," he finally says, and the line goes silent.

I keep pacing furiously. He's always done this, fucking *always*, and of course my little brother can piss me off more than anyone else in the world.

But he makes me fucking *livid*, the way he can't take responsibility, the way he constantly thinks the world is out to get him. The way he blames me for his shit.

The bedroom door opens, and Darcy's standing there, stark naked.

"You okay?" she asks, her voice soft and worried.

"Eli somehow called at four in the morning and wants me to send him five thousand dollars," I spit out, still pacing furiously. "He won't tell me why, he won't even tell me how the fuck he's *calling* me right now."

I turn, the phone still in my hand. I still feel like I could breathe black fire if I wanted to.

"And then he fucking blames *me*. That night, the night I got arrested, I was fucking protecting *him* and he fucking *knows* it and he *fucking blames me* for all his problems!"

I hurl the phone at the wall. I don't even think about it, just channel my fury and frustration and pitch it as hard as I can.

It hits with a sharp crack, falls to the floor, and Darcy flinches.

Fuck.

Her eyes dart from the phone to me, and she looks *afraid*. Of me, of what she knows I could do.

I feel like a fucking monster.

I thought I had it under control better than that, I thought I knew better than to throw something when I could have easily hit Darcy, and I didn't.

The look in her eyes stabs me deep, a needle to my heart, thin and piercing, leaving me breathless. I've got no fucking excuse, because I've flinched at thrown objects before. I know exactly what it's like to wonder if you're next, and I can't fucking believe I made her think that, for a second.

"I'm sorry," I say, rubbing my face. "Fuck, Darcy, I'm sorry."

She glances at the phone again.

"Trent, just—"

"I need to go," I say. "I'm sorry, Darce, I shouldn't have..."

I move past her, grab my pants from the floor, pull them on.

"I gotta go. I'll see you tomorrow."

She starts saying something else, but I feel fucking run through with a blade, like I can't even see or think or breathe. I just need to get out, away from Darcy because the thought that I could have hurt her, that I could lose control and *do* something, makes me sick to my stomach.

In my own suite, I sit at the kitchen table, my head in my hands. I try to force myself to think about something else, *anything* else, but it just replays over and over again:

The phone arcing through the air, the crash, her flinch, that *look*.

CHAPTER THIRTY
Darcy

Trent leaves. The door shuts behind him and I go back into the bedroom and sit on the edge of the bed, sinking in, wondering what just happened.

I sit there for a long minute. I wonder if I should just go back to bed, or at least try, see him in the morning and talk it over then. But that feels wrong, feels like I'm abandoning him when he needs me.

Fuck it, I can try. If he wants to be alone he can tell me he wants to be alone and that's fine, but I'm going to try. I stand, grab the robe, get his phone from the floor and take my room key and walk into the deep dark of the hallway.

I knock lightly on Trent's door, hoping I don't wake anyone else up. There's no answer.

I know he's in there, so I knock again, louder, and this time he pulls the door open, still shirtless, face dark.

I hold out his phone, the glass casing fractured with a thousand lines. It's pretty broken. Trent just looks at it, then at me, and swallows hard.

"I would never hurt you," he whispers.

"I know," I say.

We look at each other for a long time, and finally, he takes the phone out of my hand.

"I don't want to be someone you're afraid of," he says.

"You're not."

He's just looking at the phone in his hand, shattered almost beyond recognition.

"Maybe you should be."

I cross my arms. It's late, I'm tired, and I want to get to the bottom of whatever's actually going on.

"How about you let me decide what I'm afraid of and you focus on inviting me in and telling me what the fuck happened?"

A smile glimmers around his eyes, and he steps back, letting me in. His suite's pristine, probably because he more or less hasn't actually been living here for the past week. Trent tosses the phone onto the counter with a clatter, then walks in and flops on the couch, rubbing his face with both hands.

"I don't know," he says. "My shithead brother won't tell me. He wants me to deposit five thousand dollars into his commissary account, and he somehow got hold of a phone at four in the morning to call me, but he won't tell me how he did that or why he wants the money."

I sit next to him. Even though he's much taller than me, he tilts his head down until it's touching mine.

"It's bad, Darcy. I can't come up with anything that doesn't end somewhere bad. And..."

Trent trails off, taking a deep breath, and I shift on the couch, pull his head onto my lap.

"If I give him the money, whatever this is won't end. It'll get worse, because that's how Eli operates. But I've got no idea why he wants it. I don't know if he's trying to start some sort of toilet wine enterprise or whether he's gotten into debt with a mass murderer."

I stroke his hair. He shifts slightly, and now he's looking up at me, his deep brown eyes searching mine.

"Whichever happens, it's not your fault," I tell him. "I'm taping that to your bathroom mirror. 'What my brother does is not my problem.'"

"I wish it felt like that," he says. "But it feels like everything he does is another punch to the gut. Fuck, Darce, this all started because I wanted to protect him."

I keep stroking his hair, even though we're suddenly in new territory. I'm pretty sure I know what Trent's talking about, but this is one of the few details of his life I don't know. I just know something horrible happened, and it was all a decade ago.

"I know," I say, even though I don't, because that story can be for later.

We sit there like that for a long time, and I stroke his hair, his head in my lap.

I know I don't understand. I don't have any siblings, blood or otherwise. I've got no idea what it feels like to share your DNA with someone, to grow up with them, to be fiercely loyal like this to them even when they fuck up beyond belief.

I had foster siblings, but it's not the same. When I was fourteen and my last foster father sneaked into the girls' bedroom at night, I didn't try to protect the girl whose bed he went to. I didn't do shit.

I just laid there, thankful I wasn't on the bottom bunk, and planned out how to run away.

"He still blames me because Dad died," Trent says, his voice low and dreamy.

"He shouldn't."

"He does. I think he blames me for Mom, too."

"Because you should have been your father's only punching bag?"

"Eli doesn't make that much sense," Trent rumbles. "He doesn't have fucking reasons for it. He just does."

I still don't know what to say, because I want to tell him that his father was a monster who's better off dead and his brother's an idiot who's deserved everything he's gotten. But I don't think that's going to help right now, and it's definitely not what he wants to hear, so I don't say anything.

After a while, he sits up, sighs, stands. Holds out his hand to me, still on the couch.

"Stay over," he says.

CHAPTER THIRTY-ONE
Trent

The next morning, we finally leave Tallwood. We've got a whole squadron of vehicles waiting for us in the parking lot: our tour bus, totally nondescript and black, two moving vans for our stuff, plus a couple of passenger cars, smaller vans with odds and ends.

Darcy and I stand there, in front of the Lodge, coffee in hand, surrounded by suitcases. The morning chill is still in the air, but it makes everything feel fresh and new, cleaned out. Like Eli's late-night call was a dream aberration, a blip in the functioning of everyday life.

"Remember the van?" Darcy asks, taking a long drink. "How'd we get here from there?"

"I think this is what they call *making it*," I say, looking over the hubbub.

"I do like the part where someone else carries my luggage," she admits.

"I like the part where we sleep in beds, not the back seat."

"You're going soft," she teases. "Next, you'll lose your edge, get all sensitive, and before I know it you'll be Michael Bolton Junior."

"I don't think my hair would look that good long."

"You also can't sing for shit."

"So I wouldn't be Michael Bolton at all."

"Don't start, this is my first cup of coffee," she says, wrinkling her nose, and I laugh. I feel like right now I could put my arm around her, pull her in for a coffee-flavored kiss and it would all be perfectly natural. I feel like it would be so normal that no one else would even notice, that Gavin and Joan would skip right over it like it was part of the landscape.

I don't point out that *she* started this in the first place by calling me Michael Bolton.

• • •

Our first show on the *new* tour schedule is in a Spokane venue called the Knitting Factory, across the state. Besides the few festivals we're playing — like Grizzly — most of our shows aren't in huge arenas, by design. They're mostly in smaller venues, old theaters and spaces that only hold two thousand people, not twenty thousand.

We'd make more money playing arenas, but when we started planning out the tour we collectively decided that we fucking hated it and didn't want to do it. It means tiny dressing rooms and hanging out in alleyways before the show, cramped quarters and air conditioning systems that can't always quite stand up to the challenge of the place being at full capacity, but we'll take it.

It goes almost perfectly. Even though Gavin's mic kept cutting out during sound check and one of the amps was making the lights shake weirdly, it's all fixed by show time. When we walk on stage it's already hot and sticky in there, but the theater is packed to capacity, everyone is shouting, and it feels like we're all just different parts of the same big musical organism.

After the show is the fans. All four of us are sticky, sweaty, and tired but elated, still buzzing from a show that's gone well, and even though what I really want is to drink a gallon of water, maybe have a beer, then fuck Darcy and go to bed I'd be an asshole if I didn't talk to the fans who make it backstage.

So I autograph what feels like a thousand ticket stubs. I autograph a beer bottle, a flyer about our show, some CDs — who knew they even made those any more — and even some guy's acoustic guitar.

Toward two in the morning, when we're all out back in the alley, finally just us and the guys loading our gear, it's quiet, just the four of us standing with our backs against the brick wall.

"I'd forgotten how rough this all is," Joan says.

"Weren't you on tour last year?" Darcy asks.

"Yeah, but we tour like old people," Joan says, laughing. "Three shows a week, maximum, and we come home at least a week a month. We've all got kids and spouses and shit."

"Just tell us if you want to be sent to the hotel early," Darcy teases.

"And miss out on all the fun? Someone asked me to sign a photo of her newborn. Never had that one before."

"Please tell me she named it after you."

"Oh, God," Joan says, crossing her arms and laughing again. "I didn't ask. I don't want to know. That's a bit much."

"Someone asked me to sign her arse," Gavin offers, standing next to them.

"Did you?" Joan asks.

"Was it a nice ass?" Darcy asks.

"How'd we miss that?" I say.

Gavin shrugs, leaning against the wall.

"You were all busy," he says. "And the arse was only out for a moment."

"That won't do," Darcy says. "You gotta let that ink dry so it doesn't smudge all over your clothes. A couple minutes at least."

We all turn and look at her.

"I did refuse," Gavin points out. "I'm not signing some strange bird's rump, but if you'd like to elaborate on how the ink ought to dry, please do."

"It's not important," she says, not making eye contact with any of us.

"Bon Jovi's drummer signed my tits when I was seventeen," Joan offers.

"Bon Jovi?"

"Seventeen?"

"I'm from Jersey," she says, her voice calm but amused. "And you can't tell me you don't like *Livin' on a Prayer*."

"I don't, really," I say.

"It's a good karaoke song," Darcy admits.

"Did it rub off the moment you put your shirt back on or were you wandering around backstage in the buff for several minutes afterward?" Gavin asks.

"I don't *exactly* remember," Joan goes on. "The whole thing took some liquid courage. It's gone now, though."

"I should hope so," Gavin says.

There's a long pause. Two guys load amps into a van, and I'm glad it's not my job any more. Setting up equipment, playing a long show, and then moving it again is exhausting as fuck.

"Anyone ever signed a dick?" Darcy asks.

"That might be hard," Gavin says.

"I think it would have to be."

Joan snorts, and Darcy grins.

"I've signed tits," Joan says.

"We've all signed tits," Gavin says, and Darcy nods in agreement.

I frown.

"I've never signed tits," I say. "I've never even been asked."

"Seriously?"

"I've signed lots of arms," I say. "I signed a bald guy's head once."

I look around at the other three. Gavin looks faintly puzzled, Joan's got one eyebrow raised, and Darcy's trying not to laugh.

"Do I have 'don't show me your tits' written on my forehead?" I ask.

"Maybe you just don't seem like a tit-signer," Joan says.

"All right," says a voice behind me, and I turn. There's a burly bald guy wearing all black and sweating slightly standing there, his hands on his hips.

"We done?" Gavin asks.

"All packed in," the roadie confirms. "Locked up tight, ready for Missoula."

Joan rubs her hands together.

"Thank you," she says. "Let's all go to bed!"

As we get on the tour bus to head to our hotel, Darcy holds me back for a moment.

"You can sign my tits if you want," she says, and winks.

• • •

A week later, we're in Minneapolis, still playing shows almost every night in small, hot, crowded theaters, not that I'd change it if I could. The grind of the road is starting to feel familiar again, the same routine of play-sleep-drive-repeat, though this time it's different.

This time, Gavin's sober. We play a lot of Scrabble on the tour bus.

Liam's not there, and instead we've got Joan, who's lovely and a good drummer and wonderfully pleasant to talk to, but she's not Liam.

Oh, and Darcy and I are fucking. We still haven't told the rest of the band — we haven't told *anyone* — and I don't know if I get to use the word *girlfriend* about her or not, but I don't really care. She's in my bed every night and we've spent a couple hours on the bus perfecting the art of throwing popcorn into each other's mouths, so I don't care what word she calls me. I'll be her dinglehopper if things can stay like this.

Eli doesn't call again, either.

The shows go beautifully. There's usually some hitch — the lights don't go down quite properly, a mic doesn't work and we have to switch it, the AC's on the fritz — but there's always going to be some minor problem. It's life.

In Minneapolis, there's a bar right next to the theater, and around one in the morning, Darcy and I head over there through the back door to escape the crush of people that always follows a show, especially somewhere small like this.

They're mostly fans, but sometimes not. There's reporters, there's people who just want to sell your autograph, there's drunk guys who want to tell you how you should *really* play guitar, and sometimes I just need to fucking leave. So we do.

The bar is smallish, cozy place, mostly empty because it's a Tuesday night.

"Do you miss it?" I ask.

"Minneapolis?"

I nod, taking a sip of my beer. Darcy shrugs.

"A little," she says. "I miss the people sometimes. I joined my first real band here after I hitchhiked from Madison."

"The Screaming Zombies?"

"That's who I was with when we met," she says, also taking a sip. "This was Doll Limb Factory."

"How could I forget?"

She laughs.

"We weren't very good," she says. "But we were fun. And mostly we were loud."

"That's what's important."

"It was for us, at least," she says. "And I guess it worked, because here I am with someone else loading my gear into a truck."

We hang out for a little while, bullshitting about nothing, because somehow our relationship hasn't really changed.

Well, it has. Fucking obviously it has, but not like I was afraid it would. The parts where we talk and joke and spend time together like we're best friends stayed almost exactly the same, and it's *great*.

After a little while, Darcy hops off her stool to go pee, and I pull my phone out and aimlessly check Twitter. I'm reading dumb shit on the internet when a woman's voice interrupts me.

"Hi," she says. "Can I get your autograph?"

I put my phone away and look up, forcing a smile. Even if I just want to be left alone with my secret-girlfriend-or-whatever, if you're rude to one fan they post it on Facebook and then fucking *everyone* thinks you're a dick.

"Sure," I say. "I haven't got a pen on me, though."

"Oh, I brought one," she says, and hands me a Sharpie. She's blonde, fair-skinned, and cute in a midwestern kind of way.

"What am I signing?" I ask, because she doesn't seem to have anything.

The girl pulls up her tank top. She's not wearing a bra, and for a second, I'm so surprised I'm speechless.

Then I think: *I finally got asked to sign someone's tits*.

"Do you have anything else I could sign?" I ask.

I'm trying not to stare, but it's *surprising*. They're pierced, a little barbell through each of her nipples, and if I'm being really honest they're nice tits.

I've got absolutely no desire to *touch* them, but I'm only human. I notice when tits are nice.

"Come on," she says, and I flick my eyes to her face. She's pouting, her pink lips in a sad little bow. "Please? You've always been my favorite member of Dirtshine."

"I don't sign body parts," I lie.

"I watched you sign a guy's arm earlier."

They're still out, her shirt still up, and I wish she'd put them away.

"If you've got a piece of paper or something, I'd be glad to sign that," I tell her. "How about a bar napkin?"

She takes a step closer. *Still* pouting, and now she's really invading my personal space with her perky, pierced nipples.

"You could think of it as foreplay," she purrs, or at least *tries* to purr. "I'm sure you get lonely on the road and you could use something to remember Minneapolis by."

She runs one fingertip across a nipple, and I lean slightly backward on my bar stool, away from her because I'd really like this girl to put her shirt back on and stop touching herself in public.

"I'm not thinking of it at all," I say, still trying to be nice, especially because we're starting to get *looks*. I grab a bar napkin and take the cap off the pen. "Look, this'll last you much longer—"

"Oh, did you want an autograph?" Darcy's voice says behind me, a little brighter and harder than usual.

The girl in front of me falters slightly, because it's fucking obvious she thinks this is between me and her.

"Sure," she says anyway, her voice notably *not* sure.

"Great!" Darcy says, and snatches the Sharpie out of my hand. "Totally happy to sign whatever our fans want! Now just hold still, this might tickle."

She grabs one breast and just about stabs it with the Sharpie. The girl with her tits out clearly didn't have this in mind, but before anyone says anything Darcy's done and steps back to admire her handiwork.

"Perfect," she says. "Make sure you keep those out for a few more minutes, otherwise it might smudge. Great piercings. Hope you enjoyed the show!"

With that, she tosses the Sharpie at the girl, turns on her heel, and walks out of the bar's back door.

Yeah, she's *pissed*.

I quickly scribble my signature on a cocktail napkin and shove it at the girl.

"Thanks for coming out," I say automatically.

"We can still—"

"No," I tell her. She's still standing there, looking like a confused puppy dog with her tits out, when I turn and leave the bar behind Darcy.

CHAPTER THIRTY-TWO
Darcy

I shove open the door to our tour bus and climb the steps, my heavy boots stomping on the metal stairs. I head past the main part, with the couches, a table, and a kitchenette, past the bathroom, and to the back where we've got two couches set up for napping behind a curtain. I don't bother turning the lights on.

This isn't Trent's fault, I tell myself, huffing down onto a couch and putting my head in my hands. He didn't do anything besides refuse to sign a girl's boobs.

I still feel sick, the beer in my stomach churning, and I don't even know why. She didn't know about Trent and me, and he didn't do anything. Hell, I'm the one who grabbed her boob and signed it.

I just fucking hate the world sometimes, hate that other women can come up to him and act like they have a chance, and more than anything I hate how it makes me feel like some bug they need to squash so I'll get out of the way.

Footsteps at the front of the bus. The whole thing rocks very slightly, and I exhale into my hands because I know who it is.

"Can I come in?" Trent asks from behind the curtain, and I flop backward on the couch.

"Yeah," I say.

He slides the curtain open, leaning against one wall, his hands in his pockets, even his silhouette sexy as fuck.

God, I can't even blame that girl. I like it when he looks at my tits, too.

"You okay?" he rumbles.

"I'm fine."

"Liar."

"I'll be fine."

"I didn't touch her," he says.

"I know," I say quietly. "It's not you. I'm just..."

I sigh. He waits.

"Jealous?" I say.

In the dark, Trent chuckles.

"It's not funny."

"You know there's nothing to be jealous of, don't you?"

I don't answer him, just look out a darkly tinted window at the street, wishing I could explain what my problem is. Wishing I fucking knew what it was.

"Darce," he says slowly. "There's nobody but you. There's been nobody but you."

Trent closes the curtain behind himself. He walks over to me, put his hands on the back of the couch on either side of my head, and leans down.

"I've wanted this for way too long to fuck it up."

"Me too," I whisper.

"This is dangerous, Darcy, and I fucking know that," he goes on, his voice low and slow. "You're not the only one who was afraid we'd lose what we had if we became more. I waited until I couldn't fucking hold out any longer because I knew how bad it would fuck me up if I lost you."

He leans in closer, and I put one hand on his face.

"I don't think I'd make it, Darce."

"You've made it through worse."

"I haven't."

My stomach twists, because there's a litany of bad things in Trent's past.

"So I shouldn't be jealous?" I ask softly, half-teasing.

He laughs lowly, getting even closer.

"No, you shouldn't be fucking jealous," he says.

He kisses me hard, his teeth pressing into my lip before I open my mouth under his. I don't know what to say that doesn't sound fucking trite and perfunctory so I just kiss him like hell, my fingers in his hair.

"In my defense, her tits were literally right in your face," I murmur.

"She was gonna have to do a lot better," he says, his hand on my knee, his skin warm and rough through the pattern of my fishnets. "Believe me, you've got nothing to worry about."

I put my hand on his as his finger moves under the hem of my dress, grab the collar of his t-shirt in my fist.

"I'm worried that we're in the back of our unlocked tour bus," I tease.

He pushes his hand up further, so now it's totally under my skirt, his calloused fingertips at the top of my thigh. My heart's pounding in my chest, fire pooling inside me, feeling like I'm vibrating at high frequency.

"I just said," Trent growls, sliding his fingers through the holes in my fishnet, "you've got nothing to worry about."

I arch my back, and he shoves his fingers under my panties. I sigh as he strokes my wetness, pulling on his shirt even harder.

"Not even our bandmates finding you with your hand up my skirt?"

Trent nips at my neck, and I gasp.

"If you're worrying, I'm doing something wrong," he says, the pad of his thumb finding my clit. "If you're thinking about someone coming through that curtain and not this."

I hold my breath, biting my lip so I don't make noise, and I trail my hand down his chest to his jeans, the palm flat against his erection. Trent growls, the noise low in his chest as he captures my mouth with his again, the vibrations traveling all the way to my toes.

Then he steps back, pulling his hand out of my skirt, and I'm left on the couch, disheveled and akimbo before Trent holds out his hand.

I grab it. He pulls me up, launching me into his tall, hard body.

Trent kisses me, roughly. I grab onto the waistband of his jeans, wanting his body against mine, needing the delicious friction of us together even though this is a stupid time and a stupid place, and we'll be in a hotel room in thirty minutes.

Instead he grabs my wrist, pulls my arm behind my back, presses my body against his. Even in the dark, Trent's deep brown eyes are endless, bottomless pools and I'm breathless, powerless against my own desire.

"Is this because I got jealous?" I whisper, half-teasing.

"No," he says, holding me even tighter. "It's because I always want to bend you over and tear your fishnets off, and I've got the chance right now."

He lets my wrist go, spins me around, grabs my hair in one hand, pulling my head back against his shoulder as he slides the other up the back of my leg, his fingers running right across my fabric-covered clit and lips.

I shudder as scorching heat races through me. Trent grabs a handful of fishnet, and before I know it his

222

thick fingers are ripping through, so I bite my lip, my head pulled back, and find the button on his jeans, pull down the zipper, and then he's filling my hand, his hardness straining against it as he groans into my ear.

I think I'm melting with anticipation, the sensation like lava running down the inside of my skin. Even though it's been a couple of weeks since the first time we did this, it still feels breathless, brand new, like everything is for the very first time.

Except now, I know exactly how good it's going to feel, and it sharpens the anticipation to a knife point.

He pulls my panties aside roughly, slicking my wetness from my lips to my clit, and I bite back a moan. I stroke him once, feeling him pulse in my hand, and then he lets my hair go, pushes me forward. My shins hit the couch and I kneel on it, grabbing the back for stability, my skirt hiked over my hips and my back arched.

Trent doesn't tease me and he doesn't hesitate, just slides the tip of his cock between my lips and then drives himself in with a single stroke.

My fingers claw at the back of the couch and I fucking shout, all my muscles tensing at once with the sheer, perfect pleasure of suddenly being filled so deep I see stars. There's a low rumble behind me, Trent grabs one shoulder, and then I'm just lost.

It's hard and fast, so fucking good that I can barely even make a sound. This is what it feels like when Trent finally stops being gentle and fucks me like a beast, when he hits every pleasure spot inside me relentlessly, when he just fucking takes what he wants.

I'm just glad that what he wants is me. I'm glad I'm already kneeling on this couch, because otherwise my knees would have buckled. My face is on the back of the couch, the fabric between my teeth, my breathing ragged and uneven and my mind totally blank with sheer fucking pleasure.

I come like a stampede, and I think I just whimper. My toes curl in my shoes and I'm biting the back of this couch, my whole body shaking and trembling. Trent slams into me a few more times, sending a tremor though my muscles and then I can feel him throb and pulse deep inside me, his hand tightening on my shoulder as he groans, shuddering.

I'm not sure I can ever move again, but after a few moments, Trent bends over me, his forehead against the back of my head. He stays that way for a moment, kisses the sweaty back of my neck, then pulls out and flops on the couch next to me.

I collapse on top of him, the two of us sprawled and taking up the whole enormous couch. My head's on his chest and I can hear his heart still thumping away, his skin warm and slightly damp with sweat.

"Oops," I finally say, after a while.

"Oops what?" he asks, not moving a muscle.

"Oops, we had sex on the bus."

"Were we not supposed to?"

"Seems like a bad idea."

"I thought it was pretty good."

I shift slightly against him, trying to pull my skirt down.

"So I should get jealous more often?"

"You don't have to," he says, a grin in his voice. "You can just say, hey Trent, bend me over this couch and fuck me good."

"That does sound simpler," I laugh.

Then the door to the bus opens with a hiss and a squeak. We both freeze. Footsteps coming down the length, and Trent lifts his hips off the couch, shoving himself back into his jeans and zipping them up.

I pull my skirt down and scoot several inches away from Trent, trying not to laugh. The footsteps hesitate just outside the curtain.

"Is that Darcy and Trent?" Gavin's voice asks.

"Just us!" I say, hoping I sound like someone who didn't just get her brains fucked out.

"Can I come in?"

"Sure!"

The curtain moves three inches, and Gavin's eye peeks at us before he pulls the whole thing back.

"You ready for the hotel?" he asks, and if he's suspicious, he manages not to show it.

I just give him a thumbs up.

"Brilliant," he says, and heads forward again.

"Do you think he knows?" I whisper.

"I'm sure he thinks we were just having a really deep conversation back here," Trent deadpans.

I raise one eyebrow at him. He shrugs.

Fuck it, I don't care if Gavin knows, I think.

CHAPTER THIRTY-THREE
Trent

After Minneapolis, we go to Chicago, Indianapolis, Detroit, Toronto. Gavin never says anything about Darcy and me, and no one else shows me her tits.

And I think, for a little while at least, that life might be almost perfect. I'm touring with my band, playing shows every night, my best friend and I are some kind of together, and nothing really *changed*. As far as everyone else knows, we're still the same Trent and Darcy as always.

Except I wake up with her naked in my bed. That's an important difference.

About a week after the tour bus, we're at the Broad Street Theater in Boston, doing sound check at five in the afternoon, and we're stuck there because when I strum my guitar in open tuning, one of the notes is hitting exactly the frequency that makes a light fixture in the ceiling rattle.

"Okay!" one of the theater's employees calls from a catwalk, where he's doing something that involves a lot of clanking to the light. Try it again?"

226

I strum each string one by one, until the high E makes something buzz.

"Fuckin' ancient lights," the guy in the catwalk mutters.

"At least we know which note it is," Gavin says.

"Just don't play that one," Joan jokes. "How hard can it be?"

"Again?" the guy calls. I pluck the string.

"Fuck!" he shouts.

"Try wrapping some tape around it or something, mate," Gavin calls. "If you stick something to the fixture it ought to change the frequency just enough so it'll stop doing that."

There's a clatter above. Some creaking.

"Huh?" the guy calls.

"Have you got any tape?" Gavin shouts.

"Yeah?"

"Try wrapping some of it..."

My phone buzzes, and I reach into my pocket to silence it.

"But I need to secure it tighter!" the guy in the ceiling calls. "It's *buzzing*."

"It's not buzzing because it's loose, it's buzzing because of the way sound works," Darcy calls, and I can tell she wants to add *you dipshit* to the end of her sentence but doesn't.

"Can we just send Gavin up?" Joan asks, her voice low enough that the guy can't hear her.

I have a bad feeling this is going to take a while, just as my phone buzzes again. I frown.

"It doesn't matter, anywhere that the light won't melt it!" Gavin calls.

I think we'll be here a minute, so I pull my phone out of my pocket and glance at the screen.

NORTH DELANO STATE CORRECTIONAL FACILITY.

Well, at least he's calling me from the proper prison phone this time, not from a cell phone that someone probably stuck up his ass to smuggle in.

"Guys, I gotta take this," I say. "Sorry, I'll be right back."

"We'll be here," Joan says grimly, and Darcy flashes me a thumbs up. Gavin's got his arms crossed in front of his chest, futilely trying to explain resonance frequencies to the guy in the ceiling.

"Hey," I say, walking off stage. "What's up?"

There's a pause, then the person on the other end clears his throat.

"Is this Trent Ryder?" says someone who is *definitely* not Eli.

"It is."

He's in the fucking infirmary again, in a coma or something which is why he's not calling me himself...

"I'm very sorry to be the bearer of bad news, but Eli Ryder was killed yesterday," the man says.

I stop short, right in front of a brick wall, and I fucking stare at it, mind blank. I stand there for a long, long time, because suddenly the words are just a collection of sounds and it's all fucking nonsense.

"Eli?" I finally ask.

"Yes."

My ears are ringing. I feel like I've been hit in the gut, like I can't get a breath, like I can't even see.

"Killed?" I hear myself say.

"He was stabbed in an altercation," the man answers carefully.

"No, he wasn't."

Silence.

"I'm afraid he was."

"No, he fucking *wasn't* because he's an idiot and an asshole but he didn't get *fucking* stabbed in *fucking* prison," I tell him, though I've got no fucking clue what I'm saying. "Eli is *goddamn* fine and probably jerking off in his cell to some porno mag so it's in your

228

best fucking interest right now to figure out who the jackass who got stabbed *really* is and tell that poor bastard's family."

"Sir, I'm afraid that—"

"Shut your goddamn mouth," I growl. "You don't know what the fuck you're talking about, and unless you find out you'd best hang this phone up and tell Eli to call me *now*."

A brief pause. I'm shaking with fury, my mind swirling, a deep thunderstorm.

How could they do this? How could they fucking do this?

"I'll have the morgue call you later to arrange the details," he says, his voice all forced calm. "We're very sorry for your loss."

I just drop the phone on the ground and walk away, feeling like there's a layer between me and the world, like I'm walking through water, blind and dumb.

Eli's not dead. He can't be dead. He's Eli. He can be a lot of things but he can't be fucking dead.

I'm not going anywhere. There's no destination, besides *someone else*, besides *through a door*, besides *away from people who'll fucking look at me*.

I shove a door open. Broom closet, too small. I shove another one. Women's bathroom.

One more. Couch, table, lamp, looks familiar.

I slam the door behind me.

CHAPTER THIRTY-FOUR
Darcy

Jesus, this is fucking endless. Now nearly everyone on the ground is shouting at the moron in the rafters, trying to explain that he *just needs to stick something to the light*, but he won't. He's convinced that something is loose.

Poor Gavin's still trying to explain that the light fixture resonates at the exact same frequency as Trent's guitar, and sticking something to it will change that, but he may as well be explaining calculus to a wombat.

I lean back in my chair and turn to Joan.

"Is there any reason *we* can't go?" I ask.

She's got her chin propped up on one fist, leaning on her drum kit.

"Is there?" she asks. "Would they even notice?"

"They might not," I say. "I bet we could go grab a drink at the bar, come back in half an hour, and Gavin would still be here arguing."

"That's not what I'm bloody saying," Gavin shouts. "Look, every piece of metal is going to be slightly different, okay? And..."

"Let's do it," Joan says, and whirls around on her stool. I lift the bass strap over my head and stand from my chair — sorry, my *throne* — and we're just about to head off-stage when there's a crash.

We stop. We look at each other.

There's another crash, this one louder, and a tremor goes through the floor. Gavin turns and looks at us.

"The fuck was that?"

Joan and I are both looking around, but there's nothing obvious, just a bunch of sound guys staring at us.

Was that Trent? He's been on the phone for a while now...

"Where's Trent?" Gavin asks, echoing my thoughts.

"I'll go find him," I say, and head off stage, a bad feeling deep in my gut.

It had to be Eli, calling from prison. Trent's mom never calls him, he only calls her, and there's no one else he'd interrupt sound check for.

And it's not like his talks with Eli ever go well. The last time he threw a phone at the wall, so Christ only knows what that dumb, useless asshole has done to piss Trent off this time.

I round a corner. There's another loud *thump*, and I think it's coming from our dressing room. My stomach's in knots, and when I reach the door, I don't even hesitate.

Trent looks up at me from the floor, a flat, rock-hard expression on his face I've never seen before. He's sitting against the overturned couch, his elbows on his knees. The table's on its side and the floor lamp is overturned, the room half-dark.

"What happened?" I ask. My heart feels encased in stone because everything about this scene screams *bad, very bad*.

He doesn't answer.

"Trent," I say, and he finally looks up at me. Flat, no expression.

"Are you okay?" I ask, taking a step into the room, even though my senses all flood with danger.

This isn't something I know, despite years of friendship. *This* is new and it seems ugly, feels fraught. Even his eyes seem dead, distant.

"Eli's dead," he finally says.

Oh shit.

Oh *shit*.

I don't know what to do, what to say. I don't even know what face to make, but before I even know it I'm on the floor next to Trent, kneeling, and I grab him and pull him against me, holding his head to my chest. He doesn't resist, just lets me, slowly wrapping his thick arms around my waist.

"I'm sorry," I finally whisper, because I'm pretty sure you're supposed to say that even though I know it's fucking futile. I know Trent loved Eli, even if Eli was a fuckup and even if I don't understand *why*, but he did.

He doesn't respond. I pull him closer, and he lets me. After a minute Gavin and Joan show up at the door, take in the scene, look at me with questions.

"His brother died," I say.

Joan gasps, her hands going to her mouth. Gavin's mouth falls open, and they both freeze for a moment.

Then Gavin walks over and sits on the other side of Trent and puts his arm around him, and Joan sits next to me and takes Trent's hand. I don't think she knows the story, though Gavin does.

"Trent, I'm so sorry," Joan says. "I can't imagine."

Thank God someone knows what to say.

"Thanks," he whispers, the first thing he's said since I came in.

The four of us just sit there. An hour passes, my spine twisted into a pretzel, but we don't move.

And I think: *at least we've got them.*

CHAPTER THIRTY-FIVE
Trent

We play the show that night anyway. There's no reason not to. It's not like I can get on a plane before the morning and I don't even know what the fuck I'm flying back to. I know fuck-all about what to do when someone dies and I know fuck-all about how to bury my little brother, so for the next couple of hours I just want to do what I fucking know how to.

It's probably the worst show we've ever played. I'm barely there, playing mechanically. Every time I look up I'm surprised to see where we are, mentally a thousand miles away.

Gavin, Darcy, and Joan keep looking over at me every thirty seconds like I'm made of glass or some shit. The entire time I just wish they'd fucking stop. I wish I were invisible, because I don't want to be here, in front of a few thousand people, trying to pretend that I'm having a good time.

I don't want to be *anywhere*.

We play one encore, and going back on stage is like pulling teeth. The audience can tell that we're having an off-night, and I can tell that they can tell, but I don't care. Afterward I leave my guitar on the stage, walk off, and leave the theater through the alley in the back. The door closes behind me and I lean against the cool brick wall between a dumpster and a stack of pallets four feet high, an oily puddle in the middle of the pockmarked asphalt.

It's as close as I can get to nowhere, at least for now.

My brain keeps spinning and stopping, spinning and stopping. Like a turntable with a broken motor, a wheel with a slipping gear. I'll replay the last time we spoke, the night he called me and wanted money, the time before that, hearing his flat voice, and then my mind will go blank.

The last time I saw him, buying him peanut M&Ms from the vending machine, sitting across the wobbly table from him in that white cinderblock room. Mom, next to me, asking for the third time how much longer he was going to be there, then blankness.

I have to tell Mom. I'll have to tell her thirteen times, a broken fucking record. I'll have to get him buried or maybe cremated, I'll have to figure out where and how, I'll have to pick a fucking coffin and hire someone to say something nice at the service...

Then blank.

I don't know how long I stand there. I think it's a long fucking time, but it's quiet and it's dark and even though it smells like hot garbage, I can't stand the thought of being anywhere else.

After a while I shove myself off the wall. I walk to the street at the end of the alleyway, out onto the one-in-the-morning sidewalk filled with the muted splashes of flickering streetlights and drunk people weaving their way home. A taxi goes by, slowly, and without knowing what I'm doing I flag it down.

"Where to?" the driver asks.

I stare at him like he's speaking Russian. My brain refuses to process it for a long time, and once it does, I've got no idea where I want to go. Just *somewhere else*, but I know I can't fucking drive around Boston in the back of a cab for the rest of the night.

"Hey. Buddy. You back there?"

No.

"Marriott," I finally say.

"You're gonna have to be more specific."

"The closest one."

He shrugs and starts the meter. I'm just guessing that the closest one is where we're staying, but it seems like a good guess.

While we on stage, I got a voicemail from a number I don't know, but it's got a 661 area code and I know where *that* is.

"This message is for Eli Ryder's next of kin," a woman's voice says. "I'm calling with information on the process that the California Correctional System uses for deceased inmates…"

I remember Eli, the first time he got out of prison, standing outside the gates at eight in the morning. Street clothes and a plastic bag in his hand, age twenty, still young enough to fidget. We hugged when I pulled up, quick and hard and perfunctory, but we were still doing that then.

I remember my eyes stung because they were burning the fields in the valley, and because I hadn't slept since I got off work at two that morning.

The voicemail finishes. I barely heard a fucking word, so I hit play again, hold it up to my ear.

"This is for Eli Ryder's next of kin…"

CHAPTER THIRTY-SIX
Darcy

I knock on Trent's door softly, hoping he's in there because if he's not I've got no clue where to find him.

No answer. I knock again, a little louder.

Maybe he's just asleep, not somewhere else, I tell myself. *People sleep when bad things happen, right?*

I knock one more time, then turn away. He's not there, and my stomach tightens, wondering where he went in a strange city at two in the morning—

But then the door opens. Trent gives me a glance up and down, then nods, steps back, gestures me in.

"Hey," I say.

"Hey," he says, his voice full of gravel.

I almost ask *are you okay* or *how are you doing* or *what's up* but those are all idiotic and trite and I bite my tongue rather than ask something stupid. He's not okay, he's doing bad, his brother's dead, and I fucking know all that.

"Any more news?" I finally ask, once the silence gets too heavy.

He slumps onto a couch, across from the room's queen bed.

"The prison morgue called," he says, and he sounds like I'm talking to him from miles away. "They want to know where to send the... where to send him, what my plans are for him, who else they need to notify. All that."

I sit gingerly on the bed opposite him. I've never done anything like this. I've never even had a grandparent or a distant uncle die, because that would require having either grandparents or uncles.

"Can I help?" I ask. "Do you want me to..."

I have no clue what needs to be done.

"...Call funeral homes or something?" I hazard.

"It's eleven on the west coast," he says, still looking at the curtains over the window like he can see through them. "I don't think you're gonna get an answer."

"Well, tomorrow," I say. "Are they going to bury him at the prison, or can they send him to Low Valley, or..."

"They?"

"Whoever's in charge of it."

Trent gives me a weird look, a little hesitant, a little put off. I think I said something wrong but I can't pinpoint it.

"That's me. I'm in charge of it. Eli goes where I say."

I look down at my hands. I'd somehow assumed this would all be done by someone else, somewhere else, and it wouldn't all fall on Trent but I have no idea why I thought that because I don't know how either death or family work.

The one person I know who died was Allen, the roadie who was with Gavin and Liam, and I have no idea what happened to his body. I guess someone took care of it.

"Right," I say, like I knew that and had forgotten.

"There's nothing to do right now," he says, his voice hollow again. He's looking back at the window. "Go get some sleep, Darce. I'll see you in the morning. Thanks for stopping by."

It's a dismissal, clear as day. I can't help but be disappointed, because we've spent every night since that first one together.

But I know why, and I know shit happens, and I know it's not about me. So I stand up. I give him a quick kiss, and I tell him he can wake me up if he needs me, I don't care, and then I leave.

Back in my own room, in my oddly empty bed, I lie awake for a long time before I finally fall into a restless sleep, ready to wake up the moment my phone rings.

• • •

It doesn't ring all night. Sometime around sunrise I fall asleep properly and only wake up when it's almost noon.

Trent hasn't called or texted, though Gavin and Joan both have, asking if I have any updates. I guess they haven't heard from Trent either. I throw on some clothes, grab two coffees and a couple pastries from the hotel lobby breakfast, come back upstairs and knock on his door with my elbow.

He's on the phone when he answers the door, listening to someone on the other end. He doesn't smile, just nods and turns, so I follow him in.

I don't think he's slept. There are circles under his eyes, he's wearing a white undershirt, and his room has that closed-in scent of insomnia and stress, random things scattered on the floor.

But at least no furniture is upside down. At least his phone's not smashed. Everything could always be worse.

"You're not listening," he says. "I don't want him there. He's not going into Green Willows and I don't fucking *care* how many spots my mother pre-paid for there."

He pauses, listening. I put the coffees on the table and sit, sipping one myself.

"How far is Brookside Meadow from the Sunset Acres home? You know what, forget it, it doesn't matter. Brookside is fine."

Silence.

"First thing tomorrow," he says. "North Delano said they'd call you and arrange for... delivery."

Another long silence. I sip coffee and look at the curtains, wondering if I should open them or turn on the air conditioning, anything to make this room a little *better*.

"Thanks," Trent says.

He hangs up his phone, tosses it onto the bed, and sits on it himself. It's still made but slightly rumpled, like he's laid on it but hasn't gotten in. I hand him his coffee and he takes it without drinking.

"Fucking Eli," he says. "I can't believe he's dead and still a useless pain in my ass."

Trent looks at the curtain-covered window, and I look at my coffee, not sure how to answer that.

"The prison won't release his body to a funeral home without someone to authorize it *in person*, otherwise they slap him in a pine box and bury him in some potter's field they've got outside Fresno. And I can't find a funeral home that'll tell me *shit* about what to do until they've got confirmation that a body's coming in, and the second I mention that he's coming from a prison they all clam the fuck up and can't wait to get off the phone with me."

He takes a long, angry pull from his coffee, still glaring at the window.

"Not to mention I've got to buy him a burial plot, and it's confusing the shit out of the cemetery because

240

when my dad died, my mom bought four plots at once, like she thought we could all be together again or some shit. And like fucking *hell* am I burying him next to our father."

There's a pretty obvious solution, I think.

"It's all a fucking mess," he says, his jaw tightening. "I thought at least Eli's fuck ups were contained if he was in prison, but apparently fucking not. Apparently he's managed to put snarls in my life even when he got himself killed."

Another angry drink.

"Have I mentioned that part yet? Stabbed twenty-something times with a fucking sharpened toothbrush. You've gotta be a pretty bad asshole to get that kind of attention in prison, but that's what Eli was, a fucking useless idiot."

He stands up, stalks to the window, throws the curtain open.

"We're probably all fucking better off," he says, his voice sharp and bitter. "Guess he's done fucking up *now*."

I take a deep breath and get ready to state the obvious.

"So let the prison bury him outside Fresno," I say.

Trent turns, slowly, and looks at me like I'm an alien.

"What?"

"You wouldn't have to deal with all this," I point out, heart pounding, but I keep my voice calm. "You wouldn't have to call funeral homes and schedule a transfer, you wouldn't have to fly to California and give the go-ahead. You wouldn't have to go at all, just let them bury him where they want and be done with it. You don't even have to reschedule any tour dates."

Trent keeps staring at me, his gaze so intense my skin starts crawling.

"Eli's my *brother*."

"I know."

241

"I can't fucking put him in some prison graveyard."

I glance at my coffee again, even as Trent's eyes bore into me. I fucking hate seeing him like this, and I hate that his terrible brother — his brother who *killed someone* — is the one making him such a wreck.

"He was in prison," I point out.

"I'm not doing that to my little brother."

"He's dead, he won't even know."

"That's not the point," Trent says, and now he looks disgusted. "I'm not just— I can't—"

He paces away from the window, takes a couple steps to the bed, turns back.

"I can't fucking call the prison and say '*do whatever you want with his body.*' He was my *brother*, I fucking owe him better than that."

"Why?" I ask softly.

I nearly say *you remember that he killed someone, right?* But I keep my mouth shut.

"Because Eli's my little brother!" Trent nearly shouts.

"Yeah, and he made you feel awful for years and he blamed *you* because he was in prison and you know that if he could have somehow gotten you to take the fall, he would have," I say. "Why the fuck does he deserve this from you? He doesn't, he's never done anything but take from you so let them bury him in a pine box. He'd do it to you."

I know that there's something at work here that I can't quite grasp, some emotional gut-punch that I'm seeing but don't know how to feel.

But I've watched Trent worry over his brother for years, and I've watched him beat himself up whenever Eli calls, give his little brother whatever he can. Pay for lawyers, for cigarettes, drive up from Los Angeles once a month to visit him in in prison.

And I hate it. I hate that Eli's been nothing but a drain on Trent the whole time I've known him, and now that he's dead, he's *still* a drain and Trent won't just let him go.

"It doesn't matter," Trent says, his voice strange and baffled.

And he just looks at me, a look I've never seen on his face before. Like he's never really *seen* me before.

"You can't understand," he finally says.

"I understand that Eli's made you miserable for as long as I've known you," I say, trying to keep my voice gentle, even though I'm pissed. Mostly at Eli.

"That's how you can sit here and tell me to let my brother rot in the middle of nowhere surrounded by people no one loved enough to bury right," he says. "You haven't *got* a family. You haven't got anyone you'd do this for."

I open my mouth, silently. Then I close it, because I haven't got a response.

"That's how you can be fucking *heartless*," he says. "You haven't got a clue how it feels to have a sibling, to grow up with someone and then lose them."

He says it quietly but his voice is shaking with rage.

"You've got a black fucking hole where your heart goes," he says, low and flat. "Just leave."

I don't know what the hell happened. I didn't think my suggestion was that bad, but here's Trent in front of me, furious and glowering and looking at me like I'm the scum of the earth, and I feel like I can barely breathe.

Mechanically, I stand. I turn and I walk out of the hotel room, and I don't think I even say goodbye, just let the door close after me, and my feet carry me to the elevator, to the lobby, outside into the Boston summer sunshine.

I stand there, and I stare, and I wonder how the fuck I'm supposed to fix this.

CHAPTER THIRTY-SEVEN
Trent

I call the prison morgue back, tell them to hold onto Eli until tomorrow. I call the other cemetery in Low Valley, the one where my mother *hasn't* got plots already, and I reserve one though they refuse to go through with the transaction until I've seen it in person.

I book a flight into Bakersfield. It gets in after midnight, I've got two layovers, and it's nearly two thousand dollars, but I don't give a shit.

And I fold everything that I just said to Darcy into the bigger misery wrenching at my gut. I just add it to the pile of horrible things to feel miserable about, because after all I've got twelve-odd hours on planes and in airports to feel as low as I can, why start now?

I'll regret it. I knew I'd regret it when I said it but I couldn't stop myself, and now I'm going to fucking pay.

I call Nigel from the cab to Logan airport, but he's already working on postponing our next couple of shows. It's not the first time I've been fucking relieved to talk to him.

The airport is miserable. It's a fucking airport. I get selected for an extra pat-down at security and nearly miss my flight, so I don't even have time to pick up a trashy thriller from the airport bookstore and I spend the first leg, from Boston to Chicago, listening to my iPod and wishing I could stop thinking.

But I can't. Every fucking time I close my eyes his face is there: making mudpies in our dusty backyard with the hose until our father came out and yelled at us. Riding our bikes around one of the empty lots in Low Valley — there were plenty to choose from — the time my wheels slipped and I went flying into the concrete foundation of a building that never got built, breaking my arm.

How Eli was the one who stayed with me while I cried, sending one of our friends to get my mom.

Us, older. Me maybe fourteen, him maybe twelve. The first time he backtalked my dad for hitting my mom and my dad cracked him across the face. He said he'd fallen off his bike the next day at school and I felt fucking awful and powerless, even though I was still afraid of my dad.

Eli stealing candy bars and sharing them with me. Eli, always a little more of a troublemaker, showing me how to get into the storm drains where we smoked pot together after school sometimes.

Bottle rockets in the desert. Finding an old wreck of a dirt bike and fixing it up just well enough to jump it off piles of hard-packed desert rock. Sneaking out, stealing my dad's truck, and driving into Bakersfield for the night.

God, we got beat for that one.

And finally, *that* night. I was seventeen, he was fifteen, and after my mom — his favorite punching bag — my dad went after Eli, and I got in his way.

We land in Chicago. I've got five minutes to spare so I grab the dumbest paperback I can find, get on another plane. Read some bullshit until Denver, where I've got four hours so I eat some Tex-Mex and try not to think, but the thoughts of my little brother are sometimes punctuated by Darcy's face, the look on it when I told her she had a black hole.

Fuck. *Fuck.*

I put her away, think about tequila shots, but I don't. Instead I pace the airport until I get on the next plane and a few hours later, at last, we land at tiny Meadows Field airport.

Outside is palm trees and dust, the day's oppressive heat still lingering in the air, and I hate it but it feels like home.

Doesn't mean I have to like it.

CHAPTER THIRTY-EIGHT
Darcy

I show up at the theater at five for sound check, like I'm supposed to. Even though we're doing two nights in the same place, something we do sometimes in big cities, we usually do sound check twice. Better safe than sorry.

But instead of finding people inside, there are papers stuck to every door:

DIRTSHINE SHOW RESCHEDULED
WE APOLOGIZE FOR THE INCONVENIENCE

I stare at it for a moment, uncomprehending. I've been wandering around Boston all day, unsure where to go or what to fucking do, feeling awful and guilty and a little self-righteous and more than anything, like I'm a clueless idiot and like I fucked something up and I don't understand *how*.

I pull out my phone to call Nigel, only to find thirty-two missed calls from him, seventeen from Gavin, and five from Joan.

"Hey," Gavin says when I call him. "No show tonight, but we're at this place called Emilio's. Around the corner from the hotel. Come down."

• • •

Emilio's is a low-key Italian joint with checkered table cloths, cheesy decor, and an extensive menu. Gavin, Joan, and Nigel are all sitting in a huge booth in the back with a basket of breadsticks, a massive salad, and drinks.

"Right," Nigel's saying, one hand around his whiskey. "I haven't rescheduled the Washington, D.C. shows yet so with any luck at all, we'll be able to make those. They're still six days away, and it's only about a twelve hour drive so frankly, maybe we should simply head out of Boston tomorrow, that way we won't have to hurry and we could even get a spot of sightseeing in as we drive..."

I grab a breadstick and tear into it, my stomach suddenly growling. I'm not sure I've eaten anything since my breakfast pastry. I'm not really paying attention to Nigel going on about sightseeing in New Jersey or whatever the hell he's talking about, I'm just stuffing my face and trying not to feel awful.

"If it's going to be much longer than that, I'd rather fly home for a couple of days," Gavin says.

"Same," Joan agrees. "Boston is nice, but I like seeing my husband, too."

I grab another breadstick and shrug at Nigel, because I don't really care right now. Mainly, I'm fucking hungry, and besides that, I don't want to *think*.

"Did he say when he might be back?" Gavin asks.

"He didn't know just yet," Nigel says. "It sounds as if the arrangements are turning out to be quite a chore—"

"Back?" I say around a mouthful of bread. "From where?"

Three pairs of eyes look at me, suddenly awkward. Joan and Gavin glance at each other, and then Gavin leans forward a little.

"He flew back to California this afternoon," he says. "To arrange the funeral and everything."

I stop. My brain stops. After a long second, I finish chewing, swallow, and blink at Gavin.

"He left?"

"At one-thirteen," Nigel offers, looking at his phone. "He doesn't get in to Bakersfield until twelve thirty, poor man has two layovers—"

"He already left," I say. "He's gone. Out of Boston."

"Right," Gavin says.

I flatten my palms on the table, processing this.

Trent left without telling me. He's flying across the country to bury his brother and he didn't tell me he was going, he just went.

I know it's not forever. I know he's coming back, but finding out now, hours later, from Gavin fucking *stings*.

"Oh," I say.

"Sorry, I thought he'd have told you," Nigel says, lifting his whiskey to his lips. "I'd have mentioned it earlier in one of the six voicemails I left you, but I assumed you already knew."

"It's fine," I say, and grab another breadstick. I shove it into my mouth as I stand.

"Are you leaving?" Gavin says.

"Yeah, I gotta go."

"Stay and eat," Joan says. "The lasagna here is supposed to be amazing, and..."

I don't catch the rest of her sentence, just shake my head and walk out of Emilio's, back into the night. I'm still starving but I don't feel like I can face them, not now, not like this.

I know it's not a huge thing that he flew somewhere in an emergency, but for some reason it feels fucking cataclysmic. I can't remember that last time that *Nigel* knew something about Trent that I didn't. I can't remember the last time *anyone* knew something about Trent that I didn't, and that's what feels like cold lead boiling in my ribcage.

We fought, and he left, I think.

We fought, he left.

There's only so many ways to parse that, and they're all fucking wretched.

CHAPTER THIRTY-NINE
Trent

I slide the rental car into a spot marked VISITOR, and then I sit in the driver's seat for a moment. Then another one, looking out over the suburban low, flat, sprawling houses, the over-green lawns, the palms trees standing bolt upright at regular intervals. There's even a golf course just out of sight, all this green and pleasant in a way that the dusty valley floor probably shouldn't be.

We're twenty miles from where I grew up, but now I'm in a different world.

I take a deep breath. I rub my eyes, my eyelids like sandpaper against them. I did manage to shower this morning in my hotel room, even if I didn't really sleep last night either thanks to the gnawing ache in my chest.

Eli's *gone*. He's gone. Not just in prison, but really *gone*.

I open the car door into the heat before I can talk myself out of it, get out, and walk toward Sunset Acres Assisted Living. Like everything else here, in the nice part of Bakersfield, it's a low, sprawling building with lush green lawns, palm trees, and a Spanish tile roof. I put her in here after we first made it big, before I even bought myself a house.

Anything to get her out of the leaking, rotting trailer where she was living alone.

I check in at the front desk, grab a nametag, and the receptionist calls my mom's nurse that day. She's a short Filipina woman named Isabel, and I've already told her everything.

"I'm so sorry," she says, when she first sees me.

"Thanks," I say automatically. "How's she doing?"

My mom doesn't know yet. I didn't want to tell her over the phone, especially knowing that I'd just have to tell her again when I got here.

And then again every half hour, for God knows how long.

"To be honest, Gwen's had a string of bad days lately," Isabel says, like she's steeling herself. "Her seizures have gotten a little more frequent, though they're not *worse*. And her memory loss... well, it's not improving."

Fuck. I haven't called my mom in two weeks, and even though I've got excuses, none of them are good enough. Fifteen minutes is all it takes, and then she'll be happy for the next twenty that she remembers I called.

"Anything else I should know?" I ask grimly, outside my mom's door.

"Just try to be patient," Isabel says gently. "Anything you tell her, she won't remember until you repeat it ten, maybe fifteen times."

I stare the door, number 1168. I'm going to have to tell my mom her youngest child is dead ten, maybe fifteen times, and every time is going to be like the first for her.

I knock.

"Come in!" I hear my mom's voice call. I look down at Isabel, who puts one hand on my arm and nods. I'm glad that there's someone in this world who appreciates how hard what I'm about to do is, and I push the door open into my mom's suite.

She's sitting in a high-backed chair with floral upholstery, a delicate coffee table in front of her with a doily and a teacup sitting on top.

As soon as she sees me, she practically leaps to her feet, her hands twisting nervously in front of herself.

"Stan," she says, her voice brittle with anxiety.

I stop in the doorway, suddenly nauseated even though this isn't the first time this has happened. I know I look a lot like my dad, that we move the same way, that we have the same gestures, but it still nearly knocks me over.

"I'm Trent," I tell her.

She exhales, her shoulders slumping, and peers at me, her whole body a picture of relief.

"Of course you are," she says, walking toward me. "I'm so sorry, I don't know what got into me! What a pleasant surprise, dear."

We hug. She asks me how the drive in was, isn't it just hot as the dickens today, would I like some orange juice or maybe a diet coke. She's still good at this kind of small talk, the things that don't require specific knowledge, the conversations she can have by rote.

I take a glass of water, sit in a floral chair opposite hers, and I know I have to do it now or I might lose my nerve.

"Mom," I say, as gently as I can. "Eli is dead."

For one long, terrible second, my mom just stares at me, mouth open, eyes wide.

Then she just *crumples*. Her whole body slumps and collapses and she slides to the floor. I can't stand in time to catch her, but in a moment, I'm kneeling next to her, arm around her shoulders, trying to hold her up.

I just gave her a seizure, I think. *Fuck, I should have asked Isabel to come in with me, I didn't think this would happen—*

"Eli," my mom gasps. "My God, Trent, not him. Not my baby. *Not my baby.*"

I know there's nothing I can say, so I don't, I just close my eyes and rest my cheek on the top of my mom's head, letting her sob in my arms. I've seen my mom go through a lot of bad, bad shit, but I think this might be the worst.

This is one, I think.

We're on the floor for a long, long time. She soaks through my shirt with tears, and I just sit there, rocking her back and forth, wishing I could do something or *say* something that would make it better, but I can't.

After ten minutes, maybe more, she sniffles, looks up at me.

"Was he hit by a car?" she asks.

After he got out of prison the first time, Eli worked construction with a county road crew. I see what Isabel means about her memory, because she's forgotten that Eli was behind bars again.

"He was killed," I say, and explain, as gently as I can. She's quiet the whole time, still crying softly. She gets the hiccups before I finish.

"Where did I go wrong?" she asks, when I'm done telling her what I know.

I don't have answer for that either, and we go quiet again.

After a while, my mom sits up straight. She grabs a tissue, dries her eyes, and from the spark in her I can tell she's starting to forget. That she still knows something bad happened, that I'm there for an ugly reason, but I don't think she knows what it is any more.

She stands, clears the teacup from the table. I can tell she's confused, that she knows she's forgetting something, like why she's crying, why I'm sitting on the floor, but too embarrassed to say anything.

So I sit again. She offers me tea and I accept, and we spend a few minutes chatting pleasantly. She asks me vague questions about my life and I answer. I ask her how her Thursday night salsa classes here are going, and she laughs, says she never *was* so popular in her younger days.

I wonder if she knows what I'm talking about.

She sits. We sip tea as the knot in my stomach tightens. I know the second time is coming like a freight train, barreling down the track toward me now.

"Speaking of which," she says, taking a sip. "Have you talked to Eli lately?"

. . .

I have to tell my mom three more times, and when I leave Sunset Acres it isn't even noon yet. I'm already wrung out and exhausted, because telling my mom once was pretty bad. Watching her find out Eil was dead over and over again? That was fucking next-level.

It's unbelievably hot. Even the breeze is hot in a way that feels like the sun is *breathing* on me, and it's got that unmistakable scent of home: dust and farming and the pollution from Los Angeles that settles here, mixed with asphalt and tires and concrete.

I go to the prison first, half an hour north, and sign the release for Eli's body in person so the funeral home can pick it up later that day. They ask if I want to see him, but I don't. I want to remember my little brother alive, not stabbed to death and in a drawer in cold storage.

Then the funeral home. They've got a thousand questions for me and an obsequious, too-gentle manner that makes me feel like I'm being treated with kid gloves. I fucking hate it, and in the end I tell them to do whatever it takes to have a funeral as soon as possible, I don't care how much it costs.

The cemetery, where the caretaker insists on taking me for a fucking *walk* to view all the different parts of the graveyard, even though they all look pretty much the same: headstones everywhere, dead people below. The grass is pale green and just beginning to go summer-brittle, and I know that in another month it'll be brown and like walking across spikes, no matter how much they water it.

It's evening when I finally get back to my hotel room at the Holiday Inn and lie on my bed without even taking off my shoes, the exhaustion and stress finally catching up to me, even as my brain buzzes over lists of everything I have left to do.

And then, inevitably, inescapably, there she is. All day I've been seeing Darcy's face, the way she looked when I told her she had a black hole for a heart. I've been trying not to think of it, trying to focus on all the shit that needs to get done, but it hasn't worked.

I took the best thing in my life and I fucked it up. And then I didn't even tell her I was leaving.

I had time to apologize. Even if I did it in five minutes before I'd left, it would be better than this gnawing heartbreak on top of the hole that's been punched through the middle of me. For fuck's sake, I could call her *right now*.

I don't. I lie on the bed and feel fucking awful and don't call her to apologize, and it's because I'm fucking afraid.

I'm afraid she won't forgive me. I'm afraid she's angry, that she's hurt, that she's decided again that this is a bad idea.

I'm afraid that Darcy's going to break my heart the day before my little brother's funeral, and I don't think I can take it. I can take a whole lot of shit, but not *that*.

CHAPTER FORTY
Darcy

I'm fucking useless. When I leave Emilio's, I walk past a liquor store, and on impulse I buy a bottle of expensive vodka, just because it's there and I can.

And because I'm so fucking certain we're done, and a couple shots of the good stuff only makes me more certain. I said horrible things about his dead brother. I basically told Trent that he didn't deserve love, that he may as well rot away forgotten, and I can't fucking blame Trent for getting angry.

I was an asshole. A total fucking asshole, and I'm pretty fucking sure that telling me I was heartless and then leaving without a peep spells THE END in big-ass neon letters that even my dumb ass can read.

I fall asleep that night with the TV blaring. I don't even brush my teeth, even though I think about it, because who fucking needs teeth if they're heartbroken? Ten thousand dollars of dental work can go fuck itself right now.

• • •

I wake up hungover at noon, and you know the best way to cure that? More vodka and stupid television. I only get out of bed to pee and put the *Do Not disturb* sign on my door, then get right back in, feeling nauseous and drunk and like I don't want to think. Someone knocks on my door a couple times during the day, and I just ignore it.

And you know the worst part? I still fucking wish I could do something to make Trent feel better, even though I'm pretty sure I'm the last person he wants to think about right now.

• • •

By mid-afternoon, the vodka's gone. In my defense, it wasn't a huge bottle, but I'm drunk and feel like hell and I'm fucking *hungry*, so I put on pants and walk around the corner to McDonald's, where I manage to scarf down a Big Mac and fries without causing a scene.

I spend another hour in my hotel room. I'm sobering up a little, which isn't so bad, especially since the thought of *more* vodka makes me feel like I might puke.

Then, the knocking starts. I try to ignore it, but it doesn't stop. Two, three minutes, ceaseless.

Go the fuck away, I think. *I can't see people right now, I'm fucking useless, just leave*.

They don't leave. They keep fucking knocking, and finally, they win.

I open the door to Gavin's hand, mid-air, Joan standing behind him.

"What," I say, closing my eyes since it feels like the world is shifting unpleasantly beneath my feet.

"Christ on a cross," he says

I lean against the door frame and flip him off.

"What do you *want*," I say, not even putting in the effort to make it a question.

"We're intervening."

"No."

"Sorry, that's incorrect," Gavin says.

"Fuck off."

"Also no."

I shut the door in his face. Or, I try, because he sticks his foot in before I can get it closed, and even though I shove my shoulder against it, he doesn't budge.

"If you think you're going to win this you're quite wrong," he says. "I've got *loads* of experience in dealing with drunk and belligerent people, and Liam's got about eighty pounds on you."

Fuck. He's right. Even in my current, blitzed state, I know that me on my worst day is nothing compared to Liam's shitshow on any given Friday.

I yank the door open and *glare*, even though Gavin and Joan seem like they're slowly sliding off to the right, and I have to prop my head against the door frame to stop it.

"I don't want an intervention," I say. "I just want to be drunk and feel like shit."

"Noted," Gavin says. "Now come the fuck on."

• • •

They drag me down to the hotel lobby and prop me up on an ugly, modern couch that's out of the way and not far from the women's restroom. Joan sits opposite me while Gavin gets me a cup of coffee, and then they both just watch me as I take several sips, my head in my hands.

"All right," Gavin finally says. "Start."

I take a deep breath, steel myself, and swallow hard, feeling nauseous. I don't want to talk about this, but I don't really see another choice.

Besides, Gavin's one of my closest friends, and I really like Joan.

"I was awful to Trent and he's never going to forgive me," I start. "I told him to just let the prison bury Eli, because Eli's kind of a dick and he's *always* been kind of a dick and if I'm being really fucking honest it's what he deserves, but Trent was really pissed—"

Fuck, I'm crying now, and I take a big gulp of air.

"Darcy," Joan interrupts. "Can you start at the beginning?"

I take another deep breath, and realize: they don't know about anything. They think that Trent and I are just really close friends and don't know that whatever we are or were, it's definitely more than *that* now.

I clear my throat. Joan offers me a tissue and I blow my nose, then sigh.

"So, uh," I say, not really sure how to phrase this. "...Trent and I are sleeping together."

I glance nervously at Gavin and Joan. I'm expecting shocked faces, mouths open in horror, gasps of surprise, *something*.

Instead, I'm pretty sure they're both trying not to smile.

"Are you?" Gavin says, almost managing to keep a straight face.

"Oh," says Joan without an ounce of surprise in her voice.

I just stare, too drunk to come up with a *next* thing to say, and look from Joan to Gavin and back.

"You knew," I accuse, leaning back on the couch. It's kind of a mistake, so I close my eyes.

"I thought that might be the case," Joan says carefully.

"Have you got any idea how loud you are?" Gavin asks, *much* less carefully. "Apparently I ought to be asking Trent for tips, because—"

"Could you not?" I ask, eyes still closed.

"Right," he says. I crack one eye open.

He's fucking grinning, and I'm fucking confused.

"You're not pissed?" I ask carefully.

Gavin sighs.

"I might have been a bit," he says. "But then you two managed to act all right, up until now at least, so I figured it wasn't such a big deal."

I rub my hands over my face, massage my temples.

"How long have you *known*?"

"The day I came looking for Trent in your room and his trousers and pants were strewn across the floor," he says, and he looks pretty fucking pleased with himself.

Shit, and here I thought we were doing *great* keeping this a secret.

"Okay, fine, we're fucking, whatever," I say quickly. "But anyway, yesterday we got in this fight and then he just left for California and didn't even tell me, and I'm pretty sure everything's fucking over and ruined and he never wants to see me again..."

Joan and Gavin are very, *very* patient. It probably takes them a good thirty minutes to tease the full, blow-by-blow story out of my dumb, drunk self, and they're fucking *nice* about it.

When I finish, they're just quiet for a long moment. I swig the last sip of my coffee, and then just stare at the disposable cup in my hand. The silence feels ominous, like they're trying to figure out how to tell me that I'm right, I'm probably never even going to talk to Trent again.

Finally, Joan clears her throat.

"Have you talked to him yet?" she asks.

I shake my head.

"He doesn't want to talk to me," I say, miserably. "He told me I've got—"

"Darcy, he said that about twelve hours after finding out his brother died," Joan says, gently. "Grief tends to make people say things they come to regret."

"Knowing Trent, I doubt he feels very good about himself right now," Gavin points out.

I sigh dramatically, my face in my hands.

"Even after I said what I said?"

"Even after that," Gavin confirms.

"You don't think he never wants to see me again?"

"I very sincerely doubt that," Joan says.

"You're really overreacting here," Gavin says, leaning forward on his chair, leather bracelets sliding down his forearms.

I flip him off, and he shrugs.

"It's your first fight, and the first one always feels like it's the goddamn apocalypse," Joan says. "But it's usually not."

"Usually," I echo.

"This is what I mean by overreacting," Gavin teases, and I flip him off again. "Three in one day," he says to Joan.

"What's the record?" she asks him.

"I think it's five," he says. "I might get there."

"So what do I *do*," I interrupt.

"You bloody talk to him," Gavin says like it's obvious. "You apologize for hurting his feelings and he'll probably apologize for hurting yours."

I give him a weird look, because I can't believe that Gavin Fucking Lockwood, of all people, just gave me relationship advice.

"This might sound a little crazy," Joan says. "But you know what I'd do?"

I raise my eyebrows.

"Fly to California," she says. "Be there for him. He's got no one else, not really."

I glance at Gavin, wondering how much he's told Joan, and he shrugs, then nods.

"Like they say, go get your man," he tells me.

"But what if he—"

"He won't," Gavin says.

I make a face.

"You don't have to trust yourself, but fucking trust me for once," Gavin says. "I'm a fucking *expert* on winning someone back, you know."

He has a point.

"Okay," I say. "Okay, I fly to California, and I talk to him, and...?"

"That's all," Joan says.

I have to admit, it sounds... simple. *Talk to him.* How did I not think of that?

"We'd best get moving," Gavin says. "You've got a flight to catch."

CHAPTER FORTY-ONE
Trent

The funeral's at three. It's the worst time of day, when the sun's been beating down for a good nine hours, before it finally starts descending and offers just a little relief.

The grave site is at the far end of the cemetery, a decent walk from the nearest paved road through the place. I'm sweating the moment I get out of the car, and with every step I wonder why the hell I'm wearing a suit at all.

It's not like Eli's ever gonna know. It's not like my mom's gonna remember, and I don't really give a shit what the discount preacher I found last-minute thinks.

But it felt right to wear a suit to my little brother's funeral, and that feeling is pretty much I have to go on right now. With this. With *anything*.

I walk around to my mom's side of the car, offer her my hand. She has some trouble with the right side of her body, and she's having a particularly bad day today so I have to practically haul her out of the car and she clings to my arm like she's drowning and I'm her only lifeline.

We head for the grave site slowly, my mom walking very carefully around the headstones, the dips in the ground, the raised tufts of grass slowly going bone-dry. She almost trips a few times, but I catch her, and we keep going.

A small mercy: she finally remembered about Eli this morning. I think Isabel took pity on her and told her a few times as well. I should thank her for that.

Halfway to the gravesite, my mom stops. Her breathing is a little hard, and she's sweating as well under her black blouse and black pants.

"Trent," she says, her voice a little shaky and uncertain.

"Yeah?"

She works her mouth, like she's having trouble forming words, and I wait.

"This isn't where your father is buried," she finally says.

"I know."

"We should bury Eli next to his father."

I swallow hard. This isn't the first time today we've had almost this exact conversation, and I've got a feeling it won't be the last.

"I'm not burying Eli next to that man, Mom."

"They should be together."

"No, they shouldn't. Come on."

There are a thousand more things I could say. I could even get away with them, because in twenty minutes they'll be gone from her memory, but I keep my mouth shut.

I've already wrecked enough by saying something I shouldn't have this week.

Finally, we're by the grave, a few minutes early. The cemetery's set up a tent over the graveside, and mom and I sit on shaded folding chairs, Eli's coffin on a metal contraption, hovering over the open hole in the dirt.

Just looking at it, my gut clenches. Even though I didn't want an open casket — staring at my dead brother just didn't appeal to me — I have the crazy urge to open it and look inside. I just want to make sure that he's really there, that he's really *dead*, that this isn't some long, bizarre joke being played on me.

"There ought to be a service," my mom says, her voice fading again.

"We're early," I tell her. "The minister's coming."

She looks around. Her right hand has started shaking a little, and I just watch it for a long moment. Thinking that they needed me, her and Eli, and I just abandoned them. The second I could get out of that house, out of Low Valley, I did.

We sit there, quietly, for several more minutes. No one else comes, but I wasn't expecting anyone. Eli's friends are mostly in prison, or not the funeral types, and it's not like we've got any other family worth inviting.

"Trent," my mom says after a while, like she's just realized something. "This isn't where your father's buried."

"No, it's not."

"We should bury Eli next to his father."

I want to scream. I want to throw this chair into the grave, I want to kick my stupid brother's stupid coffin. I want to fucking destroy everything I can see, anything so I don't have to tell my mother again and again that it's up to me and we're not fucking burying my brother next to the man he was unfortunate enough to be descended from.

"They should be together," she says.

"I'm not burying Eli next to Dad," I say.

Finally, someone else is walking over to the grave site: another man in a suit, the same carefully somber expression I saw all over faces at the funeral home. I stand, help my mother up.

"Reverend McCarthy," he says, going to my mother first, shaking her hand tenderly like she's a child. "You're the family."

"Yes," she says, and I nod.

"I'm so sorry for your loss," he says, his face practically radiating sorrow and empathy.

"Thank you," I say.

He's not. I know he's not. I know he's paid to be here and say pretty things about someone he didn't know, but it seemed like the right thing to do, so here we are.

"Will this be all?" he asks, adjusting his glasses.

I glance around. There's another row of chairs set up behind us, but that's pretty fucking optimistic. I don't know who else would show up. Besides the obituary the funeral home ran, I don't know how anyone would even know about this.

"Yes, that's all," my mom says, sounding frailer than ever.

We sit. The reverend assumes his position near the head of the grave, taking out a leather portfolio and opening it, his face so serious it may as well be made from stone.

"Brothers and sisters," he intones. "Friends and family, we're here to celebrate and mourn the death of Eli Ryder..."

My mom starts crying. I wish I could cry, but instead I just stare at his coffin.

After this, he's going down there, I think. *I'm really never going to see him again.*

"Eli was a son, but more than a son. He was a brother, but more than a..."

The reverend glances up, though he doesn't break pace, just plows along through the platitudes. I keep staring at Eli's coffin, trying not to think about the finality of being buried, about what the phrase *six feet under* really means.

I should have had him cremated, I think. *Then he wouldn't be stuck here, at least.*

In the distance, off to my right, I finally realize something's moving. The reverend drones on about souls going home to Jesus, and I look over.

It's a person.

It's *running*.

It's Darcy.

She's in a black dress and *bolting* across the million-degree grass, dodging headstones and running hell-for-leather over where people are buried, because of course Darcy doesn't give a shit about that.

I have no idea how the fuck she got here and I really have no idea how the fuck she knew this was happening now, but the middle of the absolute shitshow of my little brother's pathetic funeral, I'm suddenly *happy*.

Maybe not happy. It's harder than that. But seeing Darcy right now lights up a secret, buried part of my heart, suddenly makes all this just a little more bearable.

Twenty feet away, she slows to a walk. She's breathing hard, bright red and sweaty, and she smooths her hair down and tries to catch her breath like we didn't all just watch her sprint from the road to here.

"I'll be right back," I whisper to my mom, squeezing her hand. She's frowning at Darcy as I stand and walk out from under the tent.

The reverend just keeps going. I guess I could ask him to stop, but I'm not sure I see the point.

"Trent," Darcy whispers when I'm in earshot. "I'm so sorry, I should have come—"

I wrap my arms around her and just fucking squeeze until she stops talking and squeezes me back. I don't give a shit that a funeral is a weird time for this, I don't give a shit that a man in a suit is going on about the valley of death, and I don't give a shit that my mom is glaring daggers from her seat.

I just fucking care that Darcy's here to make this dark day a little brighter.

I lead her back to the seats. She nods and half-waves at my mom, who nods back slightly.

Then she holds my hand in both of hers, and I finish burying my brother.

CHAPTER FORTY-TWO
Darcy

"And thus we say," the minister drones on, "ashes to ashes, dust to dust..."

I just sit there, rigidly, spine perfectly straight, sweat sliding down it like a waterslide as the minister talks, Eli's coffin right in front of us. There's no one else here, just me, Trent, and Trent's mom, which only made my entrance that much worse.

Don't think about it now, I tell myself, staring at the shiny wood box hovering over the void. *You got here. That's the thing. The minister barely even noticed.*

Now that I'm here, I'm not sure what I'm supposed to do. I think this might be it, though: sit next to Trent, hold his hand. Just sit here. Just *be* here. So I sit, and I hold, and I *be*, and I hope it's what he needs.

After ten, maybe fifteen minutes, the minster stops speaking, not that I've really been paying attention. Solemnly, he takes two carnations from a plastic vase next to the grave, hands one each to Trent and his mom.

They rise. Trent's mom holds onto him as he helps her to the coffin, and they put the carnations on top. She's sobbing, practically all her weight leaning on Trent, like having to bury Eli like this has completely broken her. Even though I've never met her or Eli before, I'm crying too, just watching them.

The minister goes over to them, all professional sympathy, says something to each. Then he comes over to me, still sitting in a folding chair and sweating.

"My condolences," he says, and shakes my hand.

I swallow the lump in my throat, force myself not to say *it's okay, I didn't actually know him.*

"Thanks," I say, and he nods, then walks out into the sun and away. Trent and his mom are still graveside, his arm around her. If he moves I think she might just crumple, and suddenly I feel like I'm intruding.

I stand and walk back into the sun myself, give them about twenty feet of space, look at the shared headstone of a couple who died sometime in the 1980s. Phyllis and Phillip.

That must have been confusing, I think.

I stare at Phyllis and Phillip for a long time. They were both born in the 1906, though she outlived him by nearly ten years. I wonder if they bought the headstone when he died or when she did. If it was when he died, did half of it just sit blank for all that time, just waiting?

"Hey," says Trent's voice behind me, and I turn.

He's standing there, in a suit, his hands in his pockets, and he's also sweating like hell.

"Hey," I say, suddenly all nerves. I bite back *I'm so sorry for everything I said* and *I didn't mean it how it sounded* and *are we okay? Can we please be okay?* Because none of this is about me.

"How are you doing?" I ask instead.

"Pretty shitty," he says.

I just nod.

"It was a nice ceremony," I say, a little at a loss for words. "I thought the minister was really good, some of the stuff he said was really touching, and putting the flowers on the coffin at the end was really beautiful..."

Trent looks me up and down. The corner of his mouth twitches up, like he's amused.

Then in one big step, he wraps me in his arms for the second time in half an hour, and even though we're both disgusting and it's stiflingly hot, it feels *good*.

"Thanks," he says, his voice low and gruff. "I know you're bullshitting me, because he was terrible, but thank you."

I squeeze him back as hard as I can.

"I really am sorry about Eli," I whisper. "That's not bullshit."

"I know."

After a long time, he lets me go. His mom is still standing graveside, looking small and frail, and we both look over at her as Trent takes my hand.

"She's gonna forget this in another fifteen minutes," he says. "I'm glad you were here, so at least someone else remembers that this happened."

Just then, she looks over, but her face is different from before. It's not the same mask of anguish and pain. She's still crying, but she looks confused, lost, like she's not quite sure why she's where she is.

"Does she remember that Eli's dead?"

"She does. I had to remind her four times yesterday."

"Jesus, Trent."

"That's not the worst part," he says, his voice low and quiet, nearly slipping away in the hot wind over the cemetery. "When she first saw me, she thought I was my father. Just for a second, but it was there."

"You're not. You know that."

"I know."

Trent's mom looks around. She takes a step back from the grave, looking at it a little uncertainly, clasps her hands in front of her, and Trent looks down at me.

"I should go get her," he says. "We're going to dinner. Come."

"I don't want to intrude," I say carefully.

He smiles at me, faintly.

"If you don't intrude I might lose my mind," he says. "Come with us. Make me feel normal."

That can be my job, I think. *That's a service I think I can offer.*

"Okay," I say.

"If you don't mind, I'll just meet you there and introduce you two then," he says, watching his mom a little warily. Now she's looking around, then slowly and uncertainly takes a seat in a folding chair, glancing back at Trent every few minutes. "No point in introducing you twice, you know?"

• • •

I get to La Cocina first. The interior is done like it's the inside of an adobe in Mexico City or something: fake building fronts with Spanish tile, colorful banners hanging everywhere, waitresses wearing full, brightly colored skirts and serapes.

Not quite where I expected Trent to be going after a funeral, but I guess he's full of surprises.

A few minutes later he shows up with his mom, and I stand, nervously. I don't think I'm very good at meeting parents, and this is a hell of a way to meet someone's parents.

On the other hand, I'll have a second chance. And a third one.

I feel bad instantly for thinking that, but I smile as they walk over. Trent's smiling, but his mom has an expression of stone and eyes of flint.

"Mom, this is Darcy," Trent says. "I've told you about her before."

"Hi," I say, holding out my hand. "I'm so sorry about Eli."

She nods, stiffly.

"Gwen," she says, her hand frail and delicate in mine. "Thank you so much for coming. We've met before, haven't we?"

"I don't think so," I say, clasping my hands in front of me, just as polite as polite can be. "But I'm his bandmate, so we may have met briefly at some point."

"Maybe you just look familiar, then," she says, like she's slightly suspicious.

"That's probably it," I say.

"She's in a lot of photos with me, Mom," Trent says, and they sit opposite me. Trent grabs a menu. "Last time you were here you really liked the enchiladas..."

We have an almost-normal four-thirty-in-the-afternoon-after-a-funeral dinner. Gwen asks me where I'm from, I tell her, she says she's heard Madison is lovely. We have that conversation three times. We discuss Gavin's recovery a few times, she asks Trent when he's moving from Los Angeles back up to the Bakersfield area at least twice.

She only brings up Eli once, when she tells Trent that he should be buried next to his father, and he just tells her that Eli didn't want that and moves on. I can tell it's not the first time they've had this talk.

Somehow, Gwen's not what I expected Trent's mom to be like. The memory problems and the shaky hands are what I expected, sure, but from the way he talks about her, I was expecting someone much meeker, much frailer, a little more afraid of everything in the world.

But instead she seems oddly tough. She pushes her way through conversations, even when we're having them for the third or fourth time, and she's very brusque and matter-of-fact.

Also? I don't think Gwen likes me.

It's hard to tell. She just got back from her son's funeral, has serious brain injuries, and doesn't remember what I said to her fifteen minutes ago. I can't quite tell where her personality ends and the mental problems begin, but I'm getting pretty strong *Gwen doesn't like me* vibes.

After dinner, Trent turns to Gwen. She's in the middle of telling me again how the shower curtain rod in her apartment keeps coming down and the staff simply *won't* fix it right, because all it takes is one good tug and then the darned thing is on the floor again.

"Maybe you should stop yanking on the shower curtain, Mom," Trent suggests, again.

"I'm not *yanking*," she says. "I'm just trying to shower, like any decent person."

He looks at me across the table, a look I can't quite decode. It seems like it's partly a warning, partly something else. Gwen sighs and looks at the dessert menu.

"Where are you staying?" he asks me.

"Nowhere yet," I say. "It's still early, I might just drive back to LA tonight. Traffic shouldn't be too bad by the time I get into the city."

Trent reaches into his pocket, then slides a plastic Holiday Inn room key across the table.

"Room one-forty-one, if you want," he says. "I've gotta drive Mom back first."

Gwen, still reading the menu, side-eyes the fuck out of our interaction, but I ignore her, putting my hand over the key and sliding it toward myself, trying not to smile.

"Where?"

"It's the one on Palm and Mira Loma."

"I don't think I'm hungry for dessert," Gwen announces, and I slide the key card into my purse, heart beating faster.

CHAPTER FORTY-THREE
Trent

"I don't think I like that girl," my mom says as we drive into the parking lot of Sunset Acres.

I knew it was coming, just from her silence on the way over. Of *course* the one thing my mom remembers of today is that she doesn't like someone.

"Darcy?" I ask, just to remind her of *that girl's* name.

"She's rude," my mom says, frowning slightly at my car's windshield as I slow, looking for a parking space. "And she has a dirty mouth."

I can tell she doesn't remember *why* she thinks Darcy's rude, but apparently Darcy made an impression. Probably by sprinting into the middle of my brother's funeral.

My mom can think whatever she wants. She clearly doesn't remember the actual event.

But I don't think I've ever been happier to see someone. Fuck that it was at a shitty funeral with a terrible minister in the hundred-degree heat, and fuck that no one came because my brother didn't have anyone else who wasn't in prison.

She came. I said something fucking *terrible* to her and then disappeared, and she sprinted across graves anyway. It's better than I deserve and I know it.

"I know, Mom," I say. "I like her anyway."

"I don't think she's right for you," my mom goes on as I swing the rental car into a parking space. "Don't you think she seems kind of damaged?"

I shut the car off, the lights still shining at the building in front of us, and I think: *whatever I say, she won't remember in fifteen minutes.*

But then I look over at her, and she looks back at me. She looks twenty years older than she is, a slight dent in her skull on her left side, her right hand shaking very slightly in her lap, and whatever horrible thing I could have said to her flies right out of my head.

"Yeah, she's kind of damaged," I say. "And I love her anyway."

I turn off the headlights, undo my seatbelt.

"Well—"

"You stayed married to Dad for twenty-five years, and now you're in assisted living at fifty-six because of what he did to you," I say, my voice deadly quiet in the dark. "I think you're a pretty shitty judge of character, and I don't care what you have to say about Darcy."

That pisses her off. She gets out of the car, shaky but furious, and walks slowly to the front door of Sunset Acres.

I shouldn't have said that, I think. *I should have let it pass. She just buried Eli.*

I get out. I follow Mom in, nodding at the nurses and their sympathetic faces. When we get to her suite, she lets me walk her in, then sits in a chair and turns her head away from me, giving me the silent treatment.

It's the brain damage. I know it is, because she didn't use to be like this, so I kiss her on the head, which she ignores.

"I'll see you tomorrow, Mom," I say, and walk out of her suite.

Silence, but God help me, I don't care.

•   •   •

Outside room one-forty-one at the Holiday Inn, I lean against the frame and pause for a minute. My day is swirling through my brain, and I try to gather my fragmented thoughts together into some semblance of... something.

I should say *something*, do *something* after she showed up and practically rescued me even *after* I treated her terribly, but I don't know what. Every inch of me is tired, every bone in my body, and I don't want to think or talk.

I'm lost, adrift, and all I want is to be there, with her. I'm broken and she makes me feel whole. I'm wandering through the dark and she's my North Star.

Finally, I knock on the door. Darcy opens it, and I still don't know what to say to her.

Instead, I kiss her. In the doorway, in the hall of a Holiday Inn in Bakersfield, California, I kiss Darcy like my life depends on it, because it feels like it might.

I put everything I have into it, because suddenly I understand that this is *it*, that Darcy is *it*. All the shit that happened today, all the shit that's happened the past weeks, the past month, my whole *life* and what I want is her, plain and simple.

She pulls back, breathing hard, looks at me. The door's still open, so I nudge her inside, let it close behind me.

"Trent," she says, as I slide my fingers down her back, then lean my forehead against hers.

"I'm sorry," I say, eyes closed.

I have no plan, no outline, so clue what I'm about to say.

"It's okay," she whispers.

"I didn't mean it," I go on. "I should never have said it. I know you've got a heart because it's all I've ever fucking wanted, Darcy."

I kiss her again, just to make myself stop talking for a moment, before I pour my soul out right here in this hotel room that smells like disinfectant and air conditioning. She wraps her hand around the back of my neck, her fingers every bit as hard and desperate as I feel.

"I shouldn't have said that about your brother," she gasps, the next time our lips come apart. "I wasn't thinking, I can just be an asshole sometimes—"

"I know," I tease, and nip at her lip. I'm pushing her slowly back toward the bed, our bodies practically melded together. "You're an asshole sometimes, you swear too much, you've got spikes a mile long, and I love you anyway."

I kiss her harder, forcefully. The backs of her knees hit the bed and I can't believe I just told her I love her, but it's true, so fuck it.

I do, and I have, and I think I probably always will.

Darcy's knees buckle and then she's sitting on the bed, her hand closed around the front of my button-down shirt, tie and jacket long gone, and she pulls my face down to hers.

"I cried for a day because I thought you were gone," she says, her voice low and rough, like it's hard for her to say. "It was fucking pathetic, Trent. I was fucking heartbroken because since forever it's always been *us* and then, suddenly, it wasn't."

She drags me in with more strength than I knew she had, kisses me fiercely.

"It's us, Darce," I say. "It's us and that's all. That's it. The end."

We kiss.

"Me and you and that's what matters," I promise.

She looks up at me, eyes wide and hair wild, lips just barely parted, and there's something vulnerable and tender in her face, her heart right there on the surface, alive and pounding and more delicate than she's ever let on.

And in that moment, I fucking *need* her. I need her more than I've needed anything, more than I need oxygen. I need her skin against mine, need her fingers in my hair, need her shouting and raking her nails down my back, because I've handed Darcy my heart and all I can do is hope she doesn't break it.

I push her backward, climb between her legs. She unbuttons my shirt, shoves it off me, drags the rest of my clothes off as I pull her out of her dress and she writhes under me.

We kiss again, Darcy up on one elbow, pushing herself against me. I push her back and taste her throat, kiss her neck. I nip at her collarbone and she gasps, my face buried in her.

More. I need *more*, Darcy so intoxicating that I'm lightheaded. I take one nipple in my teeth and she *growls* at me, sinking her fingernails into my shoulder, pinpoints sending streaks of electricity through my body. My cock so hard it might just explode off my body.

I kiss Darcy one more time, and she wraps her legs around me, reaches down, and grabs my cock in her hand. I moan into her mouth and she bites my lip, stroking me hard. I know she's trying to guide me in, lifting her hips and pulling me down, but I resist for half a second.

"Don't fucking tease me," she whispers. "I need you, Trent."

In one movement, I push her hand off my cock, push her legs off me, roll her over onto her stomach. She looks over her shoulder, saucy, grinning, as I slide one hand up her spine, push her knees apart, and kneel between them.

"Good," I say in her ear, running my fingers over her slick entrance, making her shudder. "Because I need you and I need *this*."

And I push myself inside her, slowly. I want to savor every fucking inch of this heaven, want to let this erase the hell of Low Valley and North Delano State and funerals and brain damage and I just want to be here, inside her, with the one person I've ever really loved.

She curls and arches underneath me, brings one knee up, grabs the bedspread with her hand, and she *moans* with this slow, breathy moan until I'm buried inside her, our whole bodies lined up skin to skin.

There's nothing else. Nothing else at all.

"This what you needed?" I whisper in her ear.

"*Fuck* yes," she whispers back. "Fucking *just* like that, Trent, *please*."

I do it again, *just* like that, and with her other hand she reaches back and grabs my hair, pulling my head close to hers. We're intertwined, over and under and in each other, and it's everything I needed.

She's everything I needed.

I don't speed up, I don't slow down, I just fuck her slow and steady and deep. It might be a minute or an hour, marked in sighs and whispers, in the way her body moves under me, in the way she flutters around me.

I think I'm falling apart, pieces coming off me, like I'm flaking to bits, and I don't care. I just keep going until Darcy's flutters get harder, tighter, until her gasps become moans. Until her breathing gets ragged, and she's suddenly pushing back against me harder.

And then I push myself into her as hard as I can and she comes around me, clenching and jolting and crying out, and seconds later I lose control too, burying my face in the back of her neck and just letting go.

CHAPTER FORTY-FOUR
Darcy

I almost think Trent's fallen asleep when he finally pulls out of me, kisses my shoulder, then rolls over and flops down face-first next to me on the bed, his arm still slung over my back.

"I'm glad you came," he says.

I wriggle a little, getting closer to him, get my hair off my face.

"You mean just now, or..."

"I meant to California," he says, but he's smiling. "For as long as I live, I'll never forget you running across those people's graves."

I scrunch my face, because it occurred to me *afterward* that dead or not, it isn't polite to run over people.

"Mostly because I'll never forget feeling like there was a glimmer of light in the world again," he says, his eyes searching mine. "I've never been gladder to see someone."

"I'm sorry I didn't come sooner."

"I did say something horrible to you. And you didn't even know I'd gone."

"They told me later," I say, and reach out, tracing a swirling tattoo across his shoulder blade. "I'm sorry for saying you shouldn't bury your brother because he wasn't perfect."

"Eli was a *long* way from perfect," Trent says. "And I get it. You haven't got anyone like that."

"I've got you guys," I say softly. "And I know it's not exactly the same, but I remember when Liam and Gavin OD'd all the press was about what terrible people they were, how selfish, how they were lowlife scum who didn't deserve hospital resources because they'd done this to themselves and oh, my God, Trent, I wanted to fucking murder everyone I saw."

"Was that when you called some reporter a worthless fucking cockhound?"

I stop, mouth slightly open.

"Was it?"

"You definitely said that at some point. I think it was in the hospital after Gavin woke up."

"What does cockhound even mean?"

Trent grins, his face half-mashed against the hotel bedspread.

"Why are you asking me? You said it."

"*Anyway*, I knew then that the people saying all that shit were kind of right, that they did it to themselves, but I still wanted to punch anyone who said anything bad about them."

Trent's fingers are tracing slow, lazy circles on my back, and even though it's barely seven-thirty I'm fighting sleep.

"I know I don't really have a family, but I've got you guys, and it's sort of close. If they found Liam in a ditch in Yorkshire tomorrow, I'd want him buried right even though I haven't even seen him in a year."

Trent wriggles closer, plants a kiss on my forehead. I think we might have just made up from our first fight.

Briefly, I wonder if I should call Joan and Gavin and give them a 'first fight solved' report, since they're the ones who took away the vodka and told me to stop being a child.

Maybe tomorrow.

"Is it too early to go to bed?" Trent asks, his lips still millimeters from my head.

"It's still kinda light outside," I say, half drifting off myself.

"We've got blackout curtains."

"A 7:45 bedtime isn't very rock and roll," I murmur.

"I think sleeping when you want is *very* rock and roll," Trent laughs. "Besides, I think I've gotten seven hours of sleep in three days."

"I haven't slept since yesterday," I admit, though I don't mention that I slept until noon *that* day. "I had to be at the airport at three in the morning to catch my five a.m. flight."

Hungover, five-in-the-morning flights: I don't recommend them.

"Five a.m.," Trent teases. "Shit, you were serious."

"Of course I was *serious*," I tease back. "I stomped over a bunch of graves and horrified your mom because I was late."

"Next time, just get me a subscription to a sock-of-the-month club or something."

"There's a sock-of-the-month club?"

"Probably."

I should get up, go wash my face and brush my teeth, but this is so perfectly comfortable and cozy that I don't want to move, but I finally prop myself up on my elbows.

"By the way, Gavin and Joan know. Probably Nigel too, by now."

Trent stretches, rolls over, and yawns, his arms behind his head.

"You finally told them?"

285

"Turns out they knew," I say.

I don't say *because apparently I'm really loud and they've just been polite for the past month or so*.

"Is Gavin pissed?"

"Nah."

"Are you?"

I just laugh.

"No," I say.

We finally get up and brush our teeth at the same time, both standing naked in front of the mirror, foaming at the mouth. I know I didn't fix everything by showing up. There are a thousand tiny things to do when someone dies, even if they were in prison, and it's not like Trent's mom can really help with anything.

And Eli's still dead. Once all the legalities are over and done with, that's still going to be true, and it's going to be true forever.

But I'm here, and we're brushing our teeth together naked. I don't know what to do for Trent besides be here, so I'm doing it, and I'm gonna keep doing it for as long as he can stand me.

. . .

We sleep for almost thirteen hours and get up at nearly nine in the morning, groggy and sleep-drunk. That day and the next are full of bureaucracy and circular, maddening nonsense: Trent needs a death certificate to get the order for the prison ward to sign off on Eli's belongings, only to discover that the prison has a policy of only issuing death certificates through the local hospital, where Eli never went, and of course the prison infirmary doesn't have the capacity to issue a death warrant, despite having signed over a dead body two days before.

It's mind-boggling, maddening, and since I'm not the next of kin there isn't all that much I can do to help. Trent's fucking worn out and exhausted from all this, from having to deal with a ton of bullshit, from seeing his mom and repeating every conversation three times. Every so often I'll find him just staring into space, and I *know* what he's thinking about.

I don't really know what to do, but I try to give him space sometimes but I try to be there when he needs me. He gives me a temporary pass to his mom's nursing home, so I take Gwen out for a manicure and pedicure, even though I can tell she doesn't like me.

It's the second one I've gotten in my life, and I can tell she doesn't approve of the electric blue color I pick. We make repetitive, awkward conversation for a couple of hours. It's hard to tell what she remembers and what she doesn't: the fact that Eli's dead, yes. The fact that Trent has a girlfriend, yes. But I she doesn't actually remember the funeral, the dinner afterward, any of *that*, because her memory doesn't seem to be stories any more, just facts.

When she's not looking, I find the dent in her left temple. Trent's told me about that night, the chair leg that put it there, the hospital afterward. The way his father would always bring a massive bouquet of roses, the world's most loving and adoring husband.

How even though the hospital staff couldn't have possibly believed that Gwen was always falling down the stairs or burning herself on the stove, they never did much of anything. No one did, except Trent, and he fucking paid for it.

When I get back that night, Trent's already on the bed in his t-shirt and boxers, watching TV. He looks exhausted and beaten, but when he sees me, he smiles.

"Look what I found," he says, pointing at the TV.

I take off my shoes and jeans, climb onto the bed next to him.

"Which part is haunted?" I ask, watching footage of a rolling green golf course, ominous music playing over it.

"Just wait," he says.

I wait.

Slowly, from one side of the screen, a golf cart rolls onto the grass and stops. There's no one driving it. The music crescendos, and then the picture freezes, turns black and white.

"You're kidding me," I say, grinning.

"Just wait," Trent says again, and something pops up on the screen:

THE SIXTH HOLE SPECTER?

We both *lose our shit*. Trent snorts, he laughs so hard, and I laugh so hard I cry and then get the hiccups. By the end of the episode — which, yes, is about a *haunted golf cart* — Trent's sitting between my legs, leaning back against my chest, and I'm stroking his hair.

It feels oddly familiar, a mirror-reversal of Tallwood, of all the time we spent watching dumb shit while my back was too fucked up for me to do anything.

And despite everything that *has* changed, this feels the same.

CHAPTER FORTY-FIVE
Trent

I wake up face-down on the pillow, one hand on Darcy's ass. I don't know how it got there, but I don't move it.

Eight-thirty in the morning. It's an hour I don't see too often, given that my usual bedtime is around four in the morning, so I squint at the clock, double-checking.

Yup. Eight thirty-two.

Next to me, Darcy rolls over, pillow lines on her face and hair everywhere.

"When's our flight?" I mutter.

"Nnnggh."

"Not until later, right?"

Darcy's been a fucking angel. It's a weird thing to say about someone who's anything but sweet and swears like a sailor, but it's true. The last few days have been impossibly rough, but she's been here helping out however she can: getting us fed, making arrangements, getting plane tickets back to the east coast, even hanging out with my mom.

My mom who doesn't like her, and even though Darcy hasn't said anything, I can tell she knows.

"I lied," Darcy murmurs.

"Don't tell me it's earlier."

She pushes herself onto her elbows and yawns, stretching.

"It's tomorrow," she says.

I'm too barely-awake to process this, so I just stare at her, waiting for an explanation.

"I have a surprise for you," she says.

"What is it?"

"It's a *surprise*."

"What kind of a surprise?"

"God*damn* it, Trent, it's a surprise."

I don't normally like surprises, but right now, I'm in no mood to not like anything Darcy does. She wants to surprise me, she can surprise me.

An hour later, we actually get up. Darcy grabs us both coffee from the lobby, and we get dressed drinking it, even though she still won't tell me what the surprise is.

All she'll tell me is that no, I shouldn't wear my suit, and no, I don't need anything special.

Instead of the hotel breakfast, we head to a diner on the north side of Bakersfield. It's another hot fucking day in the Central Valley, in the upper nineties by the time we've eaten sausage and pancakes.

When we get back in the car, Darcy drives north.

"Fresno," I guess.

"Why would I take you to Fresno?"

"Visalia."

"What's that?"

"Another town that's kinda like Fresno," I say.

"How pissed would people in either place be if they heard you say that?" she asks, grinning.

I laugh, leaning back in the passenger seat, air conditioning blasting full-force on my face.

"Probably kinda pissed," I admit.

North of Bakersfield, though, she gets on the sixty-five freeway, not the ninety-nine, so we're clearly not going to Fresno or Merced or anywhere that I'd assumed. The two roads go the same direction, north, only the sixty-five veers further east, toward the Sierra Nevada.

"Are we going to the mountains?" I ask.

Darcy doesn't answer, just flicks on her blinker as she passes a truck at eighty-five miles an hour, but there's a smile around her eyes.

"We could be going anywhere," she says. "Just chill."

In the next town, we stop at a cafe, where Darcy gets us sandwiches and chips and still won't tell me what's going on.

We're definitely going to the mountains.

• • •

After a while, we turn east from the dead-straight highway sixty-five onto another dead-straight road, and I laugh.

"I knew it," I tell her.

"Maybe I'm taking you to Fresno by a really roundabout route," she points out, but she's grinning.

"I've only been up here a couple of times, believe it or not," I say, watching the Sierra Nevada grow slowly closer through the windshield. "We weren't exactly the 'go hiking' or the 'family vacation' types, and after everything happened and I moved away, it just never occurred me to. Even after I joined the band and moved to L.A., I never went."

"Well, I hope you still like big-ass trees as much as you did the one time when you were a kid," she says.

"I told you about that?"

"You told me you visited an aunt once and really loved the big trees and never went back," she says, her voice suddenly softer. The foothills are closing in, the landscape getting taller and greener, the road bending slightly. "I thought about taking you into L.A. or something, but I feel like we'd just end up running errands or checking on my cat, and I thought you needed an *actual* surprise day trip."

"I'm surprised you remembered that," I say.

She gives me a weird look, then tears her eyes away, back to the road, which is suddenly getting winding and curvy.

"I remember a lot of the stuff you tell me," she says, her voice slightly puzzled. "Why wouldn't I?"

Because it seems like the small, unimportant details of my own life, I think. *Because there's so much of it I don't really want to remember that it baffles me anyone would try.*

"It's just bullshit details is all," I say.

Darcy laughs, braking as she steers around a big curve in the road. In the past ten minutes we've driven from wide, flat farmland, to the low, muted brush of the foothills and now we're in full forest, deep greens and patches of sunlight everywhere. It's only taken a little over an hour to get here, but I always forget how close this is from Low Valley.

It just seems so... different.

"Sometimes the bullshit details are the important part," Darcy says, swinging around another curve in the road. "That's what makes all this shit... I don't know. Real?"

I lean my head back against the headrest. She's playing music on the car's stereo, something chill and acoustic, the sort of folk-rock she's been kinda into lately. For a second I almost reach out to take her hand, kiss it, maybe kiss her, but then she swings around a sharp bend in the opposite direction and I decide to let her drive for now.

Finally, we turn off at the Trail of 100 Giants, bump down the rough paved road, and finally park in the gravel lot. We're alone there, since it's midday on a week day.

"There," she says, yanking up on the parking brake and looking over at me. "You guessed right."

"I didn't guess this exactly," I protest.

"You guessed big-ass trees in the mountains."

"I just guessed the mountains," I say, and lean in toward her. "You supplied the big-ass tree part."

I put my hand on her face and kiss her. I don't know how she knew, but the second we drove into the forest I knew she was right: this is what I need.

Just a little while with her, nature, some big trees, and nothing and no one else. With my lips on hers I can feel the past couple days begin to melt away, to feel like something that happened to some other poor bastard, somewhere else.

"C'mon," she says, finally pulling back. "I planned a whole picnic, sort of."

• • •

Darcy did forget drinks, though luckily there's a water fountain near the parking lot. We grab our sandwiches and head along the easy trail.

It's a sequoia grove, as the name might have given away. These trees are fucking *massive*. Somewhere around here, some enterprising soul carved a tunnel through one big enough to drive a car through.

Trees big enough you can drive through them. They're some big-ass trees.

And we just stroll, talking about absolutely nothing. We hold hands and speculate about whether birds like sequoia trees or think they're too big, about why the pinecones are so small if the trees are so enormous, about whether Nigel will freak out if he finds we took an extra day just for fun.

Darcy offers to guilt-trip him about 'the whole dead brother thing,' and even though it still feels so fucking heavy, I can't help but laugh.

We find a picnic table, sit, and eat our sandwiches.

"So, are these trees big enough?" she teases, dangling a tomato slice between two fingers.

"These aren't even the trees we visited when I was a kid, you know," I tease back. "Those were just big regular trees."

"I didn't even have to do all this?" she grins, chomping on the tomato. "I could have driven for like thirty minutes less, pointed to something out the car window, and been like, 'good enough, let's go back to the Holiday Inn'?"

"I didn't say this wasn't *better*," I point out.

Darcy chews on a bite of sandwich for a moment, thinking.

"You were visiting your mom's sister, right?" she asks suddenly.

I just nod.

"She didn't come to Eli's funeral?"

I stare into my sandwich for a long moment, like maybe roast beef and horseradish will tell me what the fuck to say to *that*.

And then I think: *it's Darcy. You can't surprise her.*

"I didn't even know how to contact her," I admit. "I tried. I looked up every Darlene Wright in a five-hundred-mile radius, but I don't think I found her. My mom didn't have her number any more. I don't know if that was even still her name, because if she'd been divorced and remarried a couple of times since the last time I saw her, I'd believe it."

"That bad, huh?" Darcy says softly.

I half-laugh.

"You know my family," I say.

"I don't, really," she says.

"You know how Eli was," I tell her, putting my sandwich back down on the paper, looking away at a huge reddish tree. "I loved him, but he was how he was. My mom stayed married to a man who beat the daylight out of her once a week for twenty-five years, and she doesn't like you because she thought you were rude to come to the funeral."

Darcy turns faintly pink, but I just shake my head at her and go on.

"She took my dad's side after I finally hit him back," I tell her. "It was their word against mine, and when we got to court Eli wouldn't testify."

"He wouldn't testify...?" she says, slowly.

I raise one eyebrow.

"When my father pressed charges against me for hitting him back," I say.

Darcy's eyes are white saucers with a blue dot. She's already put her sandwich down on the paper, one hand covering her mouth as she chews quickly and swallows.

"He *pressed charges*?" she says, incredulous.

I blink, staring at Darcy, and Darcy stares back, because I'm almost positive I've told her the story before. I've told her *everything*, and this is pretty fucking important. It's how, despite everything, I became the outcast in my own family.

"I've told you all this, right?" I ask, slowly.

Maybe I haven't. Maybe I just think I have because I've told her everything else.

She shakes her head slowly.

"I don't think so," she says. "And I remembered about the trees..."

"Oh," I say, looking at the table. "Fuck."

"You don't have to," she says quickly, putting one hand on my arm. "Trent, it's okay, you can tell me whenever you want, it doesn't have to be now..."

I just laugh, shaking my head.

"I can't believe I didn't tell you years ago," I say. "You sure you want to know this?"

Darcy just rolls her eyes.

"Fucking of course," she says.

Eight Years Earlier

The door slams, and it shakes the whole trailer. Eleven at night on a Tuesday, and Eli and I look at each other across the bedroom because it's never a good fucking sign when he's home early. Means he got kicked out of somewhere and he's likely to be in a worse mood than usual.

I look back down, turn up the volume on my battered Discman. It's old as fuck and every CD skips like crazy, but lately it feels like the only thing that's been getting me through.

Sidewinder screams in my ear, so loud that Eli glances up at me again. I've got a battered copy of *To Kill a Mockingbird* open on my lap, and he's at the beat-up desk we share with a math textbook open, but we both know we're not finishing any homework tonight.

The shouting starts. I half-wonder what it is this time, but I also know it doesn't fucking matter, and I lean my head back against the headboard of my twin bed, trying to ignore it, listening to the rough, choppy melodies, thrashing guitars.

There's a clatter. Sounds like something got knocked off the stove, but my mom doesn't even scream. Deep down, I know I should be more scared. That I should have some kind of reaction beyond *oh, this again*, that I should go get involved.

But I've fucking called the cops. More times than I can even remember. Enough to figure out that it doesn't fucking matter if I call the cops, because even if they take him away, he's back in a couple of days and then he's pissed at *me*.

I've learned my lesson. Stay out of his way, keep working part-time at the grocery store, graduate Low Valley High in June and get the fuck out of this house.

Something shatters, and this time my mom yelps. My eyes fly open, because *that's* unusual, usually she's quiet as a mouse and goes down fast, because she's learned that if she stays on the floor, he's less likely to bend down and hit her and probably doesn't have the balance to kick.

And then she *screams*. I grind my teeth together, my fists in balls, and I try to turn the music up again but it's already all the way up so I have to fight the impulse.

You won't do anything, I tell myself again and again. *This is just what happens. There's no changing it.*

Heavy footsteps, sounds like from the kitchen to the living room. Coming closer, the whole trailer shaking, the metal walls rattling. My eyes still shut, and he roars something fucking incomprehensible, even over the music.

"Stan!" she screams, and she's closer too. Like he's got her.

I'm fucking seventeen years old but I want to hide under my bed right now. Build a blanket fort or some shit, go somewhere small and safe where I don't have to hear any more. Except that place doesn't exist, so I just sit there, on my bed. Trying to breathe.

"Stan, don't," my mom sobs, and I swear my heart catches in my chest. I hold my breath.

Eli slams his textbook closed, and my eyes fly open.

He scrapes back the folding chair we use to do homework in. Throws his pencil on the desk, onto the nearly-blank piece of paper he was using.

"Fuck this," he mutters, stomps out of the room.

I'm up in half a second, throwing my headphones on the bed, *To Kill a Mockingbird* in a pile on the floor.

"Don't," I call after him, but I can tell it's too late.

The trailer's fucking tiny and before I'm even out our bedroom door, he's running into the living room, shouting at the top of his lungs. Past him, our father's got Mom by the hair, and she's on the floor, conscious but practically a rag doll.

"The fuck is wrong with you?" Eli shouts, stopping a couple of feet away. "Do you get tired of hitting people who can fucking hit you back? You get your ass kicked at Downtowners tonight so you had to come home and take it out on her?"

He's fifteen, skinny, though he's on the football team this year. Gets into dumb kid fights, but he's never fought a full-grown man like our father, someone who gets into drunken brawls at least once a week.

"Eli," I say again, forcing my voice calm. "Leave it."

I've fucking tried this before, tried talk him down, get him to stop, but my father's got a trump card: he'll hurt his own child. I think he fucking *likes* it. Neither of us stand a chance.

"Fuck off, Trent," Eli spits over his shoulder. "I can't take this anymore, why don't you—"

He takes a right hook to the jaw and stumbles sideways, caught by complete surprise. He holds one hand to his mouth and comes away with blood, his face *astonished*, but before he can even process it my father's dropped my mother's hair and he's on Eli. Another punch to the gut, my kid brother doubled over.

I have to do something. *Fuck*, I have to do something and I don't know what, he's already broken my nose once—

My father shouts again and now Eli's off his feet, in the air. Held up by two big hands around his neck, against a wall, clawing at them. My mother is on the floor, not even watching, and in one sickening moment I know I'm not getting out of this, that I can't avoid it any fucking longer.

Our bathroom's to my right, the mirror dirty and cracked and a ring around the shower that no scrubbing will ever get rid of.

On the toilet there's a pipe wrench, because something's always fucking broken and leaking, and without thinking for even a second I lean in and grab it.

He's still roaring. Eli's gasping, kicking, and I feel the weight of the heavy wrench in my hand and I close my fist around it, step into the living room, and I swing it like a baseball bat, right at his fucking temple.

There's a *thud*. It's surprisingly soft, and they both go tumbling to the floor. Eli's gasping, choking, heaving for breath as he gets onto his hands and knees. My father's unconscious or maybe dead, one leg bent under him oddly.

My mother just looks at me, and I know she saw the whole thing.

I drop the wrench. My hands are shaking, but I talk myself through it, slowly and calmly. I cross the room. I call 911. I haul Eli up off the floor, and we go sit together on the tailgate of my father's pickup in our shitty dirt driveway, and we wait.

CHAPTER FORTY-SIX
Darcy

Present Day

I knew. I mean, I didn't *know* know but I knew there was something and I knew I'd never quite asked for the full story.

I'm sitting on the table, Trent on the bench, leaning back against me as I stroke his hair. We're facing yet another giant tree, both watching it.

"I really thought I'd told you all that," he says.

"Not like that. Not as a whole story," I say. "I knew the bits and pieces, but I didn't know the *story*."

Trent sighs, tilts his head back, looks up at me.

"So you know the rest, right?" he asks. "Dad pressed charges, Mom sided with his version of events. Eli sided with me but wouldn't testify, I think because he knew he was going back there no matter what he did."

I bite my lip and look away. I've learned my lesson not to say bad things about Trent's family, but Jesus Christ do I want to right now. Hell, I want to drive back to Low Valley, dig up Eli's body, and feed it to the dogs.

I want to find his old house, the trailer, and fucking set fire to it. I want to stop payments to Gwen's assisted living home and let them kick her out onto the streets.

Trent could never do any of that. Somehow, he came out of there the way he is, fucking kind and gentle and caring despite everything, but I could fucking do it. I could fucking do it to all of them.

"But I got lucky with a judge who took several years of domestic violence calls as evidence, and gave me three years of parole instead of sending me to prison," he says. "I moved out, stayed with friends in a fucking filthy apartment where the rats ate the cockroaches. Got my GED. Became a bouncer, picked up a guitar, and you know the rest."

I kiss the top of his head, because *the rest* isn't simple either but it's the part of the story I know. A couple years later, Stan finally got into a drunken fight with the wrong guy and died in a parking lot. Eli did the shit that he did, and despite *fucking everything*, as soon as he could afford it Trent paid for his mom to live where she does.

"I'm glad I didn't know that story before I met your mom," I say quietly.

"Now you know why I don't care that she doesn't like you," he says, his voice rumbling through my body. "She's got absolutely shit judgement. Fuck, it's probably a good sign that she doesn't like you."

We sit there. I run my hands through his hair, and neither of us says anything. I'm not sure there's anything left to say, but I can tell that right here, right now, Trent's at peace for once.

Everything's not fixed. He's not fixed and I'm not fixed. Someday his mom's going to die, too, and something like this will happen all over again, but that time I won't fuck it up. He puts out my fires — literally

— and I put out his, and it's the way it's been for a long time and the way it's going to be.

"Want to keep walking and looking at trees?" he finally asks.

I kiss the top of his head one more time, and for a split second, I thank every deity I can think of for this moment.

"Of course," I say.

•   •   •

The next day, we drive the two hours to LAX and fly from there rather than deal with the Bakersfield airport. Trent takes his rental car back, puts his luggage into mine and climbs in.

As I drive south, out of Bakersfield, he's oddly quiet.

"How much time have we got?" he suddenly asks.

"Before we need to be at the airport?"

"Yeah."

"Three hours."

There's a long, long pause. I glance over and he's looking out the window, so I take one hand off the wheel and put it on his.

"Would you mind driving through Low Valley?" he suddenly asks. "It's on the way."

"I can do that," I say. "Why?"

"Because I want to know it's the last time I'll ever see it," he says. "Eli's gone, my dad's gone, my mom is... how she is, and I've got no fucking reason to ever go back, but I kind of want to see it one last time, just to say *good fucking riddance*."

I get it. I go back to Madison, Wisconsin every so often to play shows, and sometimes I walk around, remembering being a teenage runaway and living half on the streets, half on the floors of older punks, anyone who would give me shelter for a night. And if I think I could never go back, I might.

303

He only speaks to give me directions. All the roads here are flat, straight, and dusty; all the corners ninety-degree angles ruled only by stop signs. If it weren't for the smog and the golden glow of the air itself, I'd be able to see forever.

And then, suddenly, a green sign on the side of a two-lane road announces LOW VALLEY, Population 13,093, even though nothing else changes. One side of the road is dusty and fallow, the other has low green plants baking in the sun.

"Here we are," Trent says.

"Where to now?"

"There's not much to see," he says, but we drive anyway: past a small high school with a single athletic field, past a few trailer parks, past low-slung abandoned houses. Past two blocks of downtown, where half the storefronts are boarded up, a couple are tattoo shops, and only one seems to be open and selling anything.

I think it's about what I expected from what he told me, but it's so odd to suddenly be here, in the exact place that Trent's hated for as long as I've known him.

"Has it changed?" I ask as we roll past cracked tan stucco, an abandoned gas station.

"Not really," he says. "I got busted once by the owner for stealing gum from that store. Guy nearly broke my arm. Back behind there is the lot where we used to skateboard, though there were always a couple of us sharing one board."

I look over and he cracks a smile, just barely.

"Adam Laredo was a fucking skateboard hog," he says. "Wonder what happened to that kid. Right there's where I got this fucking awful dragon tattoo, and I'm probably lucky I didn't get hepatitis, too."

Then it's over. It's not a big town and we just hit the end, from dried-out buildings to the dried-out fields. For some reason, I pull off the road and park.

"What, you want more?" Trent asks.

I turn my head, look through the car's rear window. "You're not kinda sad to leave it behind?"

"Not even some," he says. "This place gave me the worst years of my life."

I reach over and take his hand, leaning against the headrest of the front seat.

"Yeah, but it made you who you are now," I say. "Maybe I should be a little more grateful to Low Valley."

Trent laces his fingers through mine, squeezes hard, grins.

"I'd much rather think about the future, Darce," he says. "Maybe this place ended up bringing me to you, but maybe I'd have gotten here anyway. And what's important is that I got to you and you got to me, right?"

I think of Wisconsin snow drifts, of freezing my ass off for days at a time, and I think of a too-hot trailer filled with shouting, and then I think: fuck all that.

"Right," I say, smiling. "Fuck Low Valley. I love you."

"I love you too," he says, and we kiss as the hot dust swirls around the car, nearly obliterating our view of Low Valley behind us.

EPILOGUE
Trent

Six Months Later

"We're Dirtshine!" Gavin shouts. "Thank you!"

The crowd screams, the lights go dark. I put my guitar down on its stand and walk off stage, my whole body still humming.

We're in another tiny venue, this one finally in Los Angeles. It's the very end of the tour, the third of three nights playing at the Music Box, which was a theater in the 1920s that now has rock shows in it.

In the vestibule just off stage, we all stop, take a breath, and wait.

"Well," Gavin says, grinning. "How long do we give them?"

Everyone else just laughs. Even though I hate encores when I go see bands — just play your show, don't make me scream for three more songs — I like them when I'm playing.

Sure, it's nice to hear everyone scream for you to come back. But taking this tiny break mid-show, seeing each other quietly when there's this manic energy all around, is oddly *nice*.

"Don't make them wait forever," Darcy laughs. "I hate that shit."

"Ava used to take smoke breaks before an encore," Joan says. "I hated *that* shit."

"Is that when she tried to set Nadine on fire?" Darcy asks.

"Surprisingly, no," Joan says. "But we did go back on stage without her a few times, and she'd come running on twenty seconds into the first song, pissed as hell."

On our last tour, there were a couple times that we went off stage for an encore only for Gavin and Liam to never come back, and I can tell we're all thinking of it, though no one says anything, because Gavin doesn't deserve it.

He's been fucking *stellar*. I haven't seen him drink so much as a glass of wine with dinner, let alone anything harder.

Honestly, I didn't quite expect the sobriety to take. Not that I don't believe in Gavin, but it usually takes a couple of tries, and even then, addicts are often always just addicts. I guess he beat the odds, though.

"Joan," he says, folding his arms across his chest. "Any final words before you become the first former member of Dirtshine we're still on speaking terms with?"

Joan just laughs.

"What, like 'fuck all you assholes, I'm leaving'?" she asks, grinning. "Are you saying I shouldn't break the streak?"

"We *do* have a reputation to uphold," Darcy says.

"And we'd hate for it to be too easy to find a new drummer," I say. "So definitely don't go telling your friends that we're lovely people and easy to work with."

"Noted," she says. "You're a bunch of difficult musicians who barely get along with each other and have chewed through every drummer you've ever had."

"Brilliant," Gavin says. "Just what we wanted."

We pause for a moment, and at the same time, we all lean toward the stage, looking out at the audience. They're still screaming and clapping and stomping, and for a moment, my heart constricts in my chest because this tour is almost over.

Going back to regular life after a tour is... well, I've never done it the normal way. Before we hit it big, we were just always on the road, and the last tour got cut short when half our band overdosed.

And I'm coming back different than I left. I've got one more girlfriend and one less brother, a fucking seismic shift in my life, and after learning how to function properly with both those things on the road, I have to learn in real life, too.

In the dark, Darcy looks back at me, raises one eyebrow. I put a hand on her back and rub my thumb over her shoulder blade, even though she's slightly damp, sweating through her dress on the hot stage.

The girlfriend part I'm excited for. I'm excited to wake up in her loft, make her breakfast, go on dates, run errands together. The brother part I'll have to get used to.

"All right," Gavin says, still looking out at the crowd. "You lot ready?"

It's what he always says right before we go out on stage, like a good luck charm.

"Let's do this," Darcy says, and we walk back out.

I pick up my guitar, slide the strap over my head, flex my fingers. The crowd's completely losing its shit, and then the stage lights come back up.

Joan counts off, and we start playing again.

• • •

After the show, we head to Darcy's place since it's the closest, along with Marisol and Dan, Joan's longtime life partner.

She's finally gotten couches and stopped making guests sit on giant pillows on the floor, and we all sprawl on those as Bowie, her cat, wanders from person to person, suspiciously sniffing shoes.

"He likes to get projects done while I'm on tour," Joan is laughing. "Once, I swear I came back and we had a new downstairs bathroom."

"It was just remodeled," Dan says, smiling softly. He's kind of quiet but very nice, an urban planner for the City of Los Angeles or something.

In other words, not the kind of person you'd think would be in a committed twenty-year relationship with a Riot Grrl, but it obviously works for them.

"And I told you all about it," he goes on, holding out one hand to Bowie, who sniffs him, glares, and then headbutts his hand. "I don't know *how* you were surprised."

"I was surprised because that was the tour where Nadine went missing in East St. Louis for three days and we thought she was *dead* when she was just doing every drug she could find with some bohemian literature professor who compared her to Anna Karenina," Joan says. "God, what a shit show."

"At least I did a nice job on the bathroom," Dan points out.

He's now friends with Bowie, who's standing on his lap and purring her face off.

"All I did was throw away ten thousand takeout containers before Gavin got back," Marisol says. "I think."

"I did find a half-empty carton of white rice below the kitchen sink," Gavin says.

Marisol makes a face.

"Shameful," he teases her. "Absolutely disgusting, worst filth I've ever seen."

"Okay, shut up," Marisol teases. "Though, honestly, it's not so bad that you were gone a lot during my first year as an associate, because I didn't have to feel guilty if I worked from eight a.m. to midnight."

"Ugh," Darcy says, and I recoil.

"I know," Marisol admits. "But it's slacking off, at least. Oh, speaking of which, sort of..."

She stands and walks to Darcy's kitchen counter, where she tossed her purse.

"Did you bring them?" Gavin calls.

"I did," Marisol says. "Figured we could just hand them out now."

We all go quiet, craning our necks as Marisol pulls a bunch of thick, off-white envelopes out of her purse.

"Ooooh," Darcy says, rubbing her hands together. "Is this *them*?"

"This is *them*," Marisol confirms. "I've spent more time than I literally ever thought I would staring down the wording of *hey, I'm getting married* and you're about to hold the end result in your *very* hands."

She comes back, handing one envelope to Joan and Dan, and one to us.

Mr. Trent Ryder and Miss Darcy Greene, it reads.

"Fancy," Darcy breathes.

"You can open it, you know," Marisol laughs. "My mom's gotten a little crazy and she wanted to me to hire someone with nice handwriting to write these out, but I just made myself re-learn cursive."

"They look fine," I offer. I had no idea that hiring someone with nice handwriting to write your wedding invitations was even a *thing*.

"Thanks," Marisol says, flopping onto the couch again. "I agree."

Darcy opens it and pulls out the card inside. It's fancy, but in a normal way. No curlicues or any of that shit.

You are Invited to the Wedding of
Marisol Gomez
and
Gavin Lockwood

Saturday, January 14
Los Angeles, California
Details to Follow

"What details are following?" I ask.

"Oh, Christ, Valerie's making us do that," Gavin says, rubbing his face with one hand. "It's at the Griffith Mansion, but she pitched a fit about us actually putting that on the invitations because according to her, I may as well invite all the paparazzi in Los Angeles. So now we've got to somehow tell all the attendees where it is only a day or two in advance so that there's not a man with a telephoto lens taking photos of our tonsils as we say our vows."

"It must suck to be famous," Darcy says wryly, and I snort.

Neither of us is as well-known as Gavin, of course, but we do keep getting followed around by people with cameras. The other day we left somewhere and got into separate cars, because *sometimes people take separate cars*, and the next day's TMZ was alight with breakup rumors.

"I should start wearing massive sunglasses and a huge hat everywhere I go," Gavin says. "That ought to help."

Darcy flips the invitation over, glances at the back, and then hands it to me, not that I know what to do with it, and leans against my arm.

"Well, congrats," Joan says. "We'll be there."

"Brilliant," Gavin says, and Marisol gives him a *significant* look.

He frowns at her, slightly, and she just raises one eyebrow.

"Now?"

"May as well," she says.

They just look at each other for a moment.

"Now you *have* to say whatever it is," Darcy points out. "We all heard that."

"The rest of us were being polite," I say.

"The rest of you are *also* curious and are glad I'm bothering them about it right now," she teases, and she's right.

There's a pause, and Gavin glances from her to me and back.

"We invited Liam," he finally says.

There's another pause.

"Oh, *shit*," says Darcy. "Is that a good idea?"

"He's alive?" I add.

Marisol gives Gavin something I can only describe as *kind of a look*, and he flops back against the couch, crossing one ankle over the opposite knee.

"Yes, he's alive, and I've got no bloody clue if it's a good idea," he says, sounding a little resigned. "But he's in some sort of program that requires him to make amends to everyone he's wronged with his addiction, and I guess I was pretty high on that list. He called a couple of weeks ago and we ended up talking for ages."

Dead silence. Liam hasn't contacted Darcy or me, and God knows he wronged *us* too. Not as badly as Gavin, but bad enough that I could use an apology.

"Liam's the original drummer," Joan murmurs to Dan.

"The guy who's in the jam band now?"

"No, the one before that, with the heroin problem," she says, trying to keep her voice down. "I told you the whole story, with the overdose and the guy who died?"

"He went back to England when he couldn't get clean," Darcy explains. "And that was the last we heard of him. Until a couple weeks ago, apparently."

"He said he'd be calling you as well," Gavin offers. "And I suppose I ought to have told you he's alive, but I thought it was best to let him explain."

Darcy's just looking at Marisol, because Liam's not exactly her favorite person. Not after what he did to her and Gavin.

"Did he apologize to *you*?" Darcy asks her.

"He actually did," Marisol says slowly, like she's trying to pick her words carefully. "And we ended up talking for a really long time, and... I'm not exactly sure how I feel about him in general, but I'm good with him getting invited to the wedding. Who knows if he'll even come."

I haven't seen Liam in a year and a half. I think the last time was our first show with Eddie, nearly eighteen months ago. He showed up drunk and high and God knows what else, screaming about how we couldn't be Dirtshine without him, and I haven't seen him since.

Gavin and Marisol did, though, which is why he called them to apologize first. Whatever apology he owes me, he owes *them* about ten times that.

"I give it a fifty-fifty chance," Darcy muses. "If he were going to show up to a wedding, it'd be yours, but he's kind of..."

For once, she trails off, like she doesn't want to be rude.

"...A self-centered fuckmuppet and a total fucking knob, even when he's not high?" Gavin fills in.

"Pretty much," Darcy says. "Though I'm not well acquainted with sober Liam."

"I did tell him if he shows up high or drunk I'll fucking have him flown straight back across the pond," Gavin says. "Which he seemed to find funny."

• • •

313

"Do you two want a ride home?" Dan offers. "I parked like a block away, it's no problem."

"Sure, if you've got room," Marisol says, and Joan laughs.

"Rock stars: they get rides from friends, just like us!" she says.

"Rock stars: sometimes they're in the back seat of a Subaru," Dan jokes.

"I don't get shotgun?" Gavin teases.

We're all clustered around Darcy's front door, hugging and shaking hands. If you'd asked me two years ago how we'd be closing out a major world tour, I'd never have said this. I'd have said that Liam and Gavin would be somewhere, nodded out, that Darcy and I would be closing down some bar, that I'd be going home without her again and probably jerking off wishing I were here.

But that's all dead wrong. Gavin's fucking engaged, I'm staying here with Darcy, and Liam's... well, Liam's alive and apparently sober or sober-ish, and we're all saying a very civilized goodbye.

I'm not mourning the alternative. We did that for long enough, and now we're here, and I'm good with it.

"Night!" Darcy says brightly, as the others all leave, then shuts the door behind herself and leans against it, puffing out her cheeks.

"I guess that's over," she says.

I just kiss her on the forehead, because I'm not exactly sure what to say. The tour's over, yeah, but that's about it.

"Now we have to figure out how to be a regular couple," I tease.

"You mean one who's not together every minute of every day?"

"One who spends time together *not* on a tour bus or in a hotel room."

"Strange," Darcy says. "Are we gonna have to learn to fight over the dishes and stuff like that?"

"I bet we can just transfer our argument over who used the fuzzbox last and packed the cables wrong," I say.

"Which was you," Darcy points out.

It wasn't. There's no fucking way it was me, I *always* pack cables properly because I'm not a madman.

I don't say that.

"It might not be all bad," I tease.

"I didn't mean it that way," she says.

"I know."

"I think it's gonna be good," she says, her voice suddenly quiet. "I think it'll be really good."

"I think it'll be spectacular," I say.

"MRROWWWW," Bowie shouts as she headbutts my leg, and Darcy laughs.

"She wants us to go to bed," she says. "We're *way* behind schedule, according to her."

"Bowie, we're having a nice talk," I tell the cat. "Give us a minute."

She sits and stares up at me with one green eye and one blue eye.

"MARP," she says.

"I love you," Darcy says. "And I'm kinda glad I caught on fire because it ended this way, even though that part did suck."

"I'm not glad you caught on fire, and I love you too," I say.

I kiss her, slowly, and even though by now this is perfectly familiar, it still sends a tingle all the way down to my toes. I know Darcy better than I've ever known *anyone*, and somehow, it only makes me love her more.

She pushes her fingers through my hair, pulling me closer, and I slide one hand around her waist. Even though I know her burn is fully healed, I'm *still* careful with her back, still try not to be rough with that spot.

Darcy bites my lip. She pulls on my shirt, and I step in closer, pressing her fully against the door.

"MRAAAHHHH," Bowie insists, and we both start laughing.

"I think she's telling us to go to bed," Darcy says, grinning.

I grab her ass and squeeze.

"Is that what she wants or what *you* want?" I ask, and Darcy just laughs.

"C'mon," she says, taking my hand and slipping through my arms. "It's not such a bad idea."

With that, she pulls me into her bedroom.

THE END

About Roxie

I love writing sexy, alpha men and the headstrong women they fall for.

My weaknesses include: beards, whiskey, nice abs with treasure trails, sarcasm, cats, prowess in the kitchen, prowess in the bedroom, forearm tattoos, and gummi bears.

I live in California with my very own sexy, bearded, whiskey-loving husband and two hell-raising cats.

53539121R00200

Made in the USA
San Bernardino, CA
20 September 2017